HIDDEN AWAY

MASTERS OF MARQUIS

BOOK 7

GOLDEN ANGEL

CONTENTS

PROLOGUE

"I'm sure it'll be fine." Famous last words, but there was no way Rae was going to admit to Domi that she was anxious about being the only single woman on the Jack-and-Jill wedding party trip to the Hideaway Resort. Her bestie was the bride, she was the maid of honor, and it was her job to make sure Domi had a great time during her bachelorette party, not spend it worrying about Rae. Especially not worrying about Rae's single status. "We're not doing group stuff together every day, right? And at night, I can go find a Dom to have fun with."

Hideaway Resort was a special destination for Kinksters—rather than a club, it was an entire island where they could indulge in their kinky sides at any time of day or night without risking judgment or misunderstandings. It had all the amenities of an all-inclusive resort, but like a kink club, it also had Doms and submissives on staff who were happy to scene with visitors. No sexual contact was required, but it was allowed. She could easily find a Dom to scene with—possibly a fellow guest at the resort or one of the Doms working there.

Just because she'd be yearning for a very specific Dom, who was also going to be on the trip, meant nothing.

Master Brian, who just happened to be the groom's best man, was not for her.

He was a Daddy Dom. She was a sub who refused to call anyone but her father 'Daddy.'

Neither of them was willing to compromise. It didn't matter how attracted they were to each other; that was a barrier that couldn't be overcome unless one of them was willing to give.

Rae was not that person.

Neither was Brian, apparently.

So, they were going to be the only singles on a bachelor/bachelorette trip to a kinky island resort, and they were definitely not going to be scening with each other. They'd have to find other partners. And she'd have to work on not being jealous when she had no right to be.

It would have been easier if she and Damian hadn't broken up not that long ago and she'd been able to bring him with her, but it was for the best. They hadn't wanted the same things, either, and she hadn't been as unhappy to see him go as she should have been, which told her how deep her feelings had gone—or not gone.

"We don't have to spend any time doing group activities if you don't want to," Domi insisted, which was the topic that had spurred this particular conversation. "I'll talk to Mitch about it."

"Absolutely not." Rae shook her head, scowling at her bestie. "The whole point of this was that you and Mitch wanted to be able to do a Jack-and-Jill shower so you could enjoy being at the resort together. *Not* doing things separately just because you think I can't get along with Brian for a week."

"It's not that you guys can't get along. It's just that I don't want you to be unhappy while we're there." Reaching across the kitchen table, Domi put her hand over Rae's, her short curls bouncing around her face as she leaned forward. "I want you to have fun."

Rae rolled her eyes to cover up the sudden surge of emotion. She and Domi had been friends for such a long time, and it was moments like this that it really hit her hard. Because of that, she was even more determined that Domi had a good time—and to prove that she was just fine being single.

"Stop worrying about me. It's your wedding and your party, and it's literally my job as your maid of honor to make sure you're the one having a good time. Not the other way around."

"Is this your way of telling me you want me to be a bridezilla?" Domi snickered, giving Rae's hand a squeeze before pulling back so she could take a sip of her tea.

"You couldn't be a bridezilla if you tried." Not that Domi was indecisive, but she made it a point to take literally everything under consideration that could possibly affect anyone in her wedding party or coming to her wedding. Which was probably why she was so intent on making sure Rae was going to be okay at Hideaway. It was the one possible obstacle left. "This is my way of telling you that you're worrying about nothing. Everything's going to be fine, and we're going to have an amazing trip."

She pushed the printed itinerary back across to Domi, who blew out a short breath. She finally looked like she might be convinced, though.

"Well, if you're sure."

"I'm sure," Rae said firmly. "It was very sweet of you to feel like you needed to run it by me beforehand but also unnecessary. The week is going to be about you and Mitch and finding a hot Dom to do filthy, filthy things to me."

That made Domi laugh and relax, the rest of the fight going out of her. Thank goodness.

Rae was speaking the truth, though. Domi had been worried about the idea of doing a whole big trip for the bachelor/bachelorette party, but everyone had reassured her and Mitch that they were thrilled to have the excuse to visit the resort. Almost everyone in their friend group had something to celebrate. Avery and Nick had just gotten engaged, Iris and Law had gotten engaged recently, and it wouldn't surprise her to find out that Kincaid and Zach were headed that way... although things had been a little tense between them lately. But they seemed to feel that a trip to reconnect was exactly what they needed.

Technically, Nick and Law weren't groomsmen, but since they were connected to Avery and Iris, Domi's bridesmaids, they'd been invited and had jumped on the chance. What kinky couple wouldn't want to get away to a kinky island resort with their fiancée?

Brian and Rae were there to make sure everything went smoothly for Mitch and Domi. That was her main goal for the week. She didn't have anything to celebrate, so she was going to make sure *their* celebration was everything they wanted it to be. It had not been a stressful wedding planning experience so far, and Rae was determined to make sure it remained that way.

"We're going to have an *amazing* time," she said firmly. "The itinerary looks great. The resort looks great. I am so excited to go."

The best part? It was the truth. Brian notwithstanding, she couldn't wait to see what Hideaway Resort had to offer. If she was lucky, there would be the opportunity for a little vacation fling that would make her forget about him altogether.

1

"And this is where you'll be staying." The little line of golf carts was slowly coming around a cul-de-sac of villas. His driver was a cute redhead named Ariel with a bright smile as she stopped in front of the pathway up to a small house. The oppressive heat of the island was enough to make him very glad for the little electric misting fan that had been handed to him upon arrival. He'd known it was going to be hot, but somehow, he hadn't expected it to be quite *this* hot. It might be more the humidity than the actual heat—Maryland was humid by August, but he hadn't been prepared for this level of moisture in the air.

"Great, thank you so much for the ride," he said, giving her his best smile. Which had absolutely nothing to do with the fact that right in front of him, Rae was being helped out of her golf cart by the far-too-handsome driver. Her braids were piled on top of her head to keep them off her neck and shoulders. Her dark skin gleamed bronze in the sunlight that danced over her exposed cleavage and back, and he didn't miss the way her driver's gaze slid over her rounded ass as she moved past him before he went to get her bags.

"Let's get you set up," Ariel chirped.

Brian yanked his attention back from Rae and her driver, who was now getting *her* bags from the cart. On the other side of him, Iris and Law were headed into their own villa. Their group took up the entire cul-de-sac, with Mitch and Domi in the first villa, followed by Zach and Kincaid, Rae, him, Iris and Law, and finally Avery and Nick.

Why he had to end up next to Rae... well, what was done was done. He sure as hell wasn't going to make a fuss about it. This trip was not about him. It was about making sure Mitch and Domi had a fun, relaxing time before their wedding. For the others, it was about allowing them to celebrate their recent engagements—or in the case of Kincaid and Zach, to hopefully work through their shit.

He was worried about those two.

There wasn't much he could do about that at the moment, though. What he could do was go into his villa and not cause any issues right at the beginning of the trip, just because being right next to Rae made his skin crawl with hyperawareness of her nearness. He could deal with it for a few days. And nights.

"Here's the main room, then the bedroom is right over here," Ariel said, waving her hand as she led him through the villa.

Brian was holding his own suitcase—he didn't care if she worked here, there was no way he was letting a woman nearly half his size carry his suitcase—as he followed her into the bedroom, setting it next to the closet. He'd unpack later.

"Bathroom is right here, and you have a walkout to the balcony for your beach view from both the bedroom and the main room."

"Everything looks great, thank you," he said honestly. The cool air inside the rooms was a relief. He wasn't sure he'd be spending much time on the balcony, though he couldn't help the impulse to step out and see the view... and as he did so, he saw movement out of the corner of his eye.

Though there were quite a few lush branches of greenery in the way, that didn't stop him from recognizing Rae... also out on her balcony. She seemed to sense him at the same time, turning her head, and their gazes clashed. Then she turned away and went back inside.

Brian's muscles relaxed. He hadn't even realized they'd tensed until he felt them unclench.

Dammit.

"Alright then, if you need anything, just call the front desk," Ariel said cheerfully behind him.

"Thank you so much," he said, turning back around to go inside and give her a tip. After he'd done so, he looked out the bedroom window—which just happened to be the one facing Rae's villa.

Just like out on the balcony, there were plenty of plants obscuring the view... but not entirely. His window looked into her main room, which had a glass door leading onto the wrap-around balcony. The curtains could be drawn, but right now, they were wide open, and if he positioned himself just right, he could see straight in through the tree branches to her balcony and past it into her villa.

Where she was standing with her hand on the arm of her driver.

Fuck.

The surge of jealousy that went through him was not promising. He thought he'd gotten past this when she'd been dating Master Damian. And it wasn't like he'd been celibate... he'd dated, too. It was just that nothing had come of any of it, and now they were both single again and here with a bunch of couples.

Taking a deep breath, he looked up at the ceiling and let it out slowly. That was probably the real issue here. Knowing they were the only two singles, it felt inevitable they should be paired up together... but they already knew that wouldn't work. Setting himself up for rejection again was not on his to-do list.

He'd tried in the past. After being one of the Doms during her Introduction classes at Marquis, the local kink club they both belonged to, he'd gotten one glorious night with her. Yes, it had been a discipline scene she'd earned through bad behavior, but he'd also seen it as his chance to show her how good being his babygirl could be.

He thought he'd done it, too.

But the next day, she'd never texted him back after he texted her, much less picked up his calls. The next time they'd run into each other at the club, she'd acted like the night had never happened.

Brian had gotten the message even before she'd started dating Master Damian.

Just thinking about trying again made his chest hurt. He'd learned his lesson in the past about giving people too many chances, and Rae had already had far too many from him.

Tearing his gaze away from her, Brian went to unpack his suitcase.

---

*R*AE

What does one wear to dinner at a kinky island resort?

Rae sifted through her suitcase. Since the weather was supposed to be hot as fuck, she'd been able to pack a lot more than she needed since no layers were needed and no cold weather clothes, which was both good and bad. Good because she had options, bad because she had too many options, and she wasn't sure what to go with.

Fetwear?

A cute dress?

Shorts and a tank top?

Sighing, she pulled out her phone and went to the girls' group chat to see what everyone else was wearing.

Within a few minutes, she had her answer—cute dress.

Okay, check.

Digging through her clothes, she grinned with triumph as she located her blue dress with the thin straps, built-in bra, and flippy skirt. It was cute, sexy, and easy access. Not that anyone was going to be accessing anything yet, but if the group decided to go to the Dungeon section of the resort after dinner, she wouldn't feel totally out of place. And she'd even be able to scene if she wanted to.

The cute driver, Jose, had indicated he would be more than happy to show her around the resort if she wanted an escort. She'd gotten pretty strong Dom vibes from him, though he'd been very respectful about his offer. Not at all like the overly bossy Daddy Dom who was in the villa next to her.

Maybe she'd find Jose later and take him up on his offer. Help clear Brian out of her head.

If she could after that little balcony eye lock.

Not that she was going out on the balcony again anytime soon.

Getting dressed, she did her hair and makeup, pulling her hair back into a high ponytail so the ends brushed against her exposed upper back. Makeup was easy—natural eye and cheeks, with a lush red lip. By the time she was done, she was feeling pretty damn hot and a lot more confident about seeing Brian.

This wasn't her usual look, but it also wasn't a look he'd be into. She knew that she dressed like a baby girl sometimes, but that was just her aesthetic, not her kink. She'd deliberately packed for this trip so her outfits wouldn't be like a mating call to the solo Daddy.

Walking out into the main room, she happened to look out the window and realized she could see into his bedroom. Not the whole bedroom, but she saw a flash of movement as he walked by the window—shirtless. She could see his shoulders, so she knew he wasn't wearing a shirt, even though she couldn't see the rest of him.

Maybe he's naked.

Maybe you're a perv. Stop watching him!

She wasn't trying to perv. She just wanted to make sure she couldn't see too much... otherwise, she might need to tell him to close his blinds. In fact, she should probably go close her blinds just so she didn't inadvertently give Zach and Kincaid a show at any point.

Doing an abrupt about-face, she went back into her room and looked out the window, just to see, but the vegetation on the left of her villa must be thicker than on the right because she couldn't see them at all. There was just less greenery between her and Brian's villa. Because, of course, the universe was conspiring against her that way.

Sighing, Rae closed the blinds, anyway, just for verisimilitude, before heading back out to her main room. She peeked through the window again, but there was no more movement. Turning, she tried to figure out how much of her space he'd be able to see.

Most of it, possibly? She was pretty sure he'd have a decent view of the couch. If he looked out the window, he'd certainly see her.

There was a curtain she could draw across the large expanse of glass if she wanted... but she didn't. Instead, she went outside to meet up with everyone for dinner. This time, when the golf carts arrived, there were fewer of them since there was no luggage to contend with. Rae sat beside the driver—not Jose—with Mitch and Domi behind her in the first golf cart. She couldn't see how everyone else arranged themselves.

Driving through the resort to the restaurant was just as nice as the drive in had been. The lush greenery was everywhere, lining all the pathways and hiding most of the small villas and places they passed.

There were some larger buildings interspersed throughout, the walls of the buildings a dark sandy color with roofs several shades darker and trimmed in blue. Ocean-blue shutters adorned the windows, just like the villas, standing out against the pale walls.

They pulled up to one of the larger buildings.

"Here we are," the driver said, jumping out to help her step out. Mitch was doing the same with Domi in the back. Domi hopped out, and he curved his arm around her, pulling her against him rather than stepping away and dropping a kiss on her nose.

Rae sighed.

They were so fucking cute, it was stupid.

"Okay, lovebirds, plenty of time for that after dinner," Iris teased, coming up beside them. The pretty brunette was wearing a dress similar to Rae's, though her skirt was a little longer and a little tighter, with slits up the sides to nearly her hips. "We need to fuel up. I'm starving!"

Laughing, Mitch and Domi broke apart as Law came up behind Iris to corral his girlfriend. Grinning, Rae kept up with Domi, comparing notes on their villas as they went into the restaurant. It sounded like they were all the same, though as the soon-to-be bride and groom, Domi and Mitch had some extra goodies waiting for them in theirs—champagne, chocolate-covered strawberries, and a welcome basket of fruit, crackers, and cookies.

Domi seemed happy and relaxed, which was good. Not that anything had been going wrong with the wedding planning, but it was still a huge event—though Rae suspected this trip might have been the cause of some of her stress. Domi asked about Rae being next to Brian, but Rae reassured her that it was no problem. The villas were completely private, after all.

She didn't mention the realization that he was able to see right into her living room or onto her balcony.

Domi didn't need to know either of those things.

Their table inside was already set up with menus, and the hostess led them straight to it, a beaming smile on her face. There was nothing about the restaurant décor that hinted at it being a kink resort, but when Rae looked around at the other diners, there were signs.

The foursome at the bar, where the men were sitting and the women gracefully kneeling at their feet, was one sign. As Rae watched, one of them reached down to feed his partner a tidbit of something.

The couple in the corner looked like a regular, cuddling couple... other than the fact the man was wearing a leather harness and collar in lieu of a shirt.

Not all the diners were exhibiting their kink, but enough were to make it clear this wasn't a regular beach resort.

Seating herself next to Domi, a frisson of awareness spread through Rae as the seat next to her was pulled out. Only one man made her react like that. It felt like the universe was mocking her as Brian sat next to her, and all the little hairs on the back of her arm stood up.

Really? He couldn't find a different seat?

But no, she realized, everyone was already sitting down around them, no one noticing that the only seat left open for Brian was the one next to her. Because why should they be thinking about that?

Gritting her teeth, Rae smiled at him as he sat down, ignoring the way her pulse suddenly sped up and the area between her legs suddenly tingled as his arm brushed against hers. There was no way she was going to say anything. It was literally the first meal of the trip. Domi was relaxed and enjoying herself, and asking him to move would make it clear that she was bothered by his presence.

The best thing to do was to show she wasn't bothered at all, which would also be best for making sure Domi didn't worry about her.

She smiled sweetly at Brian, pretending her entire body hadn't just come alive in a way that it hadn't been before.

"Settled into your villa, okay?" she asked.

He looked at her, his hazel eyes bemused.

"Yes, you?"

"Yup. Everything's great."

"Great."

That was about all the small talk with him she could muster for now, so she turned her attention to the menu, thankful for the distraction.

2

Sitting next to Rae was pure torture.

Note to self: move faster next time so I can choose my own damn seat.

It felt like the universe was shoving them together as the only two single people. Thankfully, no one else seemed to notice or think anything of it, but he was hyperaware of her beside him... and it was nearly impossible not to peek down the low-cut front of her dress to see the curve of her breast. He couldn't look at her without seeing it unless he kept his gaze trained strictly above neck level. Which was hard to do when her dress' neckline was so enticing.

Get it together, asshole.

Thankfully, there was plenty of group conversation to help distract him from the tempting beauty on his left—talking over the options for ordering, the server coming by to tell them the specials and take drink orders. Then, of course, once they had all their orders in, the conversation turned to talk of the week.

Brian leaned back, resisting the urge to put his arm along the back of Rae's chair. If she'd been any other woman, he would have. But he couldn't. It felt too... close. Zach was on his right, and Kincaid already had his arm along the back of Zach's chair. Brian felt scrunched in, but there was nothing he could do about it. He couldn't spread out.

"Tomorrow, we have our spa day, right?" Avery asked, looking across the table at Domi. She was practically bouncing in her seat. As Sous Chef and Executive Chef at the same restaurant—which was also attached to their kink club—she and Nick hardly ever got to get away together, much less for almost an entire week. Nick had his elbow resting on the back of her chair, his hand buried in her blonde hair, a fond expression on his face as he watched her profile.

All of which made Brian even more aware of his inability to put his own arm out because he and Rae didn't have that kind of relationship.

Being single in a group of couples wasn't fun. Being single in a group of couples where the only other single was someone he was desperately attracted to and couldn't have was infinitely worse. For a whole week. At least they would be separated tomorrow.

"Spa day for the ladies and beach day for us, right?" Brian asked. Having the first day separated from the women would be good. He could get a hold of being so close to Rae without being *so close to Rae.*

"Yes. We're thinking of doing a little volleyball," Mitch replied, leaning forward to see past Domi and Rae. "There's supposed to be some nets set up and equipment for anyone to use."

"Sounds good," Kincaid replied. "A little friendly competition." The heated look he shot Zach was filled with promise, and Brian wouldn't be surprised if they had a little side bet going on tomorrow. It looked like getting away from home was already doing them some good, which was a relief.

They made a good couple, but Zach struggled with his sexuality, not to mention his needs as a sadist and occasional Dominant. Kincaid was completely comfortable being bisexual and was always the Dominant in their relationship, so they had to find other ways for Zach to get his needs met. Brian hoped they could make things work, though, and not just because he didn't want a shake-up in their friend group. In so many ways, they were really good together. They just seemed to be missing some essential piece that would help everything click into place. He just wished he knew what it was so he could help.

Maybe this trip would do the trick.

Besides, he couldn't even help himself, so he wasn't really in a position to be trying to help out someone else's relationship.

"I can't wait for tomorrow," Rae said, reaching over with one hand to rub the shoulder closest to Brian. "I need a massage so bad. It's been way too long since my last one."

She's not talking to you, he told his cock, which had perked up with interest at her desire for a massage. First of all, she wasn't talking about getting her pussy massaged, and second of all, he would probably be the last person she'd accept a massage from, even if she wasn't getting a professional one tomorrow.

Despite his first instinct being to reach over and start massaging the spot she was rubbing, he managed to keep his hands to himself. It was something he would do for anyone... anyone but Rae. Because the opportunity for misinterpretation was high. Not to mention, if his arousal was stirring just thinking about giving her a massage, he could only imagine his body's reaction to actually getting his hands on her again.

Yeah.

He had a problem when it came to her, and he was willing to admit it—there just wasn't anything he could do about it.

"Is there a plan for after dinner?" he asked, mostly to help get his mind off Rae's need for a massage and the way her fingers were currently pressing into her shoulder. He could do a better job. If she'd let him.

Which she wouldn't.

Which drove him up the fucking wall.

"I think just exploring the resort," Domi said, glancing at Mitch for confirmation. He nodded, leaning in to leer at her.

"Exploring the resort... exploring you..." He winked.

"I'm pretty sure you've already explored every inch of me," she retorted with a roll of her eyes, though she couldn't keep the smile from her lips.

"I'd better make sure. Go over everything again, just in case I missed something the first time."

Next to Brian, Rae sighed. He glanced down at her but couldn't see her face. She was watching Mitch and Domi, so her head was turned away from him. He could guess, though. He bet she was feeling the same yearning he was.

Dammit.

If only he'd been able to convince her to give him a try, to let him be her Daddy Dom, this entire trip might be very different.

R_{AE}

Dinner next to Brian had been pure torture.

It had been hard to be right next to him among all the couples, all while thinking... *what if?* After sitting next to him for so long, it felt like her entire right side was tingly and extra sensitive. They hadn't been able to avoid brushing against each other multiple times, and every time someone to the right of her had talked, she'd had to look past him to see them.

Talk about brutal.

Fortunately, Domi seemed to think everything was fine, so Rae knew she was covering it up well. Linking arms with Rae, Domi gave her a little squeeze as they walked into the building with the Dungeon.

"I can't wait to see this place," Domi said, her eyes alight. On the other side of her, Mitch shot her a sideways glance before his apologetic gaze flicked up to Rae. She grinned back at him.

She fully expected him to steal Domi away at some point this evening. She would be disappointed if he didn't. And she was a big girl; she could entertain herself. She'd been going to Stronghold and Marquis long enough to be comfortable in a club situation, even if it was around strangers. Plus, she doubted all their friends were going to scene immediately.

Playing third wheel to whoever was available was also something she'd become accustomed to.

Everyone walked around as a group first, admiring the Dungeon. The building was huge, easily as big as Stronghold, but with quite a few differences. Stronghold was actually three floors, while the Hideaway Dungeon had two. The main floor was dedicated to the usual equipment, but there was a large hole in the ceiling where those on the second floor could look down onto the play area.

When they went up to the second floor, they found dedicated stations for certain kinks. Unsurprisingly, Law and Iris veered toward the station where a Dom was using electricity on his submissive. That was Law's favorite kink, and according to Iris, he was damn good at it.

Rae went with Domi and Mitch to watch a cupping scene, but when that was over, Mitch whisked Domi away down to the first floor where they could play—though not before dropping Rae next to Kincaid and Zach, who were watching a fire play scene. She stood to Kincaid's left while Zach was on the other side of him.

"This looks like fun," Kincaid murmured as the fire-whipping portion of the scene started. It was beautiful to watch, but Rae wasn't sure she would describe it as "fun."

Zach apparently agreed, going by his response. "I don't know who you think you're going to be whipping with fire, but it's definitely not me."

Beside her, Kincaid chuckled. She might be imagining things, but she thought his chuckle sounded a little strained. Before she could think too much about it, her gaze lifted to a newcomer on the other side of the scene...

Brian.

Watching her from across the moving strands of fire, his eyes were just as hot as the whip. Rae's insides clenched as their gazes clashed. He was watching her rather than the scene, and for a long moment, she couldn't look away. Eventually, she dropped her gaze, forcing herself to focus on the whipping.

The fact he could draw her attention when something so interesting was going on was a testament to how much he affected her.

And holy fuck, did she resent him for it. Dammit. He shouldn't be able to affect her like that.

But every time she raised her gaze and found him still looking at her, her body heated all over again, as if she was the one on fire. Honestly, it took a lot of the fun out of watching. She didn't want to be watching. She wanted to be doing.

Specifically, she wanted to be doing Brian.

Get over it, girlfriend. You know it's a bad idea.

They wanted two different things out of a relationship. He wanted to be her Daddy Dom, and the idea of calling someone Daddy made her want to gag. She was happy it worked for other people, but it was so not her kink. Just the idea of trying to call someone other than her father 'Daddy' made her stomach turn over with nausea. But that was what Brian wanted.

Needed.

She couldn't meet those needs, so she wasn't going to try when the outcome was inevitable heartbreak.

Right, because not trying is so much less heartbreaking.

If only he would give a little on what she called him... but as far as she could tell, it was an integral part of his needs. She'd happily call him Sir. Or Master Brian. Just nothing that implied a fatherly relationship.

She couldn't do it.

Which meant she couldn't do him. Again.

It had been hard enough walking away from him after nothing more than a play scene. She couldn't imagine how much harder it would be after actually dating.

The Dom running the scene finally finished, stepping up to his submissive and running his hand down her back, leaning forward to check in on her. The moment was heart-achingly intimate. It made Rae yearn for things she couldn't have right now. Even if she did meet someone down here, it wasn't like they could start a real relationship.

Her mood was dipping, despite being in a kinky Dungeon resort. It was time to call it a night and get some sleep, and hopefully, tomorrow, she'd have a better outlook on life... and this trip. Especially after getting a massage. Tonight, she was tired from traveling, unpacking, and... sitting next to Brian during dinner. That's why she was struggling.

Yawning, she stretched and smiled at Kincaid and Zach. The audience around them was already breaking up.

"I think I'm going to head back to my room," she told them. "I'm more tired than I realized."

Immediately, both men were frowning down at her. Zach might switch for Kincaid, but it was like her statement had flicked a switch, and he'd gone into full Dom. His and Kincaid's questions overlapped on top of each other.

"Are you okay?"

"Are you sure?"

"I'm fine," she reassured both of them. "Just tired and not really feeling up to meeting someone new and negotiating and all that. You know how it is with all the travel and everything."

"As long as you're sure you're okay." Kincaid was still frowning, and Zach wasn't much better. The two of them were tall, looming presences that made her feel all petite and protected, which was very nice in some circumstances, but right now, it just made her feel even more tired.

"I'm good." She gave them a cheeky thumbs up. "Seriously, guys. Go have fun." She yawned again, letting her jaw stretch as she covered up with her hand, so they could see she was serious. Not that she was faking the yawn—it was very real—but she might be exaggerating it a bit.

The two Doms glanced at each other. Yeesh. It was a good thing they were together instead of tag-teaming some poor woman. This amount of bossy testosterone would be hard to counter.

"I don't think you should go back to your villa on your own," Kincaid said. "We can walk you back."

"Absolutely not. You guys should stay here and enjoy yourselves," she said, crossing her arms stubbornly over her chest and shaking her head. "I don't want to interrupt your night."

"It's not an interruption," Zach countered. "We can always come back here after. It's not that big a deal."

"It's also not that big a deal for me to go back to my villa on my own. There are golf carts right out front, with drivers. It's not like I'm going to be all on my own. This isn't Stronghold or Marquis; you don't have to make sure I get out to my car okay, much less back to my villa." It wasn't like the clubs back in D.C.; they didn't need to chaperone her or anything. She hated the idea of inconveniencing them, but the desire to go was getting stronger.

They both frowned harder at her. Stubborn Doms.

"You're going back to the villas?" Brian's voice came from behind her.

Rae somehow managed not to groan. Of course, he'd come over and heard the discussion because that was how her life worked. Though the fact he'd been staring at her from across the scene should have clued her into the fact that he was paying more attention to her than he should be.

"Yes, I'm tired and need some time to decompress, unwind, and get a good night's sleep," she said firmly, turning slightly to include him in the conversation without actually facing him. "Everyone else can stay here. It's *fine*."

"I can take her back," Brian said over her head to the two Doms, as if she hadn't *just said* it was fine. "You guys stay here."

"Okay, great, that works," Kincaid said at the same time Zach thanked Brian.

Great. Decision made. It seemed like her input on what *she was doing* wasn't needed at all. Thoroughly annoyed, Rae turned on her heel and stomped toward the front door.

Freaking Doms always thinking they knew best.

3

Brian

Following the clearly annoyed Rae out of the Dungeon, Brian couldn't help but be a bit amused when she obviously was trying to get to a golf cart and take off without waiting for him.

"Hold on," he called out to the driver. "I'm headed to the same street."

The 'street' and the area in front of the building were well lit, so he had no problem seeing the glare Rae turned on him. The driver didn't see her expression, though, so she smiled sweetly. For a moment, he thought Rae might try to tell him to take another cart, but it really didn't make sense. One thing about Rae was she was willing to make a fuss when she felt it was warranted, but she didn't like inconveniencing people.

The moment passed, and she proved him right. Huffing, Rae sat down in the front seat, leaving Brian to slide onto the bench behind her. Which was fine. The important thing was that she wasn't headed off on her own the first night in a new place. Especially a kinky place. Though they'd been carefully vetted before being able to make the reservation on the island, which was reassuring, there was always the possibility of someone behaving badly.

Sure, there were security measures in place, but Brian intended to ensure they weren't needed.

"Hi, I'm Kia," the driver said cheerfully, glancing over her shoulder at Brian to include him in her introduction. She had a similar coloring to Rae, but unlike Rae, she kept her hair in two cute poufs on either side of her head. The look suited her. "So, you two are part of the same group?"

"Yes, we're here for our friends' bachelor and bachelorette party," Rae answered her. Because he was sitting behind them, he noticed that Kia relaxed, which made him approve of her even more. He got the sudden feeling that if Rae had answered negatively, Kia would have stopped the cart immediately, and he'd have had a whole new set of problems to deal with. "He has the villa right next to mine."

Brian turned his head, looking out into the darkened greenery to hide his smile just in case either woman looked back. The long-suffering tone Rae was using could have been insulting, but he liked it because he liked knowing he was affecting her just as much as she was affecting him.

He liked to torture himself that way.

"Did you just get here today?" Kia asked.

"Yeah." Rae yawned, and he was fairly sure she wasn't doing it just for effect. She was actually tired. He locked his jaw against his own threatening yawn. That shit was contagious. "I'm exhausted. We're here for a bit, though, and tomorrow the ladies are going to the spa."

"Oh, you're going to love that," Kia enthused.

Brian sat back against the bench, watching the lights through the greenery while the ladies chatted about the spa's offerings. He was feeling the tiredness of travel, too, and since he didn't have a partner to jump right into activities with, he'd already decided he wanted to leave the club and take a night to decompress and recoup. It had just been a fortuitous happenstance that Rae wanted to go at the same time.

By the time they reached the villas, he cheerfully hopped out and wished both ladies a good night. Rae eyed him suspiciously as she got out, as if she thought he was going to say something to her.

"Goodnight," he said, giving her a wave before turning away.

"Goodnight."

He resisted the urge to turn around as she called after him. He really was tired and planning on resting and going to bed. Rae had made it safely back to the villa. His responsibility as a fellow wedding party member ended there.

Though he did pause at his door, waiting until she made her way into her villa before entering his own. He couldn't entirely ignore his protective instincts, even though everything told him she would be fine.

Which was also why, a few minutes later, he glanced through the window he knew looked into her villa. Just to check on her. What he was not expecting to see was a very naked Rae on the couch, hands on her bare breasts, legs spread, and pussy pointed straight at him. Brian froze as all the blood in his body surged to his groin, emptying his brain of all thoughts.

What the fuck is she doing?

What the fuck am I doing?

Standing there like a creeper, that's what he was doing.

Look away, asshole.

As if she knew he was standing there, one hand moved away from her breast and dropped down to caress her pussy. There was a roaring noise in Brian's ears at the show she was putting on.

Wait.

She *was* putting on a show.

Could she see him? Did she know he was watching?

Did she want him watching?

I shouldn't be watching.

He wasn't sure she knew he could see into her villa, which meant he shouldn't be watching. Even if it did look like she was putting on a show. Finally managing to tear his gaze away from the sight of her fingers dipping into the slick mauve folds of her pussy, Brian set his jaw and stalked to his shower. He didn't bother trying to make it cold.

Instead, he set it to hot and stepped in, the steam rising up around him as he grasped his cock in one hand and closed his eyes.

The hot water cascaded over his skin as he began to pump, bracing himself with his other arm against the wall and resting his forehead against it while the image of her in her villa, playing with herself, played on repeat in his head.

He knew what that pussy felt like.

Knew how it tasted.

His mouth watered, wishing he could taste her again.

Groaning, Brian shuddered as he squeezed his cock tightly, his climax coming fast and hard and spilling onto the floor of the shower to be washed immediately away. If only he could wash his attraction to Rae away so easily.

RAE

He wasn't watching anymore.

Disappointment fluttered through her.

Though, truthfully, she wasn't sure he'd been watching at all. Her position on the couch made it hard for her to see. But she liked the idea.

Asshole.

Jumping into the cart with her because she was a sub who needed a chaperone back to the villas, then acting as if he didn't care at all once they got back here. He had barely even looked at her.

Which had inspired her to try to make sure he couldn't help but see her.

And she thought he had.

Pussy still buzzing, she got up and went into her bedroom. She'd brought her own assortment of toys for the trip because a girl never knew when she was going to need to take care of herself. Grabbing her trusty vibrator, she plopped down on the bed and got back into position.

She could almost imagine she was still out there in the main room on the couch with her legs spread open, touching herself to tease her next-door neighbor. She could pretend he'd not only seen her but that the reason he'd stopped watching was because he was running over to her villa, determined to get his own hands on her, to be the one to make her cum.

"Oh... fuck... Brian..." She ran the vibrator up and down between her pussy lips, buzzing the length against her swollen clit before pushing it inside her. The fluttering ears of the rabbit on the clit stimulator were currently off as she teased herself, pushing the shaft of the vibrator inside herself and stretching herself open, all while pretending it was Brian's cock.

Pretending he was on top of her, pinning her down to the sofa, and calling her a naughty girl for putting on such a show. For teasing him like that. Rae whimpered as her pussy spasmed around the hard toy, her hips pushing upward. She could feel her ass tingle, as if in anticipation of a spanking... but real punishment wasn't going to be coming her way tonight.

Instead, she could only tease herself, shuddering as her need rose higher and higher until she finally turned on the clit attachment. The buzzing vibrations on her swollen nub immediately pushed her over the edge. Rae cried out Brian's name again as she came, writhing on the bed with the toy deep inside her. Her toes curled as wave after wave of pleasure pulsed through her, sending her nearly into overload as the intense vibrations became too much.

Yet, it still wasn't as good as her night with him.

Damn him.

Rae turned off the toy and stared up at the ceiling, panting as her breath came back to her. Her pussy spasmed around the quiet vibrator, still feeling full, satisfied, yet... incomplete.

It wasn't fair that she couldn't get him out of her head. That she couldn't forget that night and how good it had felt to be his babygirl for just a little bit. Because that wasn't what she wanted. They weren't going to work together.

Sighing, she slid the vibrator out of her and started to get cleaned up for the night. Did she also walk through the main room in nothing but her bonnet? Yes, yes, she did. Though she couldn't tell if he was watching or not. When she peeked through the window, it looked like his whole villa was dark.

Which meant he could be standing there staring at her, and she wouldn't even know it.

Her skin tingled.

Bad Rae.

Clearly, she needed to get laid.

Good thing she was at a kinky island resort complete with a club. The fact her brain kept bringing up Brian was likely because he was one of the few options she knew of. Sure, there had been the driver the first day, but they hadn't really clicked, although he'd been cute.

There would be other Doms, though. And tomorrow, she'd have the energy to actually hang out around the club and find one.

She could have a hot island fling and get Brian out of her head completely.

Yawning, Rae stretched and turned out the lights. The sound of a golf cart outside had her peeking to see what was going on—it looked like Kincaid and Zach were coming back now, too. They didn't look like they'd had fun after she left, though.

Not that she could hear what they were saying, but Zach stormed up the walk and into the villa ahead of Kincaid, who stood next to the street for a long moment, staring up at the stars. Rae chewed her lower lip as she watched. Should she go out to him? The way he was standing there, slightly slumped, wasn't like the confident Dom she knew at all, and she wanted to give him a big hug.

If he and Zach were fighting like this, it was only a matter of time before they broke up. Were they trying to hold it together for this trip? Or even for Mitch and Domi's wedding?

Her chest hurt just thinking about it.

Just when she was about to grab a robe and go outside to see if Kincaid was okay, he gave himself a little shake and headed to his and Zach's villa. There was no way she was going to go knock on their door—approaching Kincaid while he was outside would have been one thing—so that was the end of that impulse.

She hoped everything was alright with them, but she also hoped whatever they had going on didn't affect Mitch and Domi's enjoyment of this trip. Which then made her feel horribly selfish that she was concerned about that instead of Kincaid and Zach, but... well, from what she'd just seen, it looked like they were already a done deal, even if they hadn't admitted it yet.

Which was going to be a bummer, regardless, but this trip was supposed to be about Mitch and Domi. She'd have to keep an eye on things, be there if either Kincaid or Zach needed someone, but also to keep it from affecting this week.

Brian on one side, Zach and Kincaid on the other... Rae sighed as she made her way back to the bedroom. She was definitely going to need her sleep.

4

———————

RAE

Any signs of trouble in paradise between Zach and Kincaid were gone by breakfast. The two were sitting next to each other, Kincaid's arm around Zach, while Zach toyed with his boyfriend's fingertips, looking like they didn't have a care in the world. She was probably the only one who knew it was a front, and she was going to keep it that way.

At least this morning, she'd managed to sit all the way down the table away from Brian. She was wedged between Avery and Iris and on the same side of the table as him, so she couldn't see him at all. Which was a relief.

Taunting him last night—if he had been watching—had been fun, but she hadn't thought ahead to the morning. Without knowing whether or not he'd seen her, she wasn't sure how to act around him. Though, if he had seen her, he was definitely acting like he hadn't.

If he had seen her and was acting like it was nothing, that ticked her off.

Maybe he hadn't seen her at all, and he wasn't acting.

Her head was a freaking mess, and it was all her fault.

I shouldn't have done it.

Sometimes, she acted before she thought things all the way through, especially when she was tired. Granted, she never did anything too crazy, but she couldn't help but wish she'd thought about what this morning would be like before she'd gotten herself all laid out and naked on the couch.

Though, if she just knew whether he'd seen her, she wouldn't be so bothered by it. But since she didn't know, she just had to act completely normal, as if he definitely hadn't seen her.

Dammit.

She wanted to know. She hated that she couldn't tell. She'd hate even more if he *had* seen her and *knew* that pretending he hadn't was driving her crazy.

Stop thinking about it!

She was making herself crazy.

It was sheer relief when breakfast was over and the groups separated.

"I am so looking forward to today," Avery said, sliding her arm through Rae's as they headed down the path to the spa. While they could have taken a golf cart, they'd all felt like walking, and the morning wasn't nearly as hot and humid as the afternoon had been. "I never get to do stuff like this." She was practically bouncing as she walked, which helped Rae refocus her attention on her friends.

"You need to tell your boss to give you better hours," Rae teased. Avery's fiancé was also technically her boss. Since they both worked at a restaurant, he was also kind of limited in the hours he could give her.

It made it hard for Avery to make it to a lot of the group stuff since she was often working in the evenings, though they did their best to schedule things for her nights off. Well, her nights off when Nick didn't also have off, since when they both had off, they spent their evening at one of the kink clubs they all belonged to.

"Yeah, my boss sucks. You should definitely tell him I said that, too." Avery giggled, her eyes sparkling, and Rae couldn't help but laugh. Avery wasn't exactly 'brat' material, but she was apparently angling for a funishment—a fun punishment—now that she was on vacation.

"I'll let Olivia know."

"She is not my boss!" Avery squealed at the mention of the Dominatrix who managed Marquis. Technically, she wasn't really in charge of the kitchen, but it was still fun to tease Avery.

"Who's not your boss?" Domi came up on Rae's other side, while Iris joined Avery's other side.

"I'm trying to get a spanking from Nick, and Rae is over here threatening me with Olivia." Avery shook her head mournfully, giving Rae big doe eyes. She was very good at looking sweet and innocent. "And here I thought we were friends."

"Hey, I was just trying to give you what you need," Rae teased back. "You said to tell your boss."

"I also said 'him,' not 'her'!"

"Semantics." Rae giggled as Avery elbowed her in the side.

They were all laughing as they got to the end of the path to the spa building. A few hours later, Rae felt like a whole new woman. She'd been rubbed, oiled, and buffed to within an inch of her life, and she was both sleepy and invigorated. All the stress from the morning—the desire to know whether Brian had been watching last night—had disappeared under the firm fingers of her masseuse.

It really didn't matter.

She wasn't going to spend her whole week focusing on him.

She was going to keep an eye on Kincaid and Zach, and she was going to find a vacation fling—possibly—and everything was going to be wonderful. Even if she couldn't find a fling, she'd find a couple of one-night or one-scene partners.

"I need food. And a cocktail. A fruity frozen one." Iris grinned as they sat down for lunch on a patio overlooking the ocean. The day was definitely heating up, but they all had wanted to sit where they could hear the waves.

"Frozen and fruity sounds like a good idea," Rae agreed. They all ended up ordering different ones and trying each other's. The mango was her favorite. Talk devolved to weddings, of course, but Rae was feeling so good after the spa, she couldn't feel left out, even though she was the only one not planning one.

She'd be perfectly fine being a bridesmaid at all of them. And at least with Law and Iris, Brian wouldn't be a groomsman, so she'd get a break there. Law had his own set of close friends. The groups had been spending some time together, but for Law and Iris' wedding, Law's friends, Connor and Q, were going to be his groomsmen, and his friend Asad was his best man.

Sadly, there were no potential hookups for her there, either. Asad and Q both had girlfriends, and Connor, well, he wasn't a Daddy Dom exactly... He seemed like he was into kink, yet he hadn't really found his place in it yet. At any rate, there was no spark between the two of them.

She sighed, her gaze scanning across the beachfront. There were plenty of people out there, some of them in bathing suits, some of them nude, but she didn't see the guys.

"What are you looking at?" Domi asked, leaning over as if to try to see what might have caught Rae's eye.

"A hookup," she said, giving her friend a half-hearted grin. "Sorry, I'll pay closer attention... what are we talking about now? Flowers?"

"No, no, let's talk about getting you a hookup," Iris said, twisting in her seat to survey the possibilities out on the beach. "We've got plenty of time for wedding talk. You've only got a few nights to find a hookup."

"She'll probably have better luck in the Dungeon this evening," Avery pointed out, though she also turned to look around. "There were plenty of single Doms walking around last night."

"Yeah, but it's fun to check out the eye candy now." Rae's gaze slipped over to the small group of men walking up to the tiki bar that was just off to the side of the patio. They all had a similar look to them—white, blond, in their thirties. They looked like they could be brothers. "What about the one in the pink shorts?"

None of her friends were discreet as they all looked over at the four men, but fortunately, the men didn't notice. Or if they did, they didn't react. Maybe they were used to being ogled. They were all pretty good-looking.

"He looks douche-y," Domi said, wrinkling her nose.

"Douche-y doesn't matter to me right now unless it's coming out of me." Rae sighed.

Silence fell around the table, and she blinked as she realized what she had just said. The frozen fruity drinks were hitting her harder than she'd thought... but it was still true.

She cleared her throat and pointed to herself.

"Drunk."

Iris pointed at herself.

"Horrified."

They all cracked up.

"Shh, shh, they're looking at us," Avery whispered, waving her hand even as she kept giggling. Unfortunately, her whispered request just made them all laugh harder.

They were saved by the food showing up at their table. Thank goodness. Rae apparently needed something in her stomach to soak up the alcohol before she even thought about attempting approaching pink shorts.

BRIAN

"Take that!" Mitch jumped into the air, spiking the ball down right between Zach and Kincaid, who both dove for it and missed. Mitch, Brian, and Law all jumped in the air, whooping. That had been the final point to win in the closest match they'd had all morning. They'd all agreed that this was going to be the final game, which meant winners took all.

"Dammit!" Zach pounded his fist against the sand and sighed, falling back. Laying on the sand next to him, Kincaid reached out to pat his shoulder consolingly while Nick stood over both of them, shaking his head in amusement.

"We almost had it," Nick said reassuringly, chuckling. Unlike

Zach and Kincaid, he didn't seem to be taking their loss that hard. They really had been close; it had all come down to the final point.

Still, everyone liked winning better than losing, and Zach and Kincaid could be more competitive than some. Definitely more than Nick, who was taking their loss with a lot more grace than the other two.

"Almost doesn't count." Kincaid made a face, pushing himself up and turning to grab Zach's hand so they could pull each other to their feet in a practiced move. Something simmered in the air between them before they turned away from each other, Zach clearing his throat as he stretched.

"Who's ready for lunch?" Mitch asked, which pretty much guaranteed that everyone was going to say yes. No one wanted to tell the groom no during his bachelor party after all, even though he was hardly pushy about it.

"Lunch sounds good." Law ducked under the net, rubbing his hand over his bald head. "I could use a break from the sun."

"You could use some sunscreen," Brian countered, holding out the tube. Law eyed it disdainfully, and Brian rolled his eyes. He was pretty sure Law had put some on before coming out, but he seemed to find it a point of pride not to reapply. "When was the last time you were actually *in* the Philippines, dealing with the sun there?"

Huffing, Law took the bottle and muttered a gruff 'thanks,' which made Mitch snicker.

"You'll be thankful later when you don't have to have Iris rubbing aloe onto your head," Brian said.

"Maybe we should get you a hat," Mitch added, grinning when Law scowled at him.

"Maybe we should get *you* a hat."

"Now, now, boys, no fighting, no biting," Brian said mildly, taking the tube back from Law and passing it over to Mitch.

"Yes, Daddy," Mitch and Law chorused, causing everyone except Brian to crack up.

Even he couldn't keep the slight smile from his face, despite not wanting to encourage them. Being called that also made his chest tighten because it was another reminder of Rae. He'd managed to go all morning without thinking about her, and it didn't make sense that she'd pop into his head over a title that she refused to call him by, but that's what happened.

Pushing her back out of his thoughts—where she didn't belong—he gave Law a stern look. The formerly grouchy Dom would have never made that joke a year ago.

"Iris has been a bad influence on you." Brian shook his head sadly. Truthfully, she'd been a fantastic influence, but he wasn't going to say that right now.

"I like sassy Law," Mitch countered, slinging his arm across Law's shoulder. "Come on, let's go get lunch."

"I'm not sassy," Law grumbled.

As they walked, Brian glanced over his shoulder. Kincaid and Zach seemed to be having some kind of intense discussion. Not wanting to draw attention to them, he turned back around. They'd work it out. Though he'd need to keep an eye on things if they were going to keep this up all week.

Not just because he didn't want Mitch and Domi's week disrupted by someone else's relationship issues but also because they were both his friends.

Thankfully, Mitch and Law were too busy bickering—and Nick trying to play peacekeeper between them—to notice what was going on behind them. By the time they reached the restaurant, whatever was happening between Kincaid and Zach seemed to be resolved. Or they were pretending it was.

5

———————

RAE

How could an afternoon shower and nap go so horribly wrong?

Well, she didn't even get to the nap, but that was part of what was wrong. After lunch, Domi had been yawning, and they'd all decided that a siesta during the heat of the day was the way to go. Plus, Rae was the only one who'd gotten to bed at a decent hour the night before. The rest of them had stayed in the Dungeon until late. Even with that, she felt kind of tired, so she figured a nap would help.

At the very least, she'd lay in bed and read. Rest up for the night ahead since she was planning on finding a Dom and, possibly, getting laid. Kink didn't have to include sex, but that's what she wanted right now. She wanted a spanking and a dick, not necessarily in that order.

Instead, she got in the shower and screamed as the showerhead nearly nailed her when it shot off of the base. The water sprayed everywhere before she managed to turn around and get it shut off... except it wouldn't shut off. The handle just spun in place, the water shooting out in every direction, and it seemed like it was getting stronger rather than weaker.

Shit. It was going to flood the bathroom if it kept up, and she couldn't turn it off. Thank goodness she'd gotten her bonnet on already or she'd be cursing for more than one reason.

Not even bothering to grab a towel, Rae dashed out to the bedroom and picked up the phone to call the front desk. The woman who answered sounded horrified, apologizing profusely and promising maintenance was on their way. As much as Rae wanted to screech at the woman to hurry, she knew there was only so much she could do, and she'd understood the situation was urgent.

Going back to her bathroom, Rae saw the spreading puddle on the floor and quickly put her towels across the doorway. Then she ran and grabbed the beach towels to do the same thing. At the very least, hopefully, she could keep it from getting on the carpet.

But she really hoped maintenance moved fast because the towels were getting wet faster than she was comfortable with. Though she also needed to get some clothes on before anyone arrived. Yeah, she was on kink island, but that didn't mean she felt comfortable being naked when the maintenance guy showed up.

That felt too much like the beginning of a porno.

Quickly, she hurried over to her suitcase and grabbed a simple sundress, pulling it over her head just as she heard a knock at the door. Phew, that was fast! Thankfully, she was dressed now.

When she yanked open the door, she had to drop her gaze about half a foot to the tiny Asian woman standing in front of her. Short and curvy, with tanned skin and long black hair pulled back in a ponytail, she was wearing grey coveralls with a white tag that said "Maintenance" in red letters. A large toolbox sat on the ground next to her

"Hi, I'm Layne!" she said briskly, eying Rae as if she was expecting trouble—or a protest. Rae bet she ran into a lot of people who didn't think she could do her job. "Heard you have a shower problem?"

"Yup, it's spraying water everywhere. Come on in." Rae stepped to the side, gesturing.

The set of Layne's shoulders relaxed slightly at Rae's lack of protest. She bent to pick up her toolbox and strode in with confidence, heading straight for the bathroom. Rae followed, curious about her reaction.

Layne stopped in her tracks as she looked through the open bathroom door. The water was still spraying everywhere, and it looked like there was about an inch of water now on the floor between the shower pan and the towel blockade. Fuck.

"Oh, wow. That is a pickle." Layne didn't wait. She put her toolbox down and started untying the laces on her boots.

Before Rae could ask if Layne's pickle reference came from a certain blue cartoon dog, there was more knocking on her door.

"I'll be right back," she told Layne, who nodded but was far more focused on getting her boots off and her pants rolled up so she could take care of the problem. Which... fair. The bathroom was definitely the priority.

Hurrying to the door, Rae opened it, and this time, she had to take a step back as she looked up. Dammit. There was just something about Brian that always made her feel smaller than she actually was. Yes, he was tall and broad-shouldered, but it was more than that, and when he was looming in her door with a frown on his face, it was like being smacked with all that delicious, protective dominance.

"Is everything okay?"

"Everything's fine," she said, which was immediately negated by a shriek from her bathroom.

"Holy shit! That's fucking cold!" Apparently, Layne had entered the bathroom and was a talker. Also completely audible through the door. Rae was just glad she'd gotten out if the water had turned cold.

"Um..." Brian looked over Rae's head, then back down at her.

"My showerhead broke. Maintenance is here to fix it."

"How'd you break it?" he asked as he stepped inside—stepping *to* the side as he did since it wasn't like she'd moved out of the way to invite him in. Exasperated, Rae glared at him.

"I didn't do anything! The head just popped off, then it wouldn't... Where are you going?" She didn't know why she bothered asking the question because she already knew the answer. He was going to see what was going on for himself because he was a bossy Dom who couldn't help himself.

Dammit. She should've shut the door in his face as soon as she saw who was standing there.

Rather than answering her, Brian strode back and into her room. Rae made another exasperated sound of frustration as she trotted in behind him, which he also ignored.

"Oh, wow," he said, coming to a halt in Rae's bedroom as he took in the scene. Layne was in the bathroom, soaking wet, with her coveralls clinging to her curves. Somehow, she'd gotten the water turned off at least, but that didn't solve the problem of what now looked like two inches of water on the bathroom floor that was slowly seeping through the towel barrier.

"I think we're going to have to turn off the water to this villa in order for me to fix this," Layne said apologetically, looking between Rae and Brian. "And I'm not sure I'm going to be able to fix it today, though I can try."

"We're also going to need someone to come clean up the water," Brian murmured, turning his head slightly back and forth as he looked everything over.

"Not my department, but yes. I'll let them know." Layne glanced between Rae and Brian. "Are you two both staying in here or..."

"No, I'm next door. She can stay with me until this is fixed."

"Hey, who says I want to stay with you?" Rae put her hands on her hips. It was just like Brian to come barging into her villa and bossing her around. At the same time, the moment he suggested she do so, her brain started pinging around her head with all the reasons why it was a good idea.

Everyone else was paired up, so she'd be a complete third wheel staying with them. She also didn't want to bother Mitch and Domi or make them feel like they needed to do anything for her—and Brian would keep his mouth shut about it. Plus... okay, as anti-feminist as it was, there was a part of her that swooned over a man who led with problem-solving. Even if she didn't actually need him to solve her problem, it was still kinda hot.

<u>BRIAN</u>

"Okay, well, I'm going to go turn off the water from the outside, and you two can figure out what you're doing in private," said the woman in Rae's bathroom, sloshing through the water to get to the door.

Her exit gave him the opportunity to take a deep breath and get himself under control.

Dammit, he should know better than to go into Daddy mode with Rae. She might like it, but she hated admitting how much she liked it. Seeing the golf cart pull up in front of her villa and the woman with a toolbox get out, he hadn't been able to resist the impulse to come over and find out what was going on. Nor had he been able to resist going into Rae's villa and offering up his own place for her to sleep.

Except it hadn't really been an offer. More like a demand. He'd seen a need and responded to it, the way he always did. And with Rae, he always forgot to have a gentler hand.

Taking a deep breath, he turned to face her.

"Rae, would you like to spend tonight in my villa, so you have a place to sleep near everyone else?" If she went elsewhere, that would stress out Domi, which would upset Mitch. He didn't think Rae wanted to go to a different villa on a different street, away from the rest of the group. She just also didn't like him making decisions for her.

Which, since she wasn't his, was fair.

Rae lifted her stubborn chin in the air, and for a moment, he thought she was going to say no just to spite him.

"Fine. Since you *asked*," she said haughtily.

It wasn't what she said so much as the way she said it that made his palm itch to spank her, even though she had good reason for it.

"Great." A night on the couch wouldn't hurt him. It was a comfortable couch. But he was already regretting the necessity because the more time he spent with Rae, the more he struggled with his desire for her. "Do you want to pack up a few things to bring over?"

To his surprise, she turned around and walked over to where her suitcase was lying on the floor, crouching down to zip up the case.

"Done," she announced, standing back up and pulling it up on its end with her. The way she handled it made it clear that it was heavy and full of her things.

Brian blinked.

"Seriously?" he asked. It wasn't like they'd been go-go-go since arriving, especially yesterday, and she hadn't unpacked at all?

"Oh, right, toiletries." Rae looked at the open doorway of her bathroom, as did Brian. It was clear the towels were getting soaked. "I'll get those later."

"Right." He took a deep breath. He wasn't going to criticize her for not unpacking. It worked out right now, and he knew she wouldn't respond well if he said something about it.

The maintenance woman walked back in, on her phone with someone, and she held up one finger to Rae and Brian as if asking them to wait. He took advantage of the opportunity to walk over and take the suitcase from Rae, who scowled at him and held on for a second before letting him take it. But she did let him take it, and a little surge of triumph went through him—which he did *not* let show on his face.

"Okay, so housekeeping has some people coming to clean up the water, but I'm definitely not going to be able to fix this today. We'll be giving you a full refund, of course, and we're so sorry about the inconvenience." The woman rattled through the words almost as though she was reading off a list, her tone matter-of-fact rather than apologetic. "You're going to be staying next door?"

"Yes."

"Villa Forty-two," Brian added helpfully, and the woman nodded.

"Great, they'll probably send you some kind of apology basket or something. I'll let them know where you'll be."

Rae took in a deep breath and let it out, sagging slightly as if the situation was now fully hitting home.

"Thank you. I appreciate your help." Reaching up, Rae rubbed her forehead, closing her eyes for a moment before opening them again, drawing on her inner patience. It was fascinating to watch. Brian wasn't sure he'd ever seen her exhibit this kind of patience. "Guess that means I'm at your place tonight. Can we not... tell everyone else?"

"Fine by me." He didn't feel like being teased for the rest of the week about Rae sleeping over, either.

"Great."

"Great." He held his hand out, gesturing in front of him for her to go ahead. Maintenance woman's gaze bounced back and forth between them, like they were a complicated math equation she was trying to figure out.

If she came up with an answer, Brian hoped she would be open to sharing with the class.

6

Since they were trying to keep Rae moving into his place a secret from everyone else, they went out the back, crossing over the beach to get her from her villa to his. Because of the way the cul-de-sac curved on the street, this gave them the least chance of being seen, as long as no one was out on the beach. Thankfully, they weren't. The coast was completely clear, literally.

"You can just set my suitcase down— Where are you going?" The exasperation in Rae's voice was clear as he kept walking, ignoring her because they were in the main room. She was gesturing toward the couch, as though she really thought he was going to let her sleep there.

Absolutely not.

Maybe it was old-fashioned of him, but if he was in a situation with a woman he wasn't sharing a bed with and there was only one bed, she was absolutely going to be the one sleeping in the bed.

"I'm going to the bedroom," he answered, even though it should be obvious. Before he could tell her that she got the bed and he'd take the couch, she was already talking again.

"Oh, so that's how it is, huh? You offered me a room, and I'm going to pay for it with my body?"

Well, that was interesting. She didn't sound defensive at all. In fact, she sounded like she was... flirting.

Pausing in the bedroom doorway, Brian turned around to look at her, one corner of his mouth lifting up in a smile when he met her gaze. She was standing next to the couch, hands firmly planted on her hips. The sun filtered in through the window behind her, making her dress a lot more sheer than he'd realized, and he wondered if *she* knew that he could see right through the fabric.

"Yes," he said, just to see how she would respond.

"What?" Her mouth popped open, eyes widening—not in horror, but in surprise and... was that interest?

"Yes, I'm offering you a place to stay. You should repay me." He was enjoying her shock enough to keep the joke going. Although he was starting to feel like maybe he wasn't really joking.

After all, she was the one who had brought it up, not him.

Really? You're going to give her another chance? Again? Have you not learned your lesson yet?

It didn't have to be another chance, though. He already knew things weren't going to work out between them, that she didn't want him. It wasn't setting himself up for rejection if he wasn't going to put himself out there.

But if she was going to be staying here tonight, maybe they could do one more night. Just for fun. Closure of a kind. One night and then goodbye.

And this is what we call thinking with your dick instead of your brain.

His inner voice was disgusted with him because he knew he was rationalizing, yet...

Rae lifted her chin, but he could tell from her expression she was intrigued. If this was the game she wanted to play... well, fuck, he wasn't strong enough to resist. It was vacation, after all, and he knew the score.

Why not give in?

"Well, that's not very gentlemanly."

"Who said I was a gentleman?" He winked at her and turned away, heading into the bedroom. If she changed her mind, he'd just sleep out on the couch.

He wasn't surprised when he heard her footsteps following him in. What did surprise him was when he turned around and found she'd stripped off her dress, leaving her utterly naked.

Brian's jaw dropped open.

"What are you doing?" he asked before he could stop himself. Obviously, he knew what she was doing, but his brain had come to a screeching halt at the sight of her bare breasts. It wasn't as if he hadn't seen boobs before, and he'd spent some time up close and personal with hers. He just hadn't been expecting her to raise the stakes like this.

Shrugging one sassy shoulder, she ran her hands down over her body, skimming her curves, as though she thought maybe he'd missed the fact that she was naked.

"You said I have to pay for my stay, right?" A little smile flirted on her lips as she sashayed toward him. "Well, I don't have any money on me at the moment... but..."

Sex chicken.

They were playing sex chicken and seeing who was going to blink first.

Well, it sure as hell wasn't going to be him.

Rae

Brian went from shocked and confused to Master Brian in the blink of an eye. He drew himself up, his gaze hardening, his shoulders squaring, and there was an ineffable change in his demeanor. Rae's breath caught in her throat as all her senses went on alert.

Girl, you knew you were stepping into the danger zone. Play with fire, and you're going to get burned.

She knew, deep down, that this was the reaction she'd been trying to get out of him. Maybe it wasn't very smart, but she hadn't been able to help herself. When he'd leaned into her teasing rather than setting her straight, her body had gone into overdrive.

How far would he be willing to take it?

She had to know.

"Stop right there." It wasn't a request; it was a command.

Rae came to a halt a few feet away from him. His gaze steady on her face, he seemed to be contemplating his next move.

He put her suitcase down.

Held one hand in the air and spun his finger in a circle.

"Turn around then. Let me see what you're offering."

Excitement tingled up and down her skin at his order. It was demanding, dirty, and made her feel oddly vulnerable through her arousal, which just aroused her even more.

Putting her hands behind her back, she held onto her forearms in one of the submissive poses she'd learned at Marquis. Her breasts thrust out in front of her, back arching a little, she kept eye contact with him as she began to turn, holding it for as long as possible before she had to turn her head away.

"Stop."

Facing directly away from him, her breath hitched in her throat at his command, her movement grinding to a halt. The fact she couldn't see him made her hyperaware, her skin tingling. She could hear his soft breathing in the silence and the padding of his footsteps as he came closer to her, yet she still almost jumped out of her skin when he ran a finger down her spine to the dip between her cheeks.

Rae gulped, her pussy clenching at the soft, almost innocuous glide of his finger, and disappointment surged when he reached her ass and barely touched the crease before pulling away.

"Bend over and touch your toes."

Oh, fuck.

If she'd been wearing panties, they would have metaphorically hit the floor with that one low command.

She didn't know why she got off on being bossed around because she sure as hell didn't like it in any other aspect of her life, but a man who knew what he was doing telling *her* what to do? Yes, please. And Brian definitely knew what he was doing.

Not for the first time, she regretted that he was a Daddy Dom... but even if she couldn't keep him, she could enjoy a night with him. It wasn't like she was going to be able to find someone else to bring back to his place, and knowing she was going to be in his villa at the end of the night meant she wasn't going to feel right about scening with someone in the Dungeon.

Besides, even if it wasn't smart, she'd rather scene with him than with a stranger.

Rae bent at the waist, vividly aware of how vulnerable the position made her, especially with her feet almost touching the way they were. It wouldn't take much to push her off-balance. She also couldn't quite touch her toes, and her fingers hung in the air about an inch above them, but she knew Brian wouldn't care.

Making the attempt and showing she was trying was more important than succeeding.

"Good girl."

The warmth in his voice as he praised her was just as good as the praise itself, washing over her and making her want to wiggle in happiness. Yeah, the poster child for feminism she was not, at least not in the bedroom.

"Yes, I think we can come to an arrangement."

"What?" Rae's mind blanked out, and she heard him chuckle, his hand coming down to rest on her lower back and curving down over her ass.

"For tonight... sweetheart. I'll be perfectly happy having you in my bed as payment for your stay."

Oh, right. For a moment, she'd almost forgotten the little game they were playing. It was hard to concentrate, especially now that his hand was so close to her pussy. When his fingers stroked through the wet folds, she shuddered, closing her eyes for a moment before they popped open again as she swayed. It would be a lot easier to hold this position with her legs spread, but she had a feeling that Brian liked her like this—vulnerable and off-balance.

She didn't hate it, either.

"Let's talk terms." His voice changed slightly as he spoke, going from the seductive, deep voice he'd been using to something more business-like. "While you're sleeping in my bed, you're mine."

"Does that go for you, too? Because I'm gonna be pissed if you scene with someone else in the Dungeon, then try to come back here to fuck me, even if you didn't have sex with them." She'd rather go sleep on the sand.

"It goes for both of us. Why would I need someone else when I have you here and at my mercy?" To punctuate his question, his fingers thrust into her pussy.

Rae rocked forward, automatically putting her hands on her knees to help her keep her balance as Brian began to move his fingers inside her, as if he was fucking her with them. She whimpered at the sensation, her body throbbing in response to his touch.

She wanted him to touch her all over. Her skin tingled to be touched, stroked, but their only point of contact was his fingers moving in and out of her pussy. It was hot as hell.

"Yes, Sir," she said, panting for breath and trying to push back against his fingers, seeking more stimulation. This whole scene was hotter than she'd expected—not that she'd expected a scene, really. She definitely hadn't expected him to play along, and once he was, she'd started going forward without really knowing what she was doing or where it was headed.

This was different from how Brian usually scened, too. He wasn't even trying to be a Daddy Dom right now, and part of her missed it as much as she loved what he was doing. The rest of her was just turned on by the way he'd fully taken charge of the situation and was making demands of her.

"And, obviously, we don't tell our friends."

Rae agreed, so that shouldn't hurt, but hearing him actually say it out loud sent a small pang through her chest. But that was dumb because she felt the same way.

"Yes, Sir." She shuddered as his other hand cupped her bottom, squeezing the soft flesh, caressing. That little bit of extra touch on her outside, while his fingers stroked her G-spot, made her want to melt into the floor.

"Good girl. Then get on your knees, and you can give me your first payment."

Holy fuck. Rae's pussy spasmed around his fingers before he withdrew them. She was so turned on, she wanted to jump him, but that wasn't what he had asked for. Besides, her knees were all too willing to drop to the floor.

She lifted her head to look up at him as he paced around to her front. His gaze met hers and held it as he lifted the fingers he'd had in her pussy to his lips and sucked them into his mouth to clean. Rae wanted to whimper again.

How the fuck had he managed to get even hotter since their last night together?

7

Seeing Rae on her knees in front of him was doing all sorts of things to Brian's imagination. The taste of her on his tongue made him want to push her onto her back and delve between her legs with his mouth, but that wasn't what the scene called for.

Playing the part of the 'hard Dom' was easier than he would have thought—maybe because of their history together, maybe because of the situation—but he wasn't having any trouble pushing back his Daddy instincts at this moment. He was, however, thoroughly enjoying watching Rae submit to him.

He sure as hell hadn't expected to be back in this position again. This time, though, he was going to do a better job of managing his expectations. He wasn't fooled. This was a one-time thing, very likely a one-night thing, that he should enjoy while it lasted, and when it was over, it would be over.

That they were on an island, away from home, actually made things easier. It was like Vegas—what happened on the island, stayed on the island.

And they weren't going to tell their friends. He could only imagine what his friends would say if they knew he was hooking up with Rae *again*. Calling him a masochist would be the least of it. But this time was different. He doubted they'd see it that way, though, which was why it was best to keep them out of it.

Plus, he didn't feel like putting up with the inevitable teasing.

"What would you like me to do now... Sir?" Rae asked coquettishly.

As an answer, Brian undid the front of his shorts, stepping closer to her as his cock sprang free, the hard length bobbing in front of her face.

"I told you, sweetheart. Your first payment. You're going to suck my cock with that pretty little mouth of yours." Normally, he would say 'suck Daddy's cock,' but it really wasn't that hard to change out 'Daddy' for 'my.' The way Rae's eyes lit up with eager expectation more than made the switch worth it.

Then her eyes narrowed.

"What do I get out of this?"

"You mean other than a place to stay?" He raised his eyebrows, wrapping his hand around his cock and stroking it as he took a step forward, so the tip was right in front of her full lips. "Well, if you're so inclined, you can play with yourself. I didn't get to see the finale of your show the other night."

He couldn't see it, but he had a feeling she blushed, her challenging gaze dropping, confirming his suspicion that, yes, she'd wanted him to watch. Then, her expression shifted, and she glared up at him.

"I knew you were watching!"

"Are you pretending you didn't want me to?" he asked. Rae pressed her lips together, which was going to make it really hard for her to suck his cock. "Open up, little girl. Unless you want to find somewhere else to sleep tonight."

Her eyes widened again, but those were the magic words—even if they were an empty threat. Rae's lips opened, and she leaned forward, taking the head of his cock between them. Brian groaned, releasing his hold on the shaft so she had access to the full length.

Fuck, that felt so damn good. As he watched her take his cock between her lips, he could see below where her hand was already between her legs, playing with her pretty pussy. Sliding one hand around the back of her neck, under her braids, he reached down with the other to cup her breast, enjoying the vibrations that danced along his cock when she moaned in response.

Thrusting gently over her tongue, he worked his cock in and out of her mouth as he squeezed her breast, pinching her nipple hard enough to make her squeal—though the sound was muffled by his dick. Which made him like it even more. He gave the tiny bud a little twist, focusing on tormenting her in order to distract himself from the growing pleasure. He wanted to make it last as long as possible.

"Fuck, babygirl, that feels so good."

'Daddy' might be on her hard limits, but he could call *her* whatever he wanted, and her eyes lit up when he called her babygirl. The suction on his dick was pure fucking heaven, and he groaned as her tongue laved the underside.

She moaned around his cock, and he could see her hand busily working between her legs... but he couldn't see enough.

Releasing her, he stepped back—though she tried to follow him with her mouth. Her eyes glazed with desire, she tipped her head back to look at him, lips still parted in erotic invitation.

"Up on the bed," he ordered. "I want to watch you play with yourself."

Her pupils dilated. He knew Rae wasn't exactly a huge exhibitionist, so that meant she liked being watched by *him*. That was an entirely different thing and one that made him feel like crowing in triumph, as if he had won something.

Holding out his hand, he helped her to her feet. The sultry look she gave him over her shoulder as she turned toward the bed was pure flirtation. His dick throbbed, and he reached down to grip it, stroking himself as Rae hopped onto the bed and laid back in position.

Feet spread wide apart and firmly planted on the mattress, knees pointed at the ceiling, she gave him a completely open view of her spread pussy. The soft, purplish brown folds glistened in the light, her swollen clit peeking from beneath its hood just below the thin strip of curly hairs on her mound. Cupping both breasts, she squeezed them before running one hand down over her stomach to dip back between her legs.

R_{AE}

Why did she like Brian watching her so much? She truly didn't know, but she loved having his gaze on her. Loved knowing he was staring at her like she was a delicious dessert he wanted to pounce on.

With his eyes glued to her body, she drew out her pleasure rather than racing for the finish line. Teasing herself rather than trying to please herself immediately. She moaned louder than she normally would, shuddering and gasping as much for his reaction as because what she was doing felt good.

"Like this?" she asked in a sultry voice, sliding her fingers between her pussy lips, dipping them inside before pulling them out to drag her wetness around her swollen clit.

"Just like that, babygirl." His eyes drank her up, heating her from the outside in. "I like watching you play with your pretty pussy."

"I thought you were going to be the one to play with it, but whatever gets you going," she responded teasingly. Sometimes, she just couldn't help her mouth.

"Oh, I'm going to do more than play with it, sweetheart. Just not yet." His eyes gleamed. "Right now, I want to watch you get off, then I'm going to cum all over you."

Rae's pussy clenched.

She'd literally never let a guy do that to her before, yet with Brian, she wanted to try it. Somehow, he made it sound hot. Maybe it was that he was letting her know ahead of time, so she could say her safeword if she needed to rather than trying to just do it. Maybe it was the idea of him marking her in some way. Maybe she was just getting kinkier with time.

Maybe a combination of all of those things. Whatever it was, she wasn't going to protest or pull out now.

Rubbing her clit harder, she moaned, arching her back with her legs held wide for him to see everything. She closed her eyes, thinking about what she must look like, what he must be seeing, as he jerked off to the sight of her masturbating.

Wondering what he was going to do to her tonight.

Remembering the last scene they'd done together when he'd put her in the sex swing at Marquis.

Rae cried out as her pleasure peaked, rubbing harder on her clit, shuddering as pleasure rippled through her. A moment later, as she still spasmed in utter erotic bliss, something hot and warm splashed against her pussy, then her skin. Brian was coming on her. Her fingers slipped through the warmth of his cum, rubbing it between her lips and over her clit, adding to the slippery sensations, and another wave of orgasm pulsed through her as she realized it.

More wet heat slid across her lower belly and inner thighs, dripping over her fingers. It was utterly filthy in the best way possible. She moaned as the crescendo of her orgasm finally peaked and began to descend, her fingers moving slower on her clit as the last shocks of pleasure tingled through her.

"Good girl," Brian rasped. Rae jerked in surprise when his hand took her by the wrist, pulling her fingers away from her pussy and lifting them up to her mouth as he loomed over her. "Now open up."

Her eyes widened, but she did as he ordered.

Utterly filthy didn't begin to describe it as the mingled flavors of his cum and her cream hit her tongue. It was salty-sweet depravity. As she curled her tongue around her fingers to lick them clean, she met his gaze. Despite his cum dripping across her body, the hunger in his eyes hadn't dissipated.

Rae sucked on her fingers, not so much because she was enjoying the taste but because she wanted his reaction. His grip tightened on her wrist—not hard enough to hurt—then he pulled her fingers away and covered his lips with hers in a hard kiss.

She moaned against his lips, wriggling, then he pulled away, cursing and looking down at his stomach.

Giggles erupted from her as she realized they were now both covered in cum.

"Oops." She grinned up at him, propping herself up on her elbows so she could look down at the white smears across her skin. They were harder to see on him, obviously, but still visible.

"It's probably for the best," he said, glancing at the clock. "We need to get cleaned up for dinner... if we're both late, it might cause some questions."

"Oh, shoot, yeah." Rae pushed herself up, jumping to her feet. The last thing she wanted was questions. This was just for one night, after all. "Um, I think I need a shower."

"Right. Ah, go ahead. I'm just going to wipe myself down." His lips quirked. "I'll take your second payment later tonight."

Heat flushed through her body at the promise.

Dammit. At some point, it would be nice if her libido didn't jump-start at a single sentence from him. Still, she didn't want him to see how much he affected her.

"I'll be ready to pay up." She winked at him and turned, sauntering to the bathroom, very aware he was watching her go. She didn't need to look over her shoulder to know he was looking; she could feel his eyes on her. Closing the door behind her, she leaned against it for a moment, taking a ragged breath.

The truth was, she wanted him in here with her, not out there. She needed to get her shit under control. Giving herself a shake, she went over to the sink and got the washcloth wet with some warm water before heading back to the door and opening it a crack.

"Here," she called. Brian walked back into the bedroom—he'd gone out to the main room for something, she supposed.

"Ah, thank you, babygirl." He smiled at her, and Rae did her best not to go all melty.

"No problem." Heck, she wasn't going to make him stand around waiting for her to shower so he could wipe himself down. That was just rude.

Closing the door again, putting some space between them, she gave herself a little shake. She was just off because she hadn't expected to be stuck in Brian's villa with him, much less having sex with him on this trip. On the other hand, she was having trouble feeling any sort of regret. Damn. She needed to be taking notes. This would make a great book... except it felt way too personal to write a book about something that was actually happening to her. Especially when her personal story wasn't going to have a happily-ever-after.

She did wish she could talk to Domi about it and get some outside perspective, but that would mean fessing up to the room issue, possibly stressing Domi out and also opening herself up to questions like *What the fuck are you thinking?*

Next week. She'd spill everything next week when they were home, and it wouldn't matter anymore.

8

____

BRIAN

Leaving Rae in his villa to get ready because he needed some distance and also because he didn't want them to appear too close together when it was time for dinner, Brian headed to the main building of the resort. The entire place was beautiful, but probably like most people, he found himself wandering into the large gift shop. The store had most of the things one would expect from a resort—t-shirts, keychains, hats, sunglasses, bathing suits, and towels, but there was also a section of sex toys. Of which there were plenty of options, though nothing too fancy.

"These are just the display items. If you want something specific, we have a whole catalogue of everything we actually have available on the island." The guy who had been behind the counter appeared on Brian's right as he looked over the wall of options. "Anything can be delivered to your room as well. If there's furniture you want, that can be delivered as well. There's no fee for the furniture unless it's damaged during use."

He vaguely remembered seeing something about that in the brochure, but he probably wouldn't have recalled it if not for the employee.

"Thanks," he said, glancing at the nametag on the blue shirt the guy was wearing. "David."

"You're welcome! Just let me know if you have any questions." David ambled away to greet a couple coming into the store. Brian glanced up to make sure it wasn't any of his friends.

Since he was on his own this week, as far as his friends knew, there was no reason for him to be buying anything from the naughty corner of the store. Thankfully, the couple wasn't from his group, but it was a good reminder to hurry up. He only had about twenty minutes before they were supposed to meet everyone for dinner at the restaurant.

Thinking about the others also deterred him from looking at the furniture. There was no way he could have furniture delivered to his villa without risking someone seeing and asking questions.

Have you thought about the fact that if you don't want your friends to know you're doing something, maybe you shouldn't be doing it?

The little voice in his head taunted him.

Maybe this was a mistake.

Maybe he shouldn't have given in to playing sex chicken with Rae.

On the other hand, who was he going to tell?

He didn't want to disrupt Mitch's trip—and if Mitch and Domi were paying attention to whatever was going on with him and Rae rather than each other, that would definitely be disruptive. Kincaid and Zach had their own issues going on. And while he was friends with both Nick and Law, it wasn't like he really knew them the same way he did the other guys. They weren't really at the 'talk about important shit' stage of friendship.

So, it wasn't so much that he didn't *want* to tell his friends as he didn't want to disrupt what they had going on this week.

Maybe next week, when everyone was home, he could demonstrate that it had been no big deal that he'd hooked up with Rae. That was probably the best way, so he could *show* them it hadn't affected him at all. Which would also cut down on the teasing.

Feeling better about his decision, Brian grabbed a pair of remote-controlled vibrating panties off the wall. Just because no one needed to know about him and Rae didn't mean they couldn't have some fun while the others were around. Tormenting her while she had to keep quiet sounded like a hell of a lot of fun to him.

They only had one night together, so might as well make the most of it.

He'd give her the remote back tomorrow.

Taking the package up to the register, he smiled at David. The other man grinned back at him, a twinkle in his eye as Brian slid the package onto the counter.

"Ah, good choice. Let me grab you some batteries."

"Thank you." He glanced at his watch while David did that. Just enough time for him to get over to the restaurant. "Actually, would you mind if I took it out of the packaging and just took the underwear and remote?"

"Of course." David slid the batteries onto the counter, not seeming to find anything odd about Brian's request. A few minutes later, the underwear was safely in one pocket while the remote was in another, and David was tossing the packaging in the trash can under the counter.

Shoving his hands in his pockets and curling his fingers around the remote and the panties, Brian whistled as he headed for the restaurant. To his surprise, the only one in the waiting area was Rae, looking around nervously. Her braids were in ponytails, and she was wearing a cute, short, pink sundress that hugged her body down to her hips before flaring out. A startled laugh burst out of her when she looked up to see him coming in.

"So much for not showing up at the same time," she muttered as he came closer.

Brian couldn't help but chuckle. He stood with his back to the door so if anyone came in, they wouldn't be able to see her. One of the benefits of her being shorter and smaller than him.

"I just got here. We can wait for everyone else, or we can be seated now."

"Let's wait for a few minutes to see if anyone else shows up." He pulled the panties out of his pocket and handed them to her. "Here. Go to the bathroom and put these on."

"What—"

"Just do it," he said, cutting her off as she started to lift them. Thankfully, she must have gotten an idea of what they were because she closed her hands around them.

"Seriously?" she hissed at him.

"*Now*, babygirl." For a moment, he wondered if she was going to say no, but then she turned on her heel and flounced away. She also peeked over her shoulder to see if he was watching her go. When their gazes connected, her head whipped back around.

Grinning, Brian gave the hostess a nod as he sat on one of the benches. She was watching him with amusement, but she just nodded back and looked down at the desk in front of her. He wondered how many crazy things she saw happening. He bet every one of the staff here had some stories to tell.

RAE

Freaking vibrating panties.

Who the hell did he think he was?

The guy who's going to be fucking you later tonight, that's who.

The amount of control she was willing to hand over to him should have scared her, but instead, she found it exciting. Hell, they were away on a private island for Kinksters. If this wasn't the time to let loose a little and do some crazy things, when was?

Heck, she could even consider it research for her books. After all, hadn't she fantasized about letting a Dom get bossy like this with her? Her ex had never been interested in doing anything like this. Might as well seize the chance while she could.

Getting into the stall, she slipped off her underwear, studying the new pair that Brian had handed her before she put them on. The crotch was definitely stiffer, and she could feel the small toy inside.

She didn't assume the small size meant it wasn't powerful, though. Some of the smallest toys could pack a real punch.

It nestled between her legs, right up against her clit, and just knowing it was there made her want to squirm. Now, what to do with her underwear... she had her room key tucked into her bra because that was all she should have needed around the resort, and of course, her dress didn't have pockets. Dammit.

She'd have to give them to Brian.

On the other hand... knowing he'd be carrying her panties around in his pocket was kind of hot.

Fine then.

Heading back out into the main restaurant, she walked with an awareness of her pussy that she didn't normally have. The underwear didn't feel that different, but she did, just knowing it was there. Knowing Brian had the remote and could turn it on at any time.

Crap. He wasn't alone at the host stand anymore. He was standing there with Mitch and Domi, both of whom were glowing. As she was coming up, Avery and Nick came in through the front door, which gave her the opportunity to sidle up to Brian and shove her underwear in his hand before she slipped away. Thankfully, he had good reaction time. As she moved to greet the others, she saw him put the wisp of fabric into his pocket.

She swore she could feel his eyes on her as she greeted the others, and her muscles kept tensing in expectation, waiting for the inevitable buzz of the vibrator between her legs. Wondering what it would feel like. Preparing to cover her reaction. Slightly terrified someone might be able to actually hear it.

The sadistic jerk made her wait.

Which was almost worse than dealing with the vibrator would be.

Rae kept her smile pasted on her face, despite her distraction, pretending she wasn't about to jump out of her skin at any second. She wished she had her notebook with her, the one that she used for keeping ideas for her books, but it wasn't like her outfit had a good place to hold it. Besides, she wouldn't have thought she needed it.

When she went to Stronghold or Marquis and got an idea, she

wrote it down when she got back to her car. She'd figured on this trip, she'd write things down when she got back to her villa, but now she was staying in *Brian's* villa. And she wasn't sure she wanted him to know she was writing about him.

Cuz it wasn't really about him, just about the things he was doing to her and how they made her feel.

She'd only written a couple books so far, but all the reviews had commented on how realistic her kink scenes seemed. There was a reason for that. Now, here she was, having a whole new experience, and she wasn't going to be able to immediately write down everything she was thinking and feeling throughout it.

Which really sucked because, holy crap, this was hot.

She should definitely put a heroine in some vibrating panties and keep her waiting for them to turn on.

"I am starving," Iris said, putting her hand on her stomach and looking past Rae. "Let's get this party started."

"Please." Domi leaned against Mitch, grinning up at him. "Especially because after dinner, we get to go back to the Dungeon."

Smiling, the hostess gathered up the menus in her arms and stepped out from behind the stand so they could follow her. As she did so, Domi separated from Mitch and linked arms with Rae, keeping her voice low as she leaned in.

"How are you doing?" she asked. "You're having fun, right?"

And that right there was why Rae was going to keep the trouble at her villa and ending up with Brian for the night to herself. Domi was supposed to be having fun with Mitch. Yes, it was technically a bachelor/bachelorette party, but they'd all known *why* Mitch and Domi had chosen Hideaway Island. They hadn't wanted to come here for their honeymoon, but they'd still wanted the excuse to come.

There was no way Rae was going to ruin it for them by being a distraction.

"I'm great. I love the resort. It's gorgeous, and I can't wait to have some fun at the Dungeon tonight." As she said the words, her knees almost buckled as intense vibrations buzzed against her clit.

That bastard.

9

Walking in a straight line had never been such a monumental effort.

The vibrations were a steady hum against her clit, a constant torment as she moved through the restaurant, her smile pasted on her lips as she pretended she wasn't being tormented by vibrating panties. Pretended she wasn't playing secret sexy games with Brian in the middle of their friends. Pretended everything was normal and nothing out of the ordinary was going on.

"Oh, good. We're having such a good time, too," Domi said, squeezing Rae's arm against hers and glancing over her shoulder at Mitch walking behind them. Thankfully, she wasn't really paying attention to Rae; otherwise, she would have noticed how distracted Rae was. "Are you sure you'll be okay at the Dungeon?"

"Totally." One-word answers were the way to go, though she was starting to get more used to the buzzing hum of the vibrator. Her panties were getting very wet as she moved, and when she reached the table, she grabbed the first chair she reached and sat down, pressing her thighs together. She hoped the damn thing was waterproof because she was soaking the fabric of the panties.

Everyone sat down around her—Brian choosing the seat across from her.

Dick.

Rae did her best not to glare at him.

Act normal.

But how did she normally act? She wasn't really sure because she'd never had to think about it before. People didn't notice how they normally acted *because* it was normal to them.

Glaring at him unprovoked probably wouldn't be normal. Or would it? Their relationship had always been a bit tempestuous at best. She probably wouldn't glare for no reason, though. She just wanted to talk herself into being able to because she wanted to glare at him really, really badly.

"Wow, everything looks good," Brian said.

To all outward appearances, his focus was on the menu in front of him, but as he said the words, his hand was in his pocket, and the vibrations against Rae's clit went from a steady hum to pulsing bursts. She barely managed to bite back her moan at the change.

Fucking hell.

She kicked him.

"Ow!" Beside Brian, Law scooted back and looked under the table, frowning as he tried to figure out who had just kicked him.

"Sorry! I was trying to stretch my leg." Rae smiled weakly at Law. Whoops. Dammit. Missed. Trying to kick Brian again was definitely out of the question. She didn't want to accidentally hit Law again, and it would also look really suspicious if she kicked someone "on accident" right after the first time.

"Everything okay?" Brian asked her with seemingly sincere concern, other than the mischief dancing in his eyes, which made her want to kick him even more.

"Leg cramp," she said through gritted teeth, glaring at him, though she tried to make it look like a smile.

"Oh, you have to watch out for dehydration here." He reached over to push her water glass toward her. "Make sure you're getting plenty of water."

"Thanks, Dad," she said sarcastically, forgetting herself before she saw the flash in his eyes. Dammit. She didn't mean to taunt him by calling him something so close to "Daddy." That was just what she would say to any Dom who reminded her of something she already knew.

Which meant he was just going to have to suck it up. She wasn't apologizing. Especially while he was torturing her with the vibrator.

Although poking at him—even accidentally—while he was in control of the vibrator was a bad idea. Rae ducked her head, biting down on her lower lip as the pulse changed to a hard burst of sensation... then disappeared. He'd made the sensation wildly intense, then turned it off.

Asshole.

The lack of vibration was now the torture. Not that she wanted to orgasm at the dinner table in the midst of all their friends, who had no idea what was going on, but... Dammit. He was fucking with her head as much as he was with her body. She was aching for sensation, for stimulation, and there was nothing.

"So, what did you all get up to today?" Mitch asked, looking around and including Domi in his glance. "How was the spa?"

"What, you mean Domi didn't already fill you in?" Iris teased. The unspoken conclusion was that Mitch and Domi had better things to do than talk about how their day had gone once they'd been reunited. Which Rae was sure was exactly what had happened.

"No, I was too busy filling her." Mitch winked at Iris as everyone cracked up, then at the waitress who had appeared beside their table and was shaking her head with amusement. They all got their drink orders in, as well as a few appetizers, before they returned to talking about what they'd done with their day.

It sounded like the guys had had a lot of fun, though Rae was glad she'd gotten to spend her morning relaxing rather than running around. She definitely would not have been as calm through the situation at her villa if she hadn't had the spa time beforehand. Sadly, the calm did not carry her through the vibrator, though her body was slowly starting to return to normal...

As if Brian knew the exact moment she was starting to relax again during the conversation, he hit the button in his pocket. He wasn't even looking at her when he did it to see how she reacted. Her breath stuttered, and she did her best to cover it by reaching for her water glass.

Staying hydrated.

Then, just as abruptly as it had turned on, it turned off again.

She'd never wanted to simultaneously strangle someone and jump their bones before, but that's where Brian was at now for her. If they weren't surrounded by their friends, who couldn't know what was happening, she might have gone over the table for him. Or under it.

It was a restaurant on kink island. They'd probably seen worse.

On the other hand, she wasn't the type to normally make an exhibition of herself, so maybe it was for the best. Brian was doing things to her that made her want to act out of character. As usual.

And he kept doing it. Over and over again.

Turning the vibrator on and off throughout the meal.

Mostly while he wasn't looking at her, but sometimes while he was. She swore his smile was more sadistic, but no one else seemed to notice.

By the time they were all done eating and headed to the Dungeon, she couldn't wait to ditch her friends and find somewhere he could finish her off. At least, he'd better finish her off, or she was going to go find someone else to do the job because, at this point, she was about to jump out of her goddamn skin.

BRIAN

The only problem with going to the Dungeon as a group was trying to get Rae alone. There were plenty of distractions, but also well-meaning friends doing their best not to let him and Rae feel like a third wheel. And as much fun as tormenting her with the vibrator was—she was starting to glare daggers at him every time he put his hand in his pocket—he was tired of remote touch.

He wanted to get his hands all over her and his cock inside her.

He was pretty sure that was what she wanted, too, though he started second-guessing himself when she walked off with a Dom who had come up and introduced himself. That had killed his erection. Watching her out of the corner of his eye, he wasn't sure what to do. They'd had an agreement after all, and he'd never known Rae to back out of an agreement, but they'd also never been in a situation quite like this before—and all his knowledge was secondhand.

Although he could always turn the vibrator on to remind her, that wasn't how he wanted to have her. He didn't want to have to remind her. Sure, it was only for one night, but trying to push her into remembering their agreement still felt like another rejection. The remembered ache in his chest from all the previous times she'd pushed him away made him think maybe it would be better to just get it over with.

It was a good thing he was watching, though, because he caught the moment when she excused herself from the Dom, then looked back at him. Brian hid his grin when she jerked her head at him and moved away through the crowd toward one of the many exits that led to the boardwalk outside.

"I'm going to go get some fresh air," he said to Kincaid and Zach, who had been hanging out with him. "You two should go have fun."

"Are you sure?" Zach asked, looking torn. He glanced at Kincaid, who was staring out into the crowd. If anyone needed to reconnect, it was those two.

"Yup, go have fun. I'll be back in soon, I'm sure." He was pretty sure he wouldn't be, actually, but hopefully, they wouldn't realize that. Kincaid was already turning back to the conversation, refocusing on his boyfriend and tilting his head suggestively at Zach.

"We could go watch the cupping demonstration," Kincaid said, his words sounding oddly like a challenge. Zach's chin jerked up, as if he was interpreting Kincaid's words the same way Brian was.

"We could do that."

Crap. Brian wasn't sure if he'd just inadvertently started something. Should he stick around and try to do damage repair? On the other hand, would he make things better or worse? He really wasn't sure.

"Okay then, let's go," Kincaid said, getting to his feet and making Brian's decision for him. As Kincaid held out his hand to Zach, who paused for a moment before taking it, Brian slipped away. He was more worried about his friends than ever, and at the same time, he didn't think there was anything he could actually do to help them. He wasn't even sure what was wrong because they weren't talking to anyone about it, as far as he knew. Which was their choice, but it felt like watching a car crash in slow motion.

He didn't take the time to watch them walk away. He had his own metaphorical car crash waiting for him.

Turning on his heel, he stalked after Rae. She'd better be alone when he caught up with her. They weren't in a relationship, but they had made an agreement. If she couldn't keep it for one night...

He spotted her as soon as he got out on the boardwalk, standing a little way down near the entrance to one of the many alcoves, leaning against the railing and looking out through the plants at the ocean. There were plenty of alcoves scattered around the resort, each one filled with different furniture and implements, most of them with obscured entrances so someone walking by couldn't peek in easily. Yet the alcoves weren't entirely private, either.

Definitely not the best choice for anyone trying to keep their hookup a secret.

Turning her head, Rae gave him a sultry look as she straightened up. Then she slid to the side and walked right into one of the alcoves.

Fuck. The comparison to a car crash was becoming all too real.

This is such a bad idea.

Not that it stopped him.

As he walked closer to the alcove, he reached into his pocket and hit the button on the remote to turn the vibrator on, not to the highest setting but not the lowest. He chose the pulse she seemed to find the hardest to deal with when she had been eating dinner. Her low moan greeted him as he stepped through the opening, brushing aside the hanging vines that acted as a 'door.'

Rae was in the middle of the space, sitting on a spanking bench, her legs pressed tightly together and her hands on her knees. She looked up at him with hot, glassy eyes full of sexual frustration and demand. Fuck him, but she looked like an angry babygirl.

"I hate you."

"But you love the way I make you feel, don't you?" he asked, walking right up to her and cupping her chin to tilt her head back. He pressed his thumb against her full lower lip, pushing in enough to feel the hard edge of her teeth and the wet tip of her tongue against it. "Answer me, babygirl."

The heat in her eyes flared, her temper fighting with her desire, and he knew the moment the latter won, and submission filled her expression.

"Yes, Sir."

10

Seated in front of Brian, his hand cupping her chin, Rae felt small and vulnerable in the best way possible. Because he also made her feel safe. Protected. Like she *could* be vulnerable. Which was part of why he was so dangerous to her, but at this moment, she appreciated it.

They'd clearly laid out the boundaries—they both knew this was just for tonight, and he knew she wasn't going to call him 'Daddy'—so she could relax and enjoy. Well, mostly relax. The alcove meant they didn't have total privacy. On the other hand, unless someone actually came in, they were unseen, and all of their friends were currently preoccupied.

And once they were done in there, they could go back out to the regular Dungeon.

If they both went all the way back to the villas, there was always the chance of being seen coming or going. This way, they were around. However, the thought of either her or Brian having to dive through greenery and out to the beach in order to avoid discovery would have made her giggle if she wasn't too preoccupied with squirming under his firm gaze.

"You don't like my present?" he asked, sweeping his thumb across her lower lip again, his eyes darkening. She wondered if he was remembering having his cock there.

"I don't like the way your present is being used. Sir." There was seriously something wrong with her, getting sassy at a time like this instead of being sweet so he'd give her an orgasm. Yet, as usual, her mouth got away from her.

She just had to push, push, push, just to see what happened.

Though, granted, a lot of the time, what happened was also something she liked, even if it did delay her orgasm. But every once in a while, it might be nice to be able to keep her mouth under control. Just so she could get what she wanted a little sooner. Or to keep herself out of trouble when she didn't really want to experience the consequences.

"Well, then. You don't have to use it." His smile widened as she groaned when he reached into his pocket. The buzzing hum between her legs disappeared, leaving her squirming again as her clit cried out in protest.

Yup, she'd just had to test him, hadn't she?

Her orgasm was looking further away than ever. Rae did her best not to whimper, not wanting him to know just how much he was getting to her. Sometimes, it felt like he saw her a little too clearly as it was.

"Up, babygirl, I want you bent over the spanking bench so I can spank that pretty ass. See if I can't spank some of that sass out of you."

"As if that's ever worked," she muttered, even as she moved. Then yelped when his hand came down on her outer thigh—more out of surprise than pain, as the sting wasn't too bad. She just hadn't been expecting it.

"I'll just have to try harder tonight, then." He raised his eyebrow at her, his gaze considering. "Stop, stand there." The order came just as she was about to turn away, and Rae froze. Brian tilted his head at her, still considering, then spun in a slow circle, looking at everything the alcove had to offer.

There was a wall where implements were hanging, most of them wooden, and several cabinets. Brian walked over to one of those as she watched, nervously wondering why he'd changed his mind. However, she didn't think he'd changed his mind about spanking her, just possibly about the order he was going to do things.

The waiting made her nervous even as it turned her on, just like it had before. Her gaze kept skipping around to all the possibilities, wondering which one he was going to choose, imagining what each of them would be like. Unlike before, her arousal was already highly primed after being teased with the vibrator for so long. It hadn't quite been edging since he'd never let her get anywhere near orgasm before backing off, but... something close. She wasn't sure there was a name for it.

Teasing. Tormenting. Torturing.

"Strip."

Rae jumped at the order. She hadn't realized she'd gotten lost in her own little world of thoughts. Now Brian was facing her, holding something in his hand that dangled with very thin chains.

Nipple clamps.

Her tiny buds puckered in anticipation.

"Even the panties?" she asked as she began to slide her dress off, revealing her breasts and hard nipples, now aching from the slight stimulation of fabric brushing against them.

"Especially the panties."

No more vibrator, then. She didn't know if she was relieved or disappointed. Maybe a little of both.

Hooking her thumbs into the underwear, she pushed them down her hips, letting them drop to the floor with the tiniest thud as the vibrator inside landed. Her clit felt extra sensitive against the night air, the slight breeze blowing coolly against her wet, swollen folds, despite the lingering warmth from the day.

"Good girl. Now, I've got something else for you to wear."

Her nipples budded even more tightly at his approach, her breasts lifting with each of her breaths. The little nubs tingled, and she resisted the urge to squirm again as he hefted one breast in his hand.

"Such pretty little nipples. They deserve some decoration." Brian's thumb swept over the hard bud, his fingers gripping her breast, and she wanted to moan at the firm touch. It was just enough to set all her senses ablaze but not enough to hurt.

Lifting the clamp to her nipple, he closed it around the base of the bud. He was using rubber-tipped tweezer clamps, and he pushed the ring around the tweezers close enough to her nipple that she cried out at the sharp ache. Tweezer clamps were hardly harsh as clamps went, but they could still pack a bite—especially when she was as sensitive as she was feeling right now, and he'd applied the clamp so quickly.

She'd barely panted through the initial sharp wave of pain before he was applying the other, leaving her nipples as twin pulsing points of erotic stimulation on her chest. When he brushed his fingers over the tips, Rae moaned and arched her back, thrusting them out at him.

"Very pretty. Now, spread your legs for me, babygirl." Brian crouched down in front of her. Rae was so distracted by the twin sensations, her body adjusting to the tight pinch on her nipples, she didn't realize at first that there was another cool chain brushing against her stomach.

Not until that same burst of pain, that same pinch, hit her clit.

It hadn't been two clamps—it was three.

Fucker.

"Oh, God..." She swayed. Firm hands gripped her hips, holding her in place so she didn't fall over. The movement pulled at her nipples and clit as the chain bounced slightly.

"Turn around." Still crouched in front of her, Brian used his hands to move her around the way he wanted. "Bend over and put your hands on the bench."

She moaned, shuddering, as the movement of bending forward made her breasts sway, which pulled on the chain, which tugged on her poor, tortured clit. The little bud was going to be so sore by the end of this. Her head hung down, her hair brushing against the insides of her arms as she panted, trying to adjust to all the new sensations coursing through her. Digging her fingers into the leather of the bench, she rocked slightly on the balls of her feet, trying to adjust.

Brian didn't give her much time to get used to it.

He had obviously gotten to his feet because the next thing she knew, his hand was coming down on her ass. Hard. Hard enough to make her jerk forward—which meant her breasts moved, which meant the chain moved, and everything *tugged* again. It wasn't just the sharp smack that hurt—it was *everything*. The effects of that one smack rippled through her, making her cry out, her nipples and clit throbbing in response.

Again, he didn't give her time to recover before his hand came down again.

Her toes tried to curl as pain and pleasure pulsed through her in equal measure. The clamps hurt, but they also felt good, the tugging stimulating her even as it made her want to whimper. The spanking also made her want to whimper in an entirely different way.

His hand came down again and again, with the same effect each time, making her pant and moan, going up on her toes as her body struggled to deal with the assault on her senses. The skin of her ass was turning hot, though somehow, that made each new smack easier to deal with. The tugging on her nipples and clit was pulling her closer and closer to orgasm,

"Still feeling sassy, babygirl?" he asked, running his hand over her roasted cheeks.

"I'm not *not* feeling sassy," she replied, with as much energy as she could. The truth was, she wasn't feeling sassy; she just wished she was. He really had spanked it out of her, as much as she didn't want to admit it.

Brian just chuckled in response, his hands still running over her bottom, then up to her hips.

"I guess I'll have to see if an orgasm or two will do it then." The sound of a condom wrapper opening crinkled behind her, and Rae shivered in anticipation.

Yes, please, Sir.

"You think you can fuck my sass out of me?" Yes, that was a challenge. One she already knew he was going to meet.

"I'm certainly going to try." His hand smacked down on her ass again, making her rock forward with a little cry as the chain and clamps went to work... and when she rocked back into place, his dick was there waiting for her. Rae cried out again as he thrust in, his hands wrapping around her hips to hold her, the thick length of his cock pushing in deep with one hard thrust. She was soaking wet. Between her own juices and the lubricant on the condom, he had no problem burying himself inside her.

His balls slapped against the swollen nub of her clamped clit, sending another wave of sensations ricocheting through her. It wasn't going to take her long to cum. She was already right on the edge, her pussy quivering around him as he began to thrust in steady, devastatingly pleasurable strokes. The clamps tugged with each one, sending her ecstasy higher and higher every time his cock impaled her.

Brian

Holy fuck, this was hot.

Scening with Rae pushed him out of his comfort zone, making him far more creative than he'd been with any other submissive he'd scened with. The drive to impress her, to make her feel things she didn't with any other Dom, was a powerful motivator.

He would have hesitated to use a chain and clamps this way when he was in the middle of being a Daddy Dom... but because Rae wasn't calling him Daddy, it was almost like he'd been given permission to unleash some of his dark desires. He didn't have to be the caretaker or the disciplinarian. He could be the filthy pervert who clamped all her most sensitive parts, then fucked her boneless while she wore them. He knew what every thrust of his cock was doing to her—he could feel it in the way her pussy clamped down around him.

The chain would be bouncing and moving beneath her, pulling at her swollen nubs, stimulating her and sending her senses into overdrive.

"Oh, fuck..." she cried out, proving his words. "Oh fuck, oh fuck, oh fuck... *Brian!*"

The ragged way she said his name as she started to climax was almost as good as hearing her call him 'Daddy' would be.

"That's it, babygirl. Come for... me." He just managed to catch himself before the word 'Daddy' slipped out of his mouth. No matter how much *he* wanted it, he wasn't going to go over her hard limits. "Come all over my cock."

"Fuck!"

She screamed out the word as he pounded into her from behind, harder, faster, driving himself to his own orgasm. He felt her start to crumble and tightened his grip, holding her in place as his balls tightened, and he slammed home. Her body spasmed around his cock as he emptied himself with a groan of pleasure, all of his pent-up need spilling out and filling the condom.

"Oh, fuck..." She whimpered the words more softly, sagging in front of him as he held them in place for the last tremors of his orgasm.

Letting out a long breath on a sigh, his muscles slowly untensed, relaxing, and he helped her straighten up, his cock sliding out of her. Before he tended to himself, he took his time removing the clamps, giving each pert nipple a kiss and a suck before kneeling before her and doing the same to her clit. She let out a little cry as he did so.

Once he got her seated on the bench to recover, only then did he go grab the wipes he'd found earlier, removing the condom and cleaning himself off before dropping it all in the trash and putting his shorts back in place. She was still naked, but he liked seeing her like that and didn't particularly want her to get dressed yet.

There was a minifridge with bottles of water, and he grabbed one for both of them, tucking one under his arm and opening the other. Sitting next to Rae on the bench—there was just enough room for both of them—he held the bottle up to her lips.

"Drink." Holding the bottle in place, he shook his head when she started to lift her hands. "No, let me do this."

Aftercare was one of the things he most enjoyed, and after putting her through such an intense scene, he wanted to be the one to take care of her. Caretaking was an essential part of why he liked being a Daddy Dom. Even if Rae wasn't going to call him Daddy, he wanted to take care of her.

Surprisingly, she didn't protest. He really must have fucked all the sass out of her. Her hands dropped down to her lap, and her lips parted, letting him hold the water for her. Satisfaction filled him as he watched her throat work, greedily guzzling down the liquid.

"Good girl." He didn't pull the bottle away until she was done.

"Thank you," she said once he took the bottle away.

"You're welcome." He opened his own bottle, thankful he had something to do because now that the scene was over, things were a little more awkward. As much as he wanted to pull her into his arms and cuddle, their current location was not really built for that.

Likely, the designer had expected that after using the nook, the participants would make use of other portions of the resort... like one of the aftercare areas. Unfortunately, those areas were a little too public for him and Rae. They were meant to accommodate multiple people.

As if the thought had drawn someone to them, a familiar voice filtered through the greenery, footsteps falling along the boardwalk outside. A low chuckle in response.

Avery and Nick.

His brain froze the moment he recognized the voices. Rae froze, too, then started scrambling for her clothes. Brian got down to help her, and she hissed at him.

"No! Go distract them!"

Right.

Because he was still mostly dressed—unlike her—and Nick and Avery were getting closer.

Shit. Were they planning on making use of an alcove? The risk of getting caught had been fun; actually getting caught would not be.

Brian jumped to his feet and hurried to the entrance, stepping out... right behind Avery and Nick, who had passed it by. They hadn't been headed to the alcove after all. He should have looked, but on the other hand, if he had and they'd seen him peeking out, that might have been even more suspicious.

As it was, they both looked over their shoulders, still holding hands, to see who had just come out behind them. His heart was pounding in his chest, and it was all he could do to push a smile on his face and act like he wasn't feeling wildly out of breath. This sneaking around thing was more stressful than he'd anticipated.

"Hey, guys. Where are you off to?" he asked, stepping toward them as if that had been his intent all along.

"Just taking a walk to enjoy the evening." The look Nick gave Avery could only be described as schmaltzy. Brian immediately realized they must have been looking for some privacy, away from the antics in the Dungeon and all the people.

"Ah, okay. Well, I won't interrupt then. I'm just headed for the Dungeon."

Thankfully, the two were so eager to get back to their late-night walk, they didn't question why he wasn't already there. They gave him a little wave and kept on moving.

When he stepped back into the alcove, Rae was gone.

11

RAE

Staring at the note that had been left on Brian's door, Rae wasn't sure how she felt. Her reaction was really going to depend on how Brian reacted when he found out. Behind her, she heard a golf cart coming up the road. She sank back into the shadows as best she could, watching to see where it was going to pull up. Going by the light on in Mitch and Domi's villa, they'd already returned, but she didn't think anyone else had.

Explaining to her friends why she was standing in front of Brian's door rather than her own wouldn't be easy. Maybe she could say she was drunk.

But she didn't have to come up with anything.

The cart pulled up in front of Brian's, and he got out of the front seat, saying something to make the pretty driver laugh. Other than her, he was the only one in the cart. Rae scowled before she smoothed the expression away from her face. He was allowed to make other women laugh. She certainly didn't have any claim to him.

Though they had agreed to be together for the night. Even though they'd already had sex, that didn't mean the night was over. Deep down, she knew he would never bring another woman back to his place, knowing that she was going to be there, but she still couldn't stop that little tendril of doubt and jealousy. There was also a touch of worry.

How was *he* going to react to the note?

As he came up the walk, Rae stepped out of the shadows. She could see his reaction when he noticed her there, the way his shoulders relaxed, his chin coming up a touch.

"Forget you didn't have a key?" he asked in a low voice that wouldn't carry, obviously being extra cautious in case there was someone around they were unaware of.

"No, I just figured you'd realize this was the most likely place I'd be." That and as soon as he'd stepped out of the alcove, she'd felt the need for a little space. A little perspective. She'd been sore, aching, and satisfied, feeling like no other Dom she'd scened with really got her the way Brian did. Her nipples and clit were still tingling, even though he'd taken off the clamps and chain.

Things had gotten a little awkward at the end. At least for her. But only because she'd wanted more than she had any right to ask for. She'd wanted him to pull her in his lap and hold her. The little hint of being taken care of when he'd been holding the bottle to her lips had satisfied an unexpected need inside her. She was longing for... things. Things she couldn't even define.

So, she'd run.

Because she'd needed to get her head on straight again.

She and Brian only worked for scenes. Occasional scenes. They'd never work as a couple. Definitely not for anything more than a night at a time.

Which was why she hadn't known how to react to the note. Cry? Cheer? Worry? It was time to find out.

"Here." She held out the note to him, trying not to appear as anxious as she felt.

"What's this?" he asked as he took it from her, looking down at it with a frown, his eyes scanning over the contents.

"Layne left it on your door... about my villa."

She knew the exact moment he got to the part about her not

being able to return to the villa this week. His frown smoothed out into an expression of astonishment, his mouth dropping open.

Her stomach tightened. Asking him to let her sleep there for a night was one thing, but there was no way he was going to want to give up his whole week, right? She wouldn't even give him the one thing he really wanted, which was probably for the best. Because they really shouldn't do more than one night together at most. That was the smarter move.

"Well, shit." He shook his head. "Alright, well, let's go in."

Wait, that was it? Rae watched him as he stepped forward and pressed his key card against the door, waiting for... something. Something more. Something to indicate what he was thinking. Did he just assume she was going to find somewhere else to go?

Or was he assuming she would stay with him the whole week?

The second one! The little dreamer in her voice said.

Bad idea.

Though, seriously, she needed to be taking notes on this. It was as improbable as the whole arriving at a hotel with a guy the heroine couldn't stand, only to discover there was only one room still available and only one bed in the room. Although, the problem with Brian wasn't that she couldn't stand him. The problem was that they liked each other, were attracted to each other, but were just *wrong* for each other. Totally different scenario.

She could totally write an enemies-to-lovers where there actually were two rooms left, but then something happened in one of them, and the heroine needed to reluctantly seek out refuge in the hero's room...

"Rae!" His stern voice snapped out her name, making her jump.

Crap. She was just standing there in front of Brian's door, under the light in plain view, daydreaming. Rae jumped forward, scurrying in as Brian frowned at her from where he was standing in the middle of the room, hands on his hips.

"What were you doing?"

"Thinking." Which wasn't really a good explanation. "Having ideas for one of my books. Sorry. I get really lost in thought sometimes when that happens." She really hoped he didn't ask her what kinds of ideas she was getting. She wasn't sure how he'd feel about her turning the circumstances of this week into a romance novel. Would he understand that she was just fictionalizing and romanticizing the situation? She didn't know.

He raised an eyebrow as he closed the door, tilting his head in consideration.

"For your books? Does that happen a lot?"

"Sometimes." Rae shrugged one shoulder, coming deeper into the room, closer to him. "I get ideas all the time. Normally, I try to write them down somewhere, but if I think them through enough, I can usually remember until I can write them down." She wasn't too worried about forgetting this idea.

Rather than answering her, Brian turned away and walked over to the side of the room. He picked up the resort's notepad and pen that were sitting there before returning to hand it to her.

"Here."

Blinking in surprise, Rae took it from him. "Um, shouldn't we talk about my villa—or lack thereof—and what we're going to do?"

"After you write down what you need to." He gestured toward the small table.

Well, fine then. Fuzzy warmth filled her as she went to sit down and write. Her friends had been mostly supportive of her writing endeavors. They bought her books and even read them. Her family... well, the reactions had been mixed. Damian, her ex, had rolled his eyes every time she'd brought them up. To be fair, he felt that way about the entire romance genre, not just her books.

That had definitely played into their breakup.

Having Brian react to her statement by immediately giving her what she needed was... well, she appreciated it as much as it made her want to kick him. Why did he have to be *almost* perfect?

Hmm. *Almost Perfect.* That would be a good name for a book.

BRIAN

Watching Rae write furiously on the notepad he'd provided her, Brian couldn't help but smile. He didn't know anything about being a writer, but he'd read her books, even though they weren't his usual genre. Actually, they'd ended up expanding what he read because he went on to read some more romances from there and thoroughly enjoyed them.

He'd always been more of a sci-fi guy, but he'd never objected to some romance thrown in with his spaceships and aliens. It turned out that he rather liked reading about kinky romance especially. Granted, he wasn't sure how he felt about seven-foot aliens with extra appendages on their dicks, but he'd given those books a try, too.

Thankfully, Rae wrote kinky contemporary romance with characters he'd found easy to relate to. She didn't have many, but he was looking forward to the next one. Not that he'd tell her that. Since she didn't talk about her writing much around the club, he wasn't sure how she felt about people she knew reading her books. But he didn't want to stop, so as long as she didn't know, then she couldn't tell him to stop.

Letting her write also gave him some time to figure out what he was going to do. Wandering over to the kitchenette, he got out two glasses and poured them both some water while he thought. It had been one thing to invite her to stay for a night, but the whole week? The problem was not that he wanted her out of his villa—the problem was how much he wanted her to stay.

On the other hand, were a few more nights really that big a deal? Had he really thought that one night with her and POOF, he'd be ready to go scene with someone else? He already knew that wasn't going to be a thing. Even if she didn't stay in his room for the rest of the trip, he was having trouble picturing himself scening with anyone else.

Picturing her scening with someone else made him want to put his fist through the wall.

The obvious solution to both problems was for her to just stay the rest of the week. That way, he wouldn't have to try to force himself to scene with someone he wasn't interested in, and he wouldn't have to see her scene with anyone else.

The downside was he wasn't going to want the week to end. He already hadn't wanted tonight to end. On the other hand, that was partly because there were more things he wanted to do with her. To her. Maybe that was the problem the last time, too.

He hadn't been able to fully satisfy his fantasies. This time, that would be all he was looking to do. No more trying to convince her that they worked together or that she needed a Daddy Dom. No more setting himself up for rejection. But having a few days to actually get his fill of her, instead of only an intense scene followed by nothing...

Plus, all the reasons he'd invited her to stay tonight still applied.

Maybe this was his sign from the universe. Last time they'd hooked up, he'd had hope that maybe it could be something more. This time, he knew it couldn't, so he could go into the situation with no expectations and, therefore, no subsequent disappointment.

"Done!" Rae said, and Brian refocused his attention on her.

Walking over to the table, he slid the glass in front of her and sat down in the chair next to hers. He didn't miss that she pushed the notepad she'd been writing on back a little, obviously wanting to keep it private. Very well, he wouldn't look, even though he was wildly curious.

"Drink," he said, nodding at the glass. First things first—keep her hydrated. He nodded again in satisfaction when she obeyed. He liked seeing her drinking the water he'd gotten for her. "So. It looks like we need to renegotiate your stay."

Something flashed in her eyes but was gone too quickly for him to be able to name it. Trepidation? Worry?

Well, he could solve that for her quickly. He smiled at her, turning it into more of a leer as he leaned forward and put his hand on her leg.

"So, sweetheart," he drawled, elongating the words more than he normally would have. "What do you have to offer to keep me interested for more than one night?"

Surprise flittered across her expression, quickly replaced by amusement and interest. She decided to play along.

"Oh, well... you mean other than my mouth and pussy? Hmmm." She widened her eyes in mock innocence that made his dick stir. "I don't know. What else could be left?" The mock innocence was turning more mocking than innocent, as he could have anticipated. Little brat.

He had to chuckle, though.

Putting his hand on her knee, he gave it a little squeeze.

"I'm sure you can think of something." His fingers moved higher, flirting with the edge of her skirt. If he found out anyone did this to a woman in real life, he'd mete out some justice, but there was something very fun about pretending to be a sleazy landlord. It also gave him the courage to do something he normally wouldn't and broach the subject of one of her hard limits. Just to see.

"Hmmm... maybe you could call me 'Daddy'?"

He leaned into letting his voice go higher at the end of the question to make it clear that this was not a demand on his part but just a testing of the waters. To his surprise, Rae didn't immediately start shaking her head or push his hand from her leg, and hope started to rise a bit...

Tapping one finger to her chin, she pondered for a long moment, making his heart start jumping before she shook her head.

"Sorry, 'not the mama' is the best I can do." She deadpanned it, sounding so much like the bald guy from that pawn shop television show that Brian couldn't help but crack up, despite his disappointment.

He wrestled with his own mirth, dispelling the image of the dinosaurs that immediately came to mind. She grinned back at him, clearly too pleased with herself. Clearing his throat, he gave her as stern a look as he could.

"Don't you dare call me that." Unfortunately, his strictness was completely undermined by his amusement and his enjoyment of how damned pleased she was with herself.

"What are you going to do to me if I do?" Her eyes were full of mischief as she asked the question, and he wouldn't put it past her to try it out just to see his reaction.

Which meant he needed to have a really good answer.

"Soap your mouth."

Eyes widening, Rae's hands flew to cover her mouth. Oh, she did not like that threat. Good to know; he marked off a little check box in his brain. It was good to have a few actual punishments on hand when dealing with a bratty sub.

"You wouldn't!" She said it in the aggrieved tone of someone who knew what they were talking about, and Brian couldn't help but chuckle.

"Familiar with the experience?"

She glared at him over her hands, which were still covering her mouth.

"My mama when I was ten, and she caught me dropping an f-bomb." Rae shook her head. "You're not doing that to me."

"As long as you don't call me 'not the mama,' you won't have to worry about it, will you?" He got to his feet, holding out his hand. "Now, let's go back to the bedroom and discuss... payment."

Slowly, suspiciously, Rae lowered her hand to his, watching him like she thought he was going to run to get the soap any moment. She wasn't adding it to her hard limits, and he didn't get the impression there was actual trauma there, but he was mentally adding it to a list of actual disciplinary actions. He wondered how she would react to writing lines, which was another fairly standard Daddy Dom punishment.

Spankings definitely didn't deter her behavior—which was nice because he enjoyed giving a good pleasure spanking. If he could keep all the non-sexual punishments for actual discipline...

You're not going to be her Dom long-term, remember? It's just for this week.

Though he wasn't kidding about soaping her mouth out if she called him 'not the mama.' A man had to draw a line somewhere.

"So... I'm staying here this week? With you?" There was something in her voice, a yearning for confirmation, for reassurance, that Brian responded to immediately.

"Yes." He said it firmly. "This week, we'll be vacation lovers."

Hand still in his, Rae stared at him, her expression inscrutable, before she nodded.

"What happens on the island stays on the island."

There was an odd ache in his chest as he nodded his head, but it didn't hurt nearly as much as he'd thought it would. Some of the ache also felt like relief. They were on the same page. They had an agreement. By the time the week was over, he'd be ready to move on, and the ache wouldn't be there at all.

"Exactly."

12

———

RAE

Banging for bunk.

That's what it was. That's all it was.

A fun vacation fling—it just happened to be with someone she knew before vacation.

Knowing it wasn't meant to last could have been a turnoff. Instead, it seemed to make both of them more desperate to get what they could from each other.

As soon as he'd agreed with her, Brian pulled her into his arms and claimed her lips with a kiss that made her toes curl. He stripped her down as he maneuvered to the bedroom. After being clamped, her nipples and clit were so extra sensitive that the barest brush against the swollen buds had her moaning and shuddering.

This time, Brian didn't hesitate, didn't tease or torment... he paused only to grab a condom. Fingers wreathed through hers, he had her hands pinned down on either side of her head as he thrust inside her, her legs wrapped around his waist. It was hot and hard, his gaze boring into hers, watching her as he fucked her hard.

She cried out as she came, the pulses of her orgasm hitting her as hard and fast as his thrusts, her swollen clit buzzing with erotic satisfaction as his dick pounded in and out of her. Every thrust rubbed him up against the poor nub, making her writhe as he kept fucking her through her orgasm. Rae tried not to make too much noise, just in case there was anyone nearby on the beach or walking by the villa, but it wasn't easy as her body buzzed and hummed beneath his.

Brian groaned, shuddering and thrusting in deep as he pressed his lips to hers, grinding his body against her clit, muffling her screams of pained pleasure as the intense ecstasy of her extended orgasm became too much to bear. She started fighting his hands pinning her. As his grip tightened around her wrists, he pulled away from the kiss, pulsing inside her as he came. Rae's cries filled the air around them, tears sliding down the sides of her cheeks and into her hair from the glut of overstimulation.

By the time he slumped over her, every inch of her skin felt extra sensitized, as though it was all one big nerve ending. She actually twitched when he began to pull away, sliding his cock from her swollen pussy; that's how sensitive she felt. Rolling to the side, Brian pressed a kiss to her shoulder before getting up, not seeming to notice the shiver that small touch sent through her. Her whole body felt like a giant pleasure spot, one that was currently drunk on bliss.

Staring up at the ceiling, Rae took in and let out a deep breath.

Holy shit.

How was she supposed to get through a whole week of sex like this, then go back to nothing?

On the other hand, her other option was 'no sex' because she honestly couldn't imagine hooking up with someone else now that she'd made this agreement with Brian. Mind-blowing sex and endless orgasms for a few days, then nothing was better than just 'nothing.'

Right?

Yawning, Rae made herself roll onto her side. She needed to brush her teeth. Get her wrap over her hair. Lotion herself. The salty air was drying her out.

The moment she moved, Brian was there, helping her up with a smile.

Getting ready for bed with him was... odd.

Far more intimate than taking his dick in her mouth or her pussy. As weird as that was, it was true. It was a side of him she hadn't seen before and one she hadn't shown of herself before, at least not to him. Sex was one thing—seeing someone's nightly routine was another.

Especially when he joined in, taking his own handful of lotion and crouching down to smooth it over her legs. His touch made her skin come to life again when all the arousal had finally started to simmer down.

Maybe it was a good thing she was stuck here all week. It would give this insane attraction some time to dissipate. Heck, half of his appeal might just be from not knowing enough about him. Definitely, the more she'd gotten to know her exes, the less she'd liked them... which was how they'd ended up being exes.

Though she was surprised when his fingers didn't start wandering.

"Are Doms supposed to do that?" she asked, amused and waving her hands at her legs as Brian got to his feet.

He raised his eyebrows, as though he wasn't sure where her question was coming from.

"Do what?"

"Get on their knees and... you know. Lotion." She waved her hand again. "Aren't I supposed to be serving you?"

Rubbing his hands together, he cocked his head at her as he moved around behind her, seeming to think about what she'd said. Looking at her in the mirror, he began to smooth lotion across her back, and her shoulders relaxed.

"Do you want to put lotion on me?" he asked after a moment.

"Not particularly. Does that make me a bad sub?" It made her feel a little bad that she didn't want to reciprocate. She would if he asked her to, but it wouldn't have occurred to her to do it first.

Master Damian, her recent ex, never tried to help her with anything. Mostly, she'd been expected to serve him. She'd liked parts of it, but it had gotten wearing, and he hadn't been willing to compromise on what he'd wanted, and neither had she.

"It does not make you a bad sub at all." Brian's tone was mild but firm. "Every kinky relationship looks different. You have to figure out what it's going to look like together. No two Doms are going to want exactly the same things, just like two submissives won't. Would you and Domi want the same things?"

"No." Rae didn't even have to think about it. She knew she and Domi liked very different things. Some of the things Damian had wanted, Domi wouldn't have hesitated to do, and some of the things Rae wanted, Domi would balk at.

It made sense when Brian said it. And it wasn't like Damian had actually said she was a bad submissive for not doing certain things... but she'd felt like he thought that. More than once. Which, ironically, had just made her want to be worse. So, that had worked out well for him.

She sighed as Brian dug his fingers into her shoulder blades, slumping forward and relaxing into his touch. With her hair already under her bonnet, she didn't have to worry about the lotion getting on them, and she could just enjoy.

"I like taking care of my... sub." There was only the slightest pause where he changed what he was originally going to say, which was probably 'little' or 'babygirl.' "It makes me happy and fulfills me. It doesn't matter who is on their knees. I'm still the one in charge."

His voice rang with confidence.

Rae had to admit, that was hot. It was the part of Daddy Doms that she *did* find appealing. She liked being taken care of. It made her feel loved. She knew that part of that came from the fact that her actual Daddy had always taken care of her. Her parents showed a lot of affection and other expressions of love. Every morning, her mom made coffee for her dad even though she didn't drink it herself, and every evening, her dad made tea for her mom even though he complained about her tea drawer.

They took care of each other, and they'd taken care of her, too, in the same way.

Yet again, Brian was almost perfect.

Almost.

"Come on," he said, sliding his fingers around her neck in a possessive movement that sent a happy little shiver down her spine. "Let's get some sleep. It's going to be an early start to the morning."

"It is?" she asked as she yawned, letting him lead her out of the bathroom. As far as she knew, it was just a day on the beach with everyone.

"If you want to make sure we're out of here before anyone can wake up and see us coming out..." He let his voice trail off.

Oh, right. They needed to keep everything about their current arrangement hidden away from their friends. Far, far away. Unless she wanted everyone's nose in their business, which she did not.

"Right. Yeah, up early," she agreed with another yawn. It was like now that her body knew she was ready for bed, she could barely keep her eyes open.

"Come on, sleepyhead, let's get you tucked in." Brian's voice was threaded through with amusement, and even though she wanted to protest at him talking to her like a child, she had to admit that being taken care of like this felt nice. She didn't have to do a thing as he got her into the bed, the sheets pulled up to her chin, then he climbed in behind her and spooned his body around hers. She loved being the little spoon and snuggled right in.

Brian

Hanging out on the beach with the full group was torture. Everyone was coupled up except him and Rae, and he wanted to be touching her... rubbing sunscreen into her back... hanging out with his arm around her...

It was better this way, though. Even if they didn't care what their friends might think or say, the less they acted like a couple this week, the easier going back to real life would be. But it did chafe that he couldn't do the things he wanted to do. Even something as simple as teasing or flirting with her.

At least he'd been able to help her get ready this morning. Her haircare for the beach had taken a good half an hour, even with his help, and then she'd covered it all up with a special cap that she had. He'd always been far more concerned about sunscreen, and she'd obediently let him slather it all over her before they'd left the villa, an expression of amusement on her face the whole time. Especially when he'd put some on the tops of her ears.

He'd enjoyed dipping his fingers under the fabric of her tiny bikini. Sure, it was just good skincare, but it was also enjoyable, knowing he could touch the parts of her no one else was going to get to see. Granted, on this beach, no one would bat an eye if she took it off, but it was the principle of the thing.

The resort had brought out picnic baskets and coolers of food for everyone, so they were all able to eat as they pleased as they arrived, under a tent with a table to sit at. There were also umbrellas and lounging chairs for anyone who wanted to sit back and relax without being in the full sun.

He and Rae sat down with food, making sure to sit well apart at the table, and it wasn't too long before they were joined by Domi and Mitch. If anyone had thought it odd that they'd made it to the beach before anyone else, no one said anything. Maybe no one thought it was weird. Or maybe they were all distracted by Kincaid and Zach, who were the last to show up.

"Did Rae do something?" Law asked, making Brian jump as the other man came up beside him.

"Um, what?"

"Did Rae do something?" Law nodded in her direction where she was laid out with Iris. Both of them were out in the sun, next to Avery, who was comfortably settled in a chair under one of the umbrellas. "You keep staring at her."

Brian barely managed to bite his tongue against protesting that he wasn't. Talk about a dead giveaway. Instead, he shrugged as noncommittally as he could, turning away from watching the ladies so he could focus on Law. That's what he would do if there was nothing going on. At least, he was pretty sure that's what he would do.

Maybe he could distract Law from thinking too hard about him and Rae.

"Just wondering if everyone's put on enough sunscreen," he teased, eyeing Law's hat. Law scowled at him.

"I didn't burn."

"I didn't say you did." Brian bit the inside of his cheek to keep from laughing.

"Hey! Who wants to play chicken?" Mitch yelled, gathering everyone's attention as he ran up to Domi and picked her up off her towel. She shrieked, kicking her legs and laughing. "Domi and I will kick your asses!"

Unfortunately, Brian didn't even get to try to figure out a way to have Rae on his shoulders without looking suspicious. Zach claimed Rae as his partner, grabbing her hand and pulling her toward the water as she laughed, leaving Kincaid and Brian on the beach staring at the others in the ocean. Brian wasn't jealous. Nope, not at all.

"Want to get on my shoulders?" Kincaid offered, making Brian snort.

"No, thanks." He shook his head in amusement. This seemed like as good a time as any to check in with the other man. It would also help him stop picturing what it would be like to be out there with Rae, her legs dangling down on his chest. "How's your week going so far?"

"Pretty good." The overly casual way he said it made it sound like he wasn't entirely sincere, and Brian didn't miss the way he kept his gaze focused on Zach. Shit, did he sound like that when he was trying to be casual about Rae? That was something to watch out for. Kincaid rocked slightly, shifting his weight uncomfortably. "It's been nice to get away from home and spend some time with Zach. Things have been hectic."

"Anything in particular? You don't have to talk about it if you don't want to." Brian hoped he would. The man had been keeping too much bottled up inside. Normally, he was a person who talked through things, but lately, he'd been keeping as quiet as Zach normally did. It was worrisome.

Kincaid shrugged his shoulder.

"The job changeover hasn't been easy. Especially having to testi-fy..." Kincaid's voice trailed off, and he cleared his throat as Brian grimaced and clapped him on the shoulder. He'd had to testify against his own partner after the man put his wife in the hospital. Kincaid still felt guilty for believing the man's tales about his cheating wife rather than realizing she was an abused wife. Some of his co-workers started shunning him after that, feeling he should have held to the blue line. Kincaid disagreed and eventually ended up accepting a job offer to be part of a private security and investigations firm. "Anyway. That's been stressful. And, well... Zach and I started talking about the holidays recently."

"Oh? What about them?"

"Where we're going to spend them." For the first time, Kincaid sent Brian a sidelong look, as if he was trying to figure out Brian's confusion.

"Right, I guess it's time to do that." Did people try to figure that out in the fall? Apparently. Some people. Maybe Kincaid and Zach had started early because of their relationship... as far as Brian knew, Zach still wasn't out to his family. Oh. *Oh.* "Are you meeting Zach's family this year?"

"No." Kincaid turned his attention back to the play in the ocean, his tone abrupt.

Ah. Well, fuck. Yeah, that could put some strain on a relationship. Both the not-meeting and the meeting. Kincaid had been out as bisexual when they'd all met, but even after they'd gotten together, Zach had not 'come out' anywhere but inside the club. Kincaid had seemed like he was happy to patiently wait, but maybe he was starting to get impatient.

They stared out at the others. Laughter drifted up to them over the crash of the waves.

"Want to get up on my shoulders?" Brian counter-offered Kincaid's earlier proposition, startling a laugh out of Kincaid, just as he'd intended.

"No, thanks." He shook his head as Rae managed to push Domi

off of Mitch's shoulders, leaving her and Zach as the victors. "Let them have their moment." He chuckled, seeming a little lighter as he watched Zach whooping and thrusting his fists in the air. Turning, Zach looked for Kincaid's approval, grinning when Kincaid began clapping his hands in applause, indicating he'd seen them win.

The two of them loved each other, it was clear. Brian had to believe that would be what mattered in the end.

Feeling Rae's gaze on him, he lifted one of his hands in the air, giving them a thumbs up. Everyone would think it was for Zach or maybe just for the winning team, but Rae would know... it was for her.

13

———————

Sneaking back into Brian's villa was becoming easier every time she did it—look around to make sure no one was watching, climb up onto the back porch, hop over the rail, and he was there waiting at the sliding glass door to let her in.

"Hey there, stranger," she said flirtatiously as she sashayed in past him. "Got a shower I can use?"

"Get in here," he replied with a growl, giving her butt a sharp smack. Rae giggled, scampering in a little faster, headed for the bathroom. She tugged the cap on her head off as she went, feeling satisfied to find there was no sand in her hair to deal with. So far, this week was going well on that front.

By the time she turned on the shower, she could feel Brian's presence behind her, even before he smoothed his hands down over her.

"Did you have fun today?" he asked.

"Of course. Didn't you?" He'd been right in the thick of things during the afternoon when the guys decided to have a boogieboarding contest. Iris and Domi had joined in while Rae and Avery were the judges.

They hadn't even had to cheat to declare Domi the winner after she'd actually managed to stand up on her board and surf for a few feet before falling off. Though Mitch had gotten points for attempting to use two boards at once to do the same. He'd failed miserably, but they'd awarded him extra points for effort.

"I did." He tugged at the bottom of her swimsuit, pulling it from her curves and sliding it down her legs. Obligingly, she stepped out. "I'm about to have more fun now."

"Do we have time for that?" she asked as he herded her into the shower. She sighed with satisfaction as the warm water sluiced over her. After being on the beach all day, she hadn't wanted hot water, but she hadn't wanted cold, either. Right in the middle was just right. Granted, once she got used to it and was no longer feeling over-heated, she'd crank the heat right back up.

"I guess we'll have to see."

Rae turned out to be right, though, since it took them longer in the shower with both of them in there. It was fun soaping each other down and giving extra special attention to cleaning off his erection, grinning as he groaned, hips thrusting forward between her soapy fingers.

"Where do you think you're going?" he growled when she let go and slid around behind him.

"You need to rinse off. I still need to do my makeup and get ready for dinner." She sidled closer to the sliding glass door, squealing when he caught her about the waist, pulling her back against him. The thick ridge of his erection pressed against her bottom, nestling between her cheeks.

One of his hands came up to curve around her throat while the other slid between her legs, his fingers sliding between her slick pussy folds. Rae whimpered, squirming against him as her whole body came to life, her hands coming up to hold on to the arm now pressed against her chest to help maintain her balance as his fingers circled her clit.

"Oh..."

"Hmmm... you're right." He rubbed his fingers over the sensitive nub, sending a spasm through her body as he whispered in her ear.

"About what?" Her hips moved, her lower body trapped between his hand and his cock, and she shuddered as his thumb stroked along the side of her neck.

"We don't have time for this."

Before his words really registered, he'd already stepped away, taking his hands and his warmth with him, leaving her stunned, aching, and tingling. She turned around to glare at him, but he wasn't even looking at her. He'd stepped under the water and had his head tipped back to rinse off, his eyes closed against the spray.

"Asshole," she muttered as she got out of the shower, stomping around as carefully as she could on the wet floor. She wanted to make her emotions heard, not slip and fall and crack her head open. Brian started whistling as he rinsed off while she wrapped herself up in a towel.

"No touching yourself, babygirl," he called after her as she yanked open the door to the bedroom. "All your orgasms this week belong to me."

Rae stomped out of the room and slammed the door behind her. Her body was still buzzing and humming. Part of her wanted to throw herself on the bed and get herself off. If he caught her, he caught her.

On the other hand, she was already learning that he was far too creative with his punishments. Besides, he definitely expected her to be bad. Therefore, she'd surprise him and be good. After all, she didn't want to be predictable.

Fifteen minutes later, she was back in the bathroom, putting on her makeup and trying to ignore the little flutters of arousal as she listened to Brian getting ready in the other room. When he walked in, she was bent slightly forward over the counter close to the mirror while she put on her mascara.

"Oh good, you're almost in the perfect position."

"Perfect position for what?" She glanced at her watch. There was no way they had time for sex right now. Not unless they were going to be very late. Which wouldn't necessarily bother her, but it would make sneaking out of his villa without being seen more difficult. The more people standing around outside waiting for them, the higher the chances someone would realize she was coming from his villa and not hers.

She pushed the mascara wand back into the bottle, eyeing him suspiciously as he came up behind her in the mirror.

"Perfect position for what?" she asked again, not liking the way he was smiling at her. That was the smile of a Dom who was up to something.

"This." He put his hand on her upper back, pushing her forward so she was bent at the waist over the counter.

When he flipped up her skirt, her breath hitched.

"I thought we didn't have time for this?" Her voice came out breathy and flirtatious, rather than challenging, the way she'd meant it to. Dammit. That was the effect he had on her.

His blue eyes flashed at her in the mirror as he glanced up from looking down at her ass.

"We have time for this." He smiled as he held up his other hand, fingers on the base of a thick black plug that was already shiny with lubrication. Rae made a sound of protest. "This is what you get for calling me an asshole."

Something in *my asshole. Of course.*

No wonder he was smiling that way. The jerk was probably appreciating the devious symmetry of the punishment.

Tugging her underwear halfway down her thighs, he left them there, leaving her bottom totally exposed while she was still mostly dressed. There was something about having her underwear only partially off that made her feel more exposed than if she was completely naked.

The tip of the plug probed her tight opening, and Rae gasped, closing her eyes against having to watch her own expression as it was inserted. She was sure Brian was, his gaze flicking back and forth between the plug slowly pushing into her and watching her in the mirror. It wasn't an overly large plug, but it was definitely big enough, she was going to feel it all night.

Sitting for dinner was going to be interesting.

The long, slow stretch of her hole had her panting as her body adjusted. She felt her face screw up, nose wrinkling, as it reached the thickest part, and she cried out at the sharp pang. Rather than pulling away and thrusting back in, Brian pushed the plug forward, and it slid inside her, the tight ring of her muscle snapping shut around the stem between the base and the bulb.

Rae moaned, panting again and shuddering as the plug settled inside her.

It felt incredibly full.

Since joining Marquis and Stronghold, she'd become far more used to anal play, but it always did something to her. Made her feel more submissive. More vulnerable. She liked the sting, the ache... she liked the feeling of taking it in order to pleasure her partner.

At first, she'd felt like that made her a bad feminist, but Domi had pointed out that feminism was about giving women the choice to do what they wanted. So, really, she was taking a butt plug for feminism.

This is what you're going to think about while you're plugged? Really?
Yup.

"Good girl." Brian patted her bottom before pulling her underwear up, both acts making her feel extra breathless and submissive. At this point, she wasn't sure she was ever going to get enough air in her lungs again.

Rae opened her eyes, pushing herself up as she did so. The plug shifted inside her and she made a face, well aware of Brian's gaze on her, enjoying the changes in her expression, reading her body language far too accurately for comfort. When she met his gaze in the mirror, he looked so smug, she'd want to kick him... if she didn't want his dick so bad.

BRIAN

Tonight, the guys and the girls were eating dinner separately, which Brian would have found a relief under normal circumstances. Normal circumstances being when he and Rae weren't hooking up.

Now, it made him antsy.

Though he did like to think of her plugged, constantly thinking about him and internally cursing him as she shifted around, trying to get a comfortable seat... and him not even available for her to glare at. He wondered if the other women would notice.

No, don't go there. That wouldn't be a good thing.

"So, I got a call from Olivia today," Law said, interrupting Brian's errant thoughts and bringing him back to the dinner table. Down the table, Kincaid's head jerked up to look at Law. He and Zach were sitting on opposite sides of the table rather than next to each other, which didn't necessarily mean anything but also might not mean anything good. Olivia was the manager of Marquis, where Law sometimes taught classes.

"Is everything okay with Cassidy?" Kincaid asked immediately. Even though he'd left the force, Brian knew Kincaid had been keeping tabs on the submissive who'd escaped her abusive Dom. Unfortunately, he'd started showing up in Cassidy's life again recently—at least, they were pretty sure it was him leaving threatening notes for her.

Law grimaced. He'd been injured after helping kick Cassidy's ex out of Stronghold. The other man had run his car into Law's on his way out of the parking lot.

"Yes and no. Olivia did tell me that Cassidy has received a few more threatening notes, but no one can prove they're from that asshole, Don." Law shook his head. "She's getting nervous. I think Patrick might suggest moving her soon if Don doesn't cut it out, but she'll have to agree."

"That might be for the best," Nick said quietly, shaking his head. "Considering that asshole just keeps popping up, I don't think he's going to go away. She might need to be the one to get away. Which sucks."

"It does. But I think Patrick might send her to his cousin, who can definitely protect her." Law sighed. "The other issue is that Julie might need some protecting."

"Is this about her secret admirer again?" Zach asked, his tone sardonic. Mistress Julie had been getting gifts at Marquis for months now, always from a secret admirer who, so far, had shown no desire to actually come forward. Law had been riled over the notes from the very beginning, but Julie had not. Everyone else tended to fall somewhere in the middle, but as the months went on, most of them had fallen into thinking it was pretty harmless.

"Yes, it is." Law glared at Zach, and his next words had all of them sitting up straight. "This time, her 'admirer' sent a present to her house."

The statement landed with a thud amid silence as the happy reverie of the week was broken.

"That's an escalation," Kincaid said after a moment.

"Yes. Exactly. *Now,* does everyone want to take it seriously?"

"Well, hold on, what did he send? And what did Julie say about it?" Zach asked, leaning forward and frowning at all of them. "We already knew it had to be someone from the club, right? So, it's not that far a stretch to think that maybe they got her address from there... and Julie's not there as much this week because you guys don't have any classes running since you're here, right?"

Law shifted in his seat, frowning even more fiercely at Zach. He also didn't answer right away. Kincaid was frowning, too, as though he wanted to protest that an escalation was an escalation, but he was looking at Zach... he didn't want to fight with his partner.

Fair enough.

"Okay, spill the tea." Mitch pointed the little pink plastic sword, still adorned with a cherry from his fruity frozen drink, at Law. "It's for the groom."

The joke—a twist on declaring something 'for the bride' and therefore mandatory—broke the tension, as Mitch had probably meant it to.

Law sighed. "Olivia says Julie isn't concerned. For the same reason Zach just said. The message said that it's the one-year anniversary of the first roses that were sent and explained they were sent to her home since they couldn't be sure she would be at the club this week." Law crossed his arms over his chest and glared. "However, Olivia is finally becoming concerned and wanted me to be kept updated and also to pass the message on to Kincaid. I figure the more eyes on Julie, the better."

"I'm not sure Julie needs protecting," Nick muttered, shifting in his chair like he wanted to cover his groin. He was the only one at the table who had been through Dom training with her. Law had been accepted into the club without going through the training class because of prior experience at another club, and the rest of them had all gone through it with Olivia. Law transferred his glare to Nick, who held up his hands in surrender. "I'm not saying I won't keep an eye out for her, man, you know I will. I'm just saying... she's a lot more dangerous than she looks at first glance."

"That doesn't mean she can't be surprised, especially when she refuses to put her guard up about this." Law looked around the table at all of them, his fierce protectiveness shining through.

It wasn't that Brian didn't feel protective. He just was more like Zach and Nick... not entirely sure it was necessary. The situation with Cassidy had Law on edge, though, and there was nothing he could do about that. That was a clearly dangerous situation that was being handled by others. He could do something about this, even though the danger was less clear.

"We'll keep her safe," he said reassuringly.

The discussion moved on to discussing what protective measures Julie might or might not tolerate. The only upside to it was that everyone was so involved in the discussion, they didn't notice how distracted Brian was, wondering about Rae and what she was doing right now.

14

———————

Brian Hyde was a pain in her ass.

Literally, right now, because she couldn't sit comfortably at all.

Okay, maybe it wasn't a pain in her ass. It was a discomfort in her ass. A nuisance in her ass. A freaking dickhead who she couldn't stop thinking about every three seconds because the moment she forgot there was a plug in her ass, she'd move in a way that forcibly reminded her.

Which was probably exactly what he'd intended.

The dickhead. Freaking devious Doms.

She couldn't even complain about it to her friends because then she'd have to explain why she'd let Brian put a plug in her ass.

It would be better when they were no longer sitting down to eat. The plug was at its most uncomfortable when she was sitting. It hadn't been nearly this distracting when she was walking.

Domi bumped her elbow against Rae's, getting her attention.

"I'm sorry," Domi said.

"What?" Rae blinked, her brain trying to loop back the conversation that had been going on around her that she'd barely been paying attention to. She didn't think Domi had said anything she needed to be sorry for. "Why?"

"I feel like a bad friend." As Domi spoke, the rest of the conversation died down, centering all the attention on her and Domi.

"We all kind of feel like bad friends," Avery confessed on Rae's other side, making her swivel her head back around in surprise. She looked across the table at Iris to see her nodding.

"But why?" she asked, genuinely confused. She had no idea where this was coming from.

It did not help when they all stared at her, confused by her confusion. What the hell was she missing?

"Um, we've been basically ignoring you the past couple days," Domi said.

"No, you haven't," Rae replied automatically.

"Okay, maybe not all day or anything, but in the evening, we go off with our men, and you've been left to fend for yourself," Iris said, her voice and expression full of apology.

Oh.

Oh.

Rae was finally starting to get an inkling of where this talk was going, but she wasn't sure how to derail it or what to do about it.

"We feel bad that we keep abandoning you without making sure you're taken care of," Domi said, reaching out to take Rae's hand in hers. "Bachelorette parties are supposed to be about the bridal party spending time together, not about us spending time with our partners."

"Yeah, but this isn't a regular bachelorette party. It's a Jack-and-Jill party." Rae squeezed Domi's fingers, giving her a bright smile. "We're supposed to spend time with the guys. It's been great. You don't need to worry about me. I don't want you to worry about me."

"It's not that we're worried, exactly," Avery chimed in again. "But we want to make sure that you're taken care of, too."

"Yeah, no woman left behind. Or without orgasm." Iris giggled. "Basically, we're going to make sure you get a hookup tonight before we all peel off."

Well, shit.

"Seriously, you all, I'm totally fine." She felt her cheeks clench around the plug as she forced herself to keep grinning at them. "I really don't want this week to be about me. It's supposed to be about Domi and about everyone enjoying themselves."

"Which is why we're trying to make sure you enjoy yourself, too," Domi replied. "Because we've all been having fun at night... and..." Her voice trailed off.

Right. Shit. They all assumed she wasn't having 'fun' at night because she wasn't telling them about any raunchy hookups or anything. Because if she had hooked up with someone, she would have told at least one of them at some point.

Except she had hooked up with someone, and she hadn't told any of them because she didn't want them to know who she was hooking up with. Yet.

Mother fucker.

Talk about being caught in a trap. She should have realized they'd become curious about why she wasn't having a hot vacation fling on sex island. She didn't know why she hadn't even considered the possibility. Maybe because she'd been too preoccupied with what was going on with Brian and her room to think about the inevitable outcome of keeping her friends in the dark.

Had she really thought they'd spend all week not paying attention to what she was doing with her nights? If she'd taken a moment to think about it, she would have known that was not how it was going to happen.

But she hadn't been thinking. Clearly.

She cleared her throat.

"Who says I'm not having fun at night?" She gave them all a little wink. The expressions around the table ranged from delighted to shocked.

"Wait, with who?"

Thankfully, she had read so many romance books, it wasn't hard to come up with a fun and plausible scenario. Granted, it was only plausible on kink island, but it still worked.

She shrugged one shoulder.

"Don't know. He was wearing a mask, and we didn't exchange names." Which didn't narrow things down for them at all. There were quite a few people wearing masks of varying sorts in the Dungeon and around the resort in the evenings. Even on an island fully devoted to the lifestyle, there were people who felt more comfortable covering their faces. "The whole point of a vacation hookup is to be mysterious, right? I don't want to know who he is, and I don't really want him to know much about me, either. Makes it easier to leave everything behind on the island in a couple days."

"When did this happen?" Iris demanded to know, leaning forward and bracing her elbows on the table so she could prop her chin up on her hands. "Tell us everything!"

Well, crap.

At least she didn't have to make up too much.

She told them about her hookup in the cabana with Brian, leaving out a few key factors—like his identity and exactly where she'd run into her 'mystery masked man.' She didn't know if Avery would put two and two together since she and Nick had run into Brian right after, but the more she could do to avoid that risk, the better.

"So, you don't need to worry about me."

"Are you going to see him again?" Avery asked, looking a little starry-eyed. "What's he look like? I mean, even with the mask, he can't have covered everything. Was he white? Black? Brown? Long hair, short hair?"

Rae shrugged, keeping it noncommittal. There was no way she was going to start trying to describe someone. The last thing she needed was for them to find a masked man running around the resort who actually fit the description. That would be worse than if they couldn't find one.

"Maybe. I'm not going to tie myself down to one mystery man, though. Maybe I'll run into him again tonight, maybe I'll find someone else to scene with, maybe I'll just watch a scene." She looked around at her friends, loving them with all her heart for their desire to do right by her and wishing that maybe they were a little less invested in that. "The main thing is that I do not want to take away from anyone else's vacation. I'm fine, I promise you. And I will find a scene or a hookup a lot easier if I'm not surrounded by three other incredibly hot women, especially if they bring all their men along with them."

Silence fell over the table as her friends considered her words. She thought it was a pretty good point. After a moment, Iris snickered.

"We are all pretty hot. We don't want to be a distraction."

"Seriously, it's been a problem in the past when a guy would meet Domi and me at the same time." Rae laughed. "They'd get so confused about which one of us they wanted to go after. We'd whisper, *stay on target* to each other when we saw it start to happen."

"Did they?" Avery asked.

"Rarely." Domi laughed. "Mitch did. But I think it was different with him and the rest of those guys because they were all leading a class with us as the students. They all got hands-on time with both of us."

"Honestly, I thought Kincaid and Domi were going to hook up for a bit," Rae admitted. "I did not see her and Mitch coming."

"Yeah, and I thought Rae and Brian were definitely going to end up together, but here we are." Domi shrugged while Rae did her best to hide her wince as her ass clenched around the plug again.

Yeah, here they were.

"What else is going on? I've spilled what I've been up to. What about you all? Anything particularly juicy?" She winked at Domi, who laughed and obliged by telling them about a medical scene she and Mitch had done last night. Working as a nurse in real life, Mitch was really good at playing doctor. Domi had gotten a very thorough exam.

Avery and Nick had apparently watched a demonstration on cupping. Nick was newer to kink than the other Doms—in fact, Avery was the experienced one in their relationship—but he was eager to learn. Cupping did sound interesting, though not really something Rae was necessarily interested *in*.

"They had some violet wand attachments here that Law hasn't used before, so we played with those, of course," Iris said, eyes sparkling when it was her turn. She lowered her voice, glancing around. "That's not the big news though. We both got phone calls today. Mistress Julie's secret admirer sent a present to her house, and Law is totally freaking out."

"Ohhh... I would be freaking out, too," Avery said, putting her hand on her chest with wide eyes. "He knows where she lives?"

"Apparently. I called Sam to find out what's going on because Law went into hyperactive protective mode. Sam's been hanging out with the Dommes sometimes lately, so I thought she might know what's going on. She said Julie's nervous but not scared." Iris shrugged. "She hasn't been in the club all week. She's taking a break since there are no classes, and apparently, it was the one-year anniversary of the first present she got. She thinks that's why they sent it to her home because they didn't want to miss the anniversary."

They all thought about that for a moment.

"That is either the sweetest or creepiest thing I've ever heard," Domi finally said. "I can't decide which."

"I think it depends on who the secret admirer is." Rae shifted in her chair, hiding her wince at the way the plug shifted inside her. *Dammit Brian.* "Did you ever see that meme going around the internet about how Christian Grey was only a hero because he was a sexy millionaire? Like, there's such a thing as book-hot, which is very different from real-life-hot."

"True, but how crazy would you have to be to be a creeper with a Dominatrix? Especially because the admirer is clearly submissive." Iris shook her head. It was a good point. "Like, sure, your biggest fantasy could be being punished, but talk about taking risks."

"I just want to know why go the secret admirer route?" Avery said, taking a sip of her drink. "It feels very high school."

"It must be someone who thinks their crush would be rejected.

Maybe that it wouldn't even be acceptable," Rae mused, thinking through possible motivations in her head. It was one of the things she loved to do and probably why she'd ended up becoming an author. She liked to try to figure out what made people tick, why they did the things they did. "Mistress Julie is straight, right? Maybe the admirer is a woman."

"Maybe they're nonbinary... maybe it's Emery," Iris suggested.

Rae considered that for a moment.

"I feel like Emery is too outspoken for that. They go after what they want, and they're not quiet about it," she said. Though, sometimes, even the most confident people kept secrets.

"That's a good point." Iris leaned back in her chair, sipping her water thoughtfully, as though she was trying to think of more options.

"Maybe they're a Dominant." Domi laughed. "That would be a good reason not to reveal themselves. They admire from afar but don't say anything because they don't want to submit. Or a switch, and they know she wouldn't go for being a sub."

"Maybe it's someone who's a friend and is afraid of ruining the friendship." Rae's brain was churning with possibilities now. She hadn't given it a lot of focused thought before, though, of course, she'd wondered from time to time. Everyone who knew about Mistress Julie's admirer must have thought about it every now and then. "Ooooh... or someone she doesn't get along with, and it's like an enemies-to-lovers kind of thing."

"Maybe it's someone just trying to cause drama."

They all looked at Iris, who seemed to immediately regret saying it. She ducked her head, avoiding all their gazes as she stabbed at a piece of meat on her plate with her fork. The fork skittered across the plate with a screeching sound, and they all flinched, including Iris.

"Everything okay?" Avery asked cautiously after a moment. "That seemed... pointed."

"I don't want to bring down the mood." Iris sighed, still not looking up from her plate. "I shouldn't have said anything. It just... popped into my head."

"I think the question is *why* it popped into your head," Domi said.

"And you're not bringing down the mood. But you can't bring up or say something like that, then not spill the tea. That's just rude."

"If you don't tell us, that will bring down the mood because we'll all be making up scenarios in our head for what you could be talking about," Rae added. Because that was exactly what would happen. "We might even blame Law."

"It's about Noelle." Iris made a face as everyone groaned in response to her ex-roommate and ex-best friend's name. "See? I didn't want to bring down the mood."

"It's not your fault. We're just tired of that bitch." So, so freaking tired. Rae shook her head. She didn't understand why some people just felt the need to constantly create drama around themselves and drag other people into it. Iris wanted nothing more than to be left alone to live her life, but Noelle wouldn't allow that. She took offense at everything Iris did, which had nothing to do with her, and was constantly claiming that Iris living her own life was somehow bullying her. "What did she do now?"

"Apparently, she's just been really insecure with Sam, insisting that I must be talking about her to Sam and saying that Sam's pulling away from her because of me. Which I'm *not*." Iris shook her head. Sam was the girlfriend of one of Law's best friends, which meant that she and Iris had become friendly, but only after Noelle had made friends with Sam. Noelle had not handled it well. "Sam knows that, but she wanted to know if I had any tips for helping Noelle believe her since we used to be friends. Which, if I did, I would tell her, but I don't know what she's thinking or why she's acting like this."

"Because she's obsessed with you and can't stand the idea of you moving on without her. She wants to turn people against you because that's the only way she can feel like a victim. Especially if she can turn friends against you. Like, I'm not saying she *is* a narcissist because I'm not qualified to make that call, but she really acts like one." Rae blew out her breath. God, she hated that bitch and wished she would just go away.

If only people could be kicked out of Marquis and Stronghold for being unlikeable. But no, they could only be kicked out for breaking rules. There were plenty of rules to make the space a safe one for everyone, but there were no rules about being a bitch outside of it. Granted, if Noelle came after Iris directly, even outside of the club, that would probably get her removed, but she was too smart for that.

She just constantly played the victim, making sure to cry loudly about how mean Iris was being to her or how Iris was turning people against her instead of acknowledging how her own behavior was making people not want to be around her. Not to mention acknowledging the reason she and Iris were no longer friends was because she'd been an *awful* friend to Iris. She'd ended the lease on their apartment without even consulting Iris when she'd gotten mad about Iris getting involved in the kink scene and making friends other than her, then acted like it was Iris' fault they were no longer friends.

If Noelle was a better person, she could have just made friends with Iris' new friends, but instead, she'd spent all her time putting Iris down in front of them, then trying to get between them and Iris. Poor Iris had put up with all of it because she'd felt bad about 'hurting Noelle's feelings' right up until Noelle had caused her to almost end up being homeless.

"I don't know anything about narcissists, but the rest of that sounds right," Domi said sympathetically. "The best thing you can do is ignore her. She's looking for attention... don't give it to her. All of your friends know and see what's really going on. She feeds off of any attention, good or bad, so it's best to just stay away from that whole situation."

"I just feel bad for Sam being stuck in the middle." Sighing, Iris rubbed her hands over her face. "And I hate thinking that there are people in the club who think I'm some kind of terrible bitch who bullied her."

"Yeah, but you didn't put Sam there. She's in the middle because Noelle won't let her be friends with both of you, and she's trying to stay friends with Noelle. For some reason." Hey, Rae had never been shy about making her feelings known, and she wasn't going to start now.

"And if some people aren't bothering to get both sides of the story, then that's on them," Avery said firmly. "It will probably come back to bite them when she does the same thing to them that she's doing to you. She's like a toxic ex. Don't feed the troll."

That got a short laugh from everyone, though it wasn't really a 'that's funny' laugh but an acknowledgment of the truth of the statement.

"I swear, I don't want to ruin her time at Stronghold or keep others from making friends with her," Iris said, her laugh dropping as quickly as it had come. "I just want to be able to enjoy the club and move on with my life."

"Which is exactly what you should do. You should ask Sam not to tell you about the things Noelle is saying anymore." Domi reached out to take Iris' hand across the table. "And trust me, we see what she's doing. We've got you."

"Thanks." Iris looked around at all of them as she squeezed Domi's hand back, her eyes a little shinier than usual. "I love you all so much."

"We love you, too. Girl hug!" Rae sang out, leaning over. They all squished around Iris, laughing for real now as they came together in support.

She loved her friends so much. They were the best.

Even if she was going to have to tell Brian he was now her masked mystery lover and not to be too surprised when he heard about it.

It was all because her friends loved her. And that was worth the bit of inconvenience when it came to having an island fling with her 'not the mama.'

15

———————

"Hey, maybe we should wingman Brian!"

Brian blinked at Iris, not understanding what she was saying or how he'd suddenly become the topic. He hadn't been paying attention to the conversation after they'd rejoined the ladies, meeting them at the entrance to the Dungeon. The other guys looked as confused as he felt, but all the women's faces had lit up—even Rae's, though hers was lit up with amused laughter rather than excitement like the other three.

"Uh, what?" he asked.

"Wingman, you," Iris repeated. "You know... help you get laid?"

He blinked again, trying to decide if he should feel insulted or not.

"You think I need help getting laid?" Insulted. He was definitely feeling a little insulted.

"You know," Rae interrupted from the back before any of her friends could answer, "I'm starting to think you all just wanted to live vicariously through someone who was looking for a hookup and not that you actually wanted to help *me* out at all."

"Hey!" Domi rounded on Rae, putting her hands on her hips and scowling, her curls bouncing around her face as she scowled. She looked like an annoyed fairy. "We just want to help everyone get laid. There's nothing wrong with that."

"I don't need any help getting laid." Brian avoided his friends' gaze as all of them looked at him with curious eyes. "Just because I don't talk about getting laid doesn't mean I need help getting laid."

And that was way too many times saying 'getting laid' in a row, but... well, he was flustered. He and Rae were trying to avoid their friends' attention to their sex lives this week, not have them actively involved in it.

"So, you have a mystery lover, too?" Iris asked, narrowing her eyes at him.

Too.

Brian's gaze darted to Rae, then back to Iris.

"Too?" he echoed, prodding for more information. Hopefully, the little glance at Rae wouldn't be too revealing. She was the only other single in the group, so it should be natural that he'd look at her when Iris mentioned having a mystery lover, right? It wasn't like he'd suspect any of the other women, who were all in committed relation-ships, might have a mystery lover.

Iris looked back and forth between him and Rae, which made his pulse race a little when Avery answered him.

"We wanted to wingman Rae, but apparently, she doesn't need us." Avery shrugged one shoulder.

Brian raised his eyebrow, looking at Rae again with curiosity. He really wanted to know what she'd told them.

His reaction seemed to satisfy Iris' suspicions because she was no longer looking back and forth between him and Rae the way she had been a moment ago.

Phew.

"She's got a mystery lover," Domi teased, nudging Rae in her side.

Rae rolled her eyes.

"Apparently, Brian does, too," Mitch said, looking at him curiously.

"I don't have a *lover.* I just don't need help getting laid." Brian shook his head. It was time for a tactical retreat. He looked at his friends, raising his eyebrows in sympathy. "Maybe you all need some help, though, if your subs are so dissatisfied with their sex lives that they're trying to direct mine."

"Hey!" Domi put her hands on her hips, standing straight up as Iris made an aggrieved sound of protest, and Avery's mouth dropped open in shock. All of his friends looked a bit struck by the comment as well, suddenly eyeing their submissives as if questioning how well the past few nights had actually gone.

"I'll leave you to it," he said, giving the guys a salute over the ladies' heads, spinning on his heel, and walking away. Out of the corner of his eye, he could see Kincaid and Zach cracking up, laughing at the turmoil he'd just caused with his verbal bomb.

It was nice to see the two of them laughing together like that, and Brian grinned as he sauntered away. He figured he'd do a loop or two of the Dungeon, then go find Rae. Shouldn't be too hard.

Of course, he was not thrilled when he found her.

She was talking to a very muscled, very tall, masked Dom. At least, he assumed the man was a Dom from the way he was holding himself as he talked to Rae, not quite looming over her but standing far too close for Brian's liking.

He worked his jaw, unclenching the suddenly tight muscle. He knew there was no actual masked mystery lover just because one had appeared now. Walking around to the opposite side of the scene she was next to—though she was talking to the mystery Dom more than she was watching the scene—Brian managed to catch her eye.

Flashing him a smile, she turned back to the Dom and said something.

To Brian's surprise, the Dom nodded and offered her his arm, and they started walking off. Together.

What the fuck?

Gritting his teeth, he began to make his way around the scene to follow them. There was no way he was going to let that go.

Rae had one hell of a spanking coming her way if she thought she was going to just walk off with some other Dom.

Unless... does she want a threesome?

Fuck.

Granted, they'd agreed they wouldn't scene with other people, but they hadn't specifically negotiated whether or not they'd add other people. He didn't want anyone but her. It had never occurred to him that she might want to try something with someone else.

Maybe the women had mentioned a masked Dom because they knew Rae's plan.

Brian quickened his steps. Rae and the mystery Dom were far ahead of him, heading out one of the side doors into the night. He plowed on ahead, dodging around some of the other patrons and getting a few looks as he went. Part of him knew he should just let her go, if that's what she wanted, but another part of him was insisting he was missing something.

Am I willing to share her?

Maybe. If that was what he had to do.

It wasn't like they were exclusive or anything.

But it sure as hell wasn't the ideal scenario.

When he burst through the door, Rae jumped at the suddenness of his appearance, staring at him from where she was standing a few feet away from the exit. The masked Dom was nowhere in sight. Brian came to a grinding halt and stared back at her.

"Where'd he go?" he asked.

"Who?" Rae stared back at him like he was crazy.

"The Dom you were with!" He had *not* imagined seeing him, dammit.

Rae's expression changed as she realized what he was talking about, though he didn't know why it took her that long. Who else could he have been talking about?

She rolled her eyes at him.

Rolled.

Her.

Eyes.

"I wasn't *with* him. I asked for an escort outside. Iris and Avery sent him over to me, and I explained that my friends were trying to hook me up with someone, and I wasn't interested, but that I didn't want them to feel like they hadn't done a good job. This way, they'll think I left with him, he was happy to help out and go to a different part of the resort for a bit, and you... well, you were supposed to get the message to follow me out here." Her eyes narrowed, and she put her hands on her hips, right above where the skirt she was wearing puffed out. "You *were* discreet about following, right?"

"Uh..." Discreet was not the word he would use. In his defense, he hadn't known what was going on.

On the other hand, if he'd taken a moment to think things through instead of just reacting, he probably wouldn't have gone storming after her the way he had. The problem was it was hard for him to think rationally when it came to Rae. For some reason, she turned his brain sideways.

Sighing, Rae looked up as if asking for patience. Little brat. She was going to be in so much trouble once he got over feeling bad about ruining her admittedly well-thought-out plan.

"Iris was still watching me." She closed her eyes and sighed again, her breasts heaving up as she took in the breath before settling back down. Even when she was exasperated, she was hot. "Okay, if Iris asks, we'll say that you saw me leaving with someone you didn't know, so you went into protective Dom mode and went after us just to make sure everything was okay."

"Uh-huh." Brian moved closer to her, and her eyes popped open, widening as she looked up at him.

"Brian. I'm trying to make a plan here."

"It's a good plan." He grinned down at her as he moved even closer. She stepped back, glaring up at him without any real heat behind it, but there were only so many steps she could take before she ran into the railing. Her hands came up to grip it as Brian crowded her personal space.

"It's not going to work if anyone comes out here and sees us," she pointed out.

"Then let's go somewhere where no one will see us."

<u>RAE</u>

Brian's villa was becoming their own little private oasis.

Once they were inside, there was no need to worry about anyone seeing them. No need to worry that someone might walk by or overhear them or anything like that. Which she was more worried about tonight because she felt like Iris might suspect something.

She could tell from the expression on Brian's face when she'd asked about how he'd acted when he followed her that he hadn't thought about being secretive at all. Which... she wasn't sure how she felt about that. Part of her loved that he'd come barreling after her, loved the idea that he might have even been jealous, yet that wasn't the plan. It wasn't the bargain.

She wasn't supposed to want him to feel jealous because they weren't supposed to be letting emotions get involved. This was a one-week thing.

Maybe he'd just been jealous because they *had* agreed to be exclusive for the week. He was feeling possessive because the week wasn't up yet. That seemed like a very Dom thing to do. Her ex hadn't been super possessive except when they were at the club around other Doms.

Brian had seen her with another Dom, and the whole Alpha instinct thing had kicked in. Or something.

It probably didn't have anything to do with her.

Which was maybe not the best thought to be having when he was bending her over the end of his couch.

"You have the most incredibly spankable ass," he said, running his hand over the anatomy in question.

That made her feel better.

The attraction between them was real, even if the possessiveness was situational. She could deal with that.

"Are you just gonna rub it, or are you gonna spank it?" she quipped, feeling a little extra sassy as she shook her ass at him, dropping her head down to lift her bottom up more. She braced for impact, but it didn't happen.

Dammit.

Instead, she clenched as he tugged on the base of the plug in her ass and twirled it, spinning it inside her. The sensations made her gasp.

"Good girls don't top from the bottom," he chided, pulling on the plug as if he was going to remove it before letting it go again so her ass spasmed around it.

"Whoever said I was a good girl?" she asked, glancing over her shoulder at him. Though she did like hearing the words, her go-to responses tended to be brat-tastic.

"You can be good when you want to be," he replied. "I think you just like pushing people to see what happens."

Ouch. That had enough truth to sting in a way that wasn't sexy at all. It was similar to what Damian had said when they'd had the fight right before they broke up.

Rae made another face at Brian before his hand came down on her ass, giving her the little jolt of stinging pain that her body was craving, and her head dropped down again.

Yes, please.

This was what she wanted.

Pain.

Pleasure.

Not uncomfortable introspection.

She wanted to *feel.*

"Good girls get fun spankings." His hand came down again on the other side of her ass, just hard enough that she went up on her toes with a little gasp as the combined plain and pleasure rolled through her. "Do you want to be my good girl, Rae?"

"Yes."

This time, his hand came down on her thigh, and she jumped, bouncing in place.

Ow, ow, ow!

Thigh spankings *hurt.*

"Yes, what, babygirl?"

"Yes, Sir. I want to be your good girl." Heat flushed through her as she said the words. Words she could not have said under normal circumstances, words she would have choked on if she'd tried to say them anywhere else, but bent over naked in front of him with a plug in her ass and her buttocks tingling from the palm of his hand, they were words that made sense.

Just saying them made her feel hotter. Wetter. More submissive. Her pussy pulsed, fluttering in response.

Good girls also got orgasms.

"You *are* my good girl." His voice was warm. Approving. Maybe even a little possessive. His hand came down again and again, heating her ass with every stinging swat, making her bounce up and down on her toes as the crisp slaps continued. Her butt clenched around the plug with each one, her pussy quivering and begging to be filled. Rae rubbed her mound against the arm of the couch, the pleasure growing, orgasm coming closer as Brian spanked her.

But before she could get there... he stopped.

She whined, but the whine turned into a moan as he gripped the base of the plug, and this time, he pulled it free in a slow but sure movement. The sudden feeling of emptiness only lasted a few moments before the lubricated tip of his cock pressed against the small opening.

Rae breathed out as he pushed in, groaning as the ring of muscle gripped the head of his cock, her muscles convulsing as he began to thrust in. There was something so intimate about taking a man in her ass, letting him have the 'wrong' hole, entering a part of her that was supposed to remain untouched. Not to mention the level of trust she had to have.

It could so easily hurt in the wrong way.

But Brian knew what he was doing. He took his time, gripping her hips and pinning her in place while he worked his cock back and forth, going a little deeper with every thrust. Rae moaned, squirming against his hands, panting as he filled her inch by excruciating inch, opening her up for his cock while her muscles tightened around him.

Just like the spanking, the pain mingled with the pleasure. With his hands on her hips and no clamps or toys, there was nothing to distract her from the sensation of his dick stretching her. Impaling her. Going deeper and deeper inside her.

The raw rasp against her sensitive nerve endings took her breath away every time the invasion receded, then pushed in again. The aching stretch of her hole as it clenched, trying to close back up, squeezing his cock, was erotic agony, sending her sensual fervor soaring higher and higher.

"That's it. Such a good girl, taking my cock up your sweet little ass."

Oh, fuck. If he kept talking like that, she was going to cum.

16

BRIAN

The tight grip of Rae's ass around his dick was fucking heaven. Brian groaned as he bottomed out, looking down to see her completely impaled on his cock. The ring of her entrance was tightly stretched around the base, her skin a paler brown where she'd been stretched open, especially against the reddish brown of her ass from her spanking.

"Good girl," he said again, enjoying the way she clenched when he did so. "Now relax, sweetheart, so I can use your pretty little ass."

She whimpered, shuddering beneath him and clenching again as he pulled out, retreating almost to the tip before he thrust back in. Rae moaned as his cock slid back up her backside, and he released her hip to give her bottom a short, sharp swat.

She clenched around him again in reaction.

"That's it, babygirl," he murmured as he began to slowly fuck her ass. *You love Daddy's cock in your ass, don't you?*

It didn't matter that he didn't say the words out loud; they had the same effect as they echoed in his head, sending a wave of hot satisfaction through him.

Brian made sure to keep his rhythm nice and steady, so she could truly appreciate the sensation of his cock moving in and out of her forbidden hole. He'd noticed that Rae responded well to anything anal. It always made her extra melty, extra submissive.

Yes, he'd been watching her more closely than he'd wanted to admit.

He could use that knowledge now, taking his time with something he knew she both enjoyed and made her into submissive putty for him to mold. He moved with deliberation, savoring every stroke, every whimper and gasp he elicited from her, every shudder of her body as he used her for their combined pleasure.

"Please," she begged as she pushed her ass back at him, meeting his strokes as best she could while he had her lower body pinned in place. She could only move so much, but her need was making her try. "Please, please, please, please…"

He could have drawn it out, but she was begging so sweetly, he wanted to reward her. Sliding his hand between her and the couch, he curved his fingers over her mound, the tips pressing against the sensitive nub of her clit.

"That's it, babygirl," he murmured in her ear as he bent over her, bracing his other hand against the couch rather than her hip. "Get yourself off."

Rae moaned again, shuddering, bucking beneath him as she rubbed herself against his fingers, frantic movements that made her clench around his cock as she moved. He did not leave her much space, holding himself completely still, making her do all the work, rubbing her clit against his hand, pushing back against his cock.

When she let out a cry, muscles going tight beneath him, her ass rippling around his cock, he stayed in place as she worked herself through her climax. Only then did he slide his hand away, getting a good grip on her hips again, before he let go of his self-control and fucked her as hard and fast as his desire demanded.

She cried out again, spasming around him, her grip on his cock trying to tighten, but with all the lube, her muscles couldn't get purchase. Brian groaned as she massaged his cock while he thrust, slamming into her harder and harder, making the frame of the couch creak as the whole thing moved an inch.

"Fuck!"

He slammed home, sinking into her to the hilt as his balls tightened and his orgasm pulsed through him. The tight ring of her ass almost worked like a cock ring, gripping his base, each jet of cum forcing its way past her entrance and deep inside her with a pleasurable spurt. Beneath him, Rae quivered, panting, a tiny hitch in her breathing as he filled her ass with his cum.

"Oh, fuck..." The words came out on a breathless moan, and she squirmed a little beneath him as Brian's muscles relaxed. Her head dropped down, resting against the seat of the couch, both of them panting as their breathing regulated.

Running his hands over her hips and the curves of her ass, Brian closed his eyes and just enjoyed having her there, touching her. He could feel her relaxing even further as he caressed her, letting her know with his touch that she'd been a very good girl. His cock slowly softened until he shifted back, and it came free.

"Okay, babygirl," he said, helping her to straighten up. "Let's go take a bath."

"You're going to dry out my skin," Rae grumbled, though she let him turn her around and start leading her toward the bathroom.

Brian chuckled.

"I will happily slather lotion all over you when we get out," he promised.

"Bet." She grinned at him as she agreed to the deal, her eyelashes fluttering a little. While he didn't think she was quite in subspace, she was definitely pleasure drunk and a little unsteady on her feet.

Wrapping his arm around her waist to help her, something fluttered in his chest when she sighed happily and nuzzled in. Seeing Rae all soft, submissive, and cuddly just flat-out did something for him. Probably because she was so rarely like that. Most of the time, she was like a prickly hedgehog, bristling suspiciously at everything he said and did. Knowing he could fuck her into a purring, cuddly kitten was satisfying.

"Bath or shower?"

"Bath." She yawned. "That way, I don't have to do as much with my hair."

Made sense.

Brian let her take care of cleaning herself up while he got the bath running. The hotel also provided bubbles, so he took advantage of that as well, and the delight in Rae's expression when she realized she was getting a bubble bath made him grin.

"Bubbles!" she squealed, all signs of sleepiness gone from her face and demeanor.

And she thought she wasn't a babygirl.

RAE

There was just something about bubbles. Sitting between Brian's legs in the tub, her back against his front, his hands slowly gliding up and down over her body—not exactly playing with her breasts but definitely not avoiding them—Rae was having fun just picking up bubbles on her palm and blowing them into the air. She should take more bubble baths at home.

Though, to be fair, part of the fun was the large muscular man she was leaning on, who was clearly enjoying her delight. Did she always need a witness to her joy? Of course not, but it did add something to the situation. And his radiant approval of her silliness felt good.

The more time she spent with Brian, the more she realized she needed to raise the bar for future boyfriends. Damian had never made her feel like this, even before they'd started the bickering that had led to their big fight. He'd always rolled his eyes when she was being silly or tried to get her to "tone it down."

He would never have enjoyed her enjoyment of the bubbles.

He definitely wouldn't have encouraged it the way Brian did as he lifted his own palmful of bubbles, hand laid out flat in front of her for her to blow into the air. Rae huffed and blew the air out, and the pile of bubbles scattered at her breath, some of them going out in front of her, some up in the air, and some to the sides. Brian's body moved behind her, and she could feel the rumble of his chuckle vibrating through her.

Happiness bubbled up inside her, just as though it was all around her in the bath. Yeah, she definitely needed to raise the bar for future boyfriends. Was it because Brian was a Daddy Dom? Maybe. Man, she hoped that wasn't the whole reason. There had to be other reasons. There were other kinds of Caretaker Doms and Service Doms who didn't want to be called Daddy.

Why couldn't Brian be one of those?

But she didn't really wish that. Rae was a big believer in being true to oneself, and if that's what he was and what he needed, well... that was that.

"How are you feeling?" he asked, dipping his hands back in the water to rub the sides of her hips.

"Good. Warm. Happy." She grinned, even though he couldn't see her. "I'm going to be even better after that massage you promised."

His hands stopped moving.

"Did I promise you a massage?" Amusement threaded through his voice.

"I was promised a rubdown with lotion; sounds like a massage to me." She squirmed against him. Not that she thought she was going to get him hard again immediately—she wasn't even sure she wanted to, she was exhausted—but she was pretty sure he would think it was cute and get her what she wanted.

She was right.

He chuckled again, his hands starting to caress her hips again.

"I suppose it does."

Yay! She was getting a massage. Rae turned her head, so she could snuggle more against him, luxuriating in both the bath and the man in it with her. This was... bliss.

She didn't want the week to end.

So, don't think about that. Think about something else.

"By the way, you really don't need to worry about me running off with a mysterious masked Dom," she teased.

The soft caresses on her hips slowed but didn't stop.

"I didn't really think I did, but I also wasn't really thinking. I just reacted," Brian admitted. That was another one of the things she liked about him. He didn't mind admitting when he'd made a mistake. "If there's a next time, I'll do my best to think before acting."

"Good. You do that." Rae squealed when his hands lifted to her breasts, gripping the slippery mounds and pinching her nipples hard in response to her sass. Her legs kicked up water and bubbles as she laughed, trying to get away, but of course, he was right behind her, so there was nowhere for her to go.

"That's enough sass out of you, little miss," he said sternly, giving each tender bud a little twist before releasing them.

Ouchies.

Rae settled back down against him, her nipples throbbing in response to the erotic abuse. Her arousal was simmering again, but her body needed a rest, so she decided not to poke at him anymore. He was liable to poke back.

"What are the ladies doing tomorrow?" Brian asked.

Rae made a little face. She didn't really want to think about tomorrow. The days were slipping by too fast. There were only two more nights at the resort.

"Beach day. You?"

"The spa." He caressed her hips again. "I'll give you a massage tonight, but then I get one tomorrow."

"Mmm, nice. I need to do them more often at home. My shoulders especially get so tight."

Without even being asked, Brian's hands drifted up from her hips, running along her arms and up to her shoulders, where he pressed his thumbs in.

"Oh, I didn't mean you had to... but don't stop." Rae moaned as she leaned slightly forward, giving him better access to her shoulders. They might be improved after her spa day, but she was never going to say no to a free massage.

Especially when the person giving it knew what they were doing. Brian's thumbs dug in on all her sorest spots. After soaking in the bath, she was feeling especially relaxed, so it was like he could dig in deeper.

"So you don't get massages often at home?" he asked.

"The accounting firm I work at brings someone in during tax season once a week to give anyone who wants one a fifteen-minute sitting massage. It's not the same, though."

"No, though that's more than most of us get. That's nice that they do that."

Rae shrugged minutely, not wanting to move too much and perhaps accidentally causing him to stop rubbing her.

"Gotta make up for the crazy hours somehow. I'm pretty sure part of the reason Domi wanted a fall wedding was so she didn't have to try to schedule anything around my insane work schedule. There's a fall tax deadline, too, but it's not nearly as bad as the spring."

"That makes sense," he murmured, moving his fingers down her back.

Rae sighed with happiness as he kept massaging her muscles, working out some of the lingering knots and tension there.

Her schedule from January through April had been another point of contention for her and Damian. Rae bet Brian wouldn't have been an ass about her long hours and that she'd been too tired to service him when she got home. He probably would have been the one servicing her.

She could totally see him getting dinner ready for her or hot tea or something on nights when she had to stay past dinnertime. Even though she didn't really need a massage, he'd jumped right to it.

Or maybe that was just part of the pre-relationship and early-relationship generosity. Damian had been a lot more involved during the chase before he 'got' her. She knew that wasn't true of all men, though—all she had to do was look at Mitch, Nick, and Law and see how they treated their partners after becoming exclusive.

Since Brian was friends with them, maybe he'd be more like them and less like Damian.

Not that it mattered.

It wasn't as if she was getting into a relationship with him.

"We should probably get out before the water gets too cold," he said, running his hands down over her back. His words seemed to echo her thoughts. *Get out before things went sour.* But then her insides warmed at his next comment. "I'll grab the lotion and rub you down."

That was really the best part of this arrangement. Things weren't going to have time to go wrong or become sour because it was a short-term thing. She could just enjoy everything he had to offer and... yeah, raise her bar for future boyfriends. She'd started out with a high bar, thanks to her father and her grandfather, but at some point over the years, she'd started to lower it.

This was a good reminder that, yes, she could have a man who treated her like Brian did.

She just couldn't have Brian.

17

___

Waking up with his arms around Rae was one of the best feelings in the world, and he was getting a little too used to it.

Only two more mornings.

Fuck, he didn't want to think about that.

Especially when Rae was nuzzling into his chest so sweetly, making soft little sighing noises.

So, instead, he rolled her onto her back and woke her up with his mouth between her thighs until she was gasping and writhing for him, her fingers entwined in his hair. Then he got his cock in her and rocked them both to orgasm.

Talk about starting the day off right.

From there, they had to say goodbye. Rae snuck out to meet up with the girls on the beach while Brian headed over to the spa. He wasn't sure what he disliked more—spending the day where he could watch her but not touch her or spending the day completely separated from her.

At the beginning of the week, he'd been relieved that Mitch and Domi had wanted the days split up between a full-group activity and gender-segregated activities. He'd been looking forward to time with just the guys and resigned to the full-group stuff. Not because he didn't like Domi or the other women, but mostly because he'd figured he'd feel like a third wheel the whole time, and it would be incredibly awkward with him and Rae as the only singles.

Now, it was still awkward, but he felt a lot more willing to put up with it if it meant he just got to be around her.

This is the second to last day here. Better get used to not being around her.

Brian pushed away the cynical little voice in his head.

Yes, tomorrow was the last day. But it was also a day they'd all be spending together, which meant he would get to see her. And they still had tonight and tomorrow night. So, even though the guys were doing their separate thing today, he still had two nights and tomorrow to watch her, even if he couldn't touch her.

Man, that made him sound like a creeper.

Maybe he had more in common with Mistress Julie's secret admirer than he wanted to think.

Except when this week ended, he was going to be willing to let go.

"Hey." The hand clapping down on Brian's shoulder made him jump, and he blinked in surprise at Mitch, who was looking at him with concern. "You okay? I called your name like three times, and you didn't answer."

"Yeah, I'm good. Just lost in thought." He yawned as he finished speaking and shrugged, giving Mitch a rueful smile. "Maybe a little tired, too."

"Late night?" Mitch asked as Law and Kincaid sauntered up behind him. Nick and Zach were following a little farther back, deep in conversation about something. Kincaid and Zach were both smiling, even though they weren't walking together, so Brian was going to take that as a good sign.

"Late night," he agreed. Early morning. Though he didn't add that last part on.

"Where did you get off to?" Law asked, obviously overhearing Brian's statement as he and Kincaid joined them. "You were in the Dungeon one minute and then gone the next."

There was a glint in his dark eyes that Brian might not have noticed if Rae hadn't specifically told him that Iris had been watching her. Maybe Iris *had* seen him storming after her. And maybe now Law was wondering, too.

It was a good thing Rae had given him a heads up about that, or he might have floundered this moment.

"Oh yeah, well, I saw Rae walking off with some masked Dom, and she was on her own. I wanted to make sure someone knew who she was with, so I followed them out onto the porch. Then I met a very nice sub before I came back in, and we ended up not making it back into the Dungeon." He shrugged one shoulder as nonchalantly as possible.

"Nice." Mitch laughed, waving as Zach and Nick finally reached them. "Though I'm sure Rae didn't appreciate you interfering."

"She didn't," Brian said, turning away from Law's too-discerning gaze. The others didn't seem to think anything of his claim, but there was something about the way Law was looking at him that made him feel like the other man wasn't buying it. Or maybe he was projecting since he knew it was a lie... Either way, it wasn't a topic of conversation he wanted anyone focusing on. He focused on Mitch instead. "How was your night?"

"Very good." Mitch grinned like the cat who got the cream, his blue eyes sparkling as he turned to head into the spa. Everyone trooped after him. "There's something to be said for staying at a resort where literally every nook and cranny is designed to cater to kink. I wish I could convince Domi to play on the beach, but she says she'll safeword unless I'm on the bottom, and I don't want sand in my ass."

"I'm guessing that's her objection as well," Brian observed wryly.

"Of course, so I can't really protest. I suggested doggy style, but she doesn't seem convinced. Still, I've got two more days to get her around to my way of thinking."

"Why not doggy style?" Nick asked, catching up with them. "Wouldn't that fix everything?"

"That's what I thought, but she pointed out that she can't always keep her arms completely straight, and she doesn't want sand burn on her nipples." Mitch shrugged. "We're going to figure it out one way or another before we leave." From the sadistic gleam in his eye, he didn't mind the idea of Domi getting sand burn on her nipples.

"Maybe she'll be more amenable on the last day," Zach suggested from behind them. "When she'll have time to go home and recover rather than wanting to keep playing during the week." The other sadist in their group, it wasn't surprising he'd be tapped into the masochist mindset.

"That's what I'm thinking, too," Mitch agreed, a little too gleefully. Clearly, he already had his plans, which meant it was very likely he was going to get what he wanted.

If only Brian's relationship had worked out that way.

Rae

"So, how was last night?" Iris asked as she settled in the lounge chair next to Rae. Domi and Avery had gone to take a dip in the ocean to cool off. Rae wasn't quite there yet, and apparently, neither was Iris, though she couldn't help but tense at the question, wondering if there was a deeper meaning behind it.

"Good." With her eyes closed, she tipped her head back, drinking in more of the sun and doing her best to appear blissfully relaxed. _Fake it 'til you make it._ "Not the same masked Dom as the other night, but I'm starting to think I have a thing for masked Doms. There's something fun about the mystery."

"Uh-huh. Law and I saw Brian running after you out of the Dungeon."

Rae was grateful that Iris waited to drop that little bomb until the other two were away from the conversation. Not that she thought Iris would keep any juicy gossip to herself, but she appreciated that Iris was at least starting out with discretion.

Or maybe she just wanted to be the first to know.

"Oh, yeah. He was annoyed I was walking off with a total stranger. Can you believe it?"

"Yes," Iris murmured in a way that felt very loaded.

Rae decided to ignore it. She didn't want to encourage any of the 'Brian really likes you' or 'you and Brian would make a good couple if you'd just give it a chance' comments that occasionally got dropped.

She was already struggling enough with what she truly wanted. She didn't need the peer pressure on top of everything else.

"Anyway... I told him you and Law introduced Marcus to me and that he needed to mind his own business, then he went off to do his own thing."

"And you had a good night."

"I had a great night." She let the ends of her lips curve up in a smile because it was true. She'd had a really great night, even if her ass was a little sore this morning.

Maybe *especially* because her ass was a little sore this morning.

"What about you and Law? Do anything fun last night?"

"We took it a little easier. Which means I need to be prepared for something big tonight." The anticipation was clear in Iris' voice. Rae was so happy for her friend that she'd found the perfect Dom for her, though she couldn't help the little streak of envy that ran through her.

Why did it seem like everyone around her was getting their happy ending except for her?

That is what happens when you're the last single standing. It had to be someone.

It wouldn't sting so much if she didn't care whether or not she was in a relationship. Some people were perfectly happy without romance, they didn't need it for their happy ending... but Rae had always wanted it. She'd dreamed of it. Her parents had set the example, and that was what she wanted, too.

Yet it was always just out of reach for her, while her friends had gotten theirs one by one.

Dammit. She hadn't started the week feeling like this. She knew it was because Brian was so close to being everything she wanted and needed, yet she wasn't going home with him the way the rest of her friends were with their men. Part of her wanted to pout that it wasn't fair. Another part of her thought maybe this was her sign from the universe... a taste of what was possible.

When she got home, she was going to get serious about getting what she wanted. No more wasting time excusing all the things about a man that she didn't like. Brian had shown her that so much more was possible. She needed to raise the bar, thanks to him.

Too bad she couldn't be everything he needed.

Something achy curled inside her chest, making her want to rub the spot, and she was glad her eyes were closed to hide the wetness that was starting to cluster there. Ugh. She needed to cut this chain of thought before she totally lost control over her emotions.

No matter which way she thought about it, the idea of calling someone "Daddy"—even Brian—was just not going to work for her. She wished it would, she really did, but even if she managed to, she doubted Brian would enjoy hearing it through gritted, reluctant teeth.

Which made him an even better man than some, who wouldn't care how she felt as long as they got what they wanted from her.

Cold water splashed over her, and Rae shrieked as she jumped up, her eyes flying open to find Avery and Domi standing in front of her and Iris, snickering. Iris was doing the same jumping-shrieking thing Rae was.

"Domi!" Rae shouted, brushing the wetness off her stomach, even though it didn't feel that bad now that it wasn't such a shock.

"Ra-e!" Domi mimicked her, elongating Rae's name into two syllables.

"The whole point of not going down to the water was not to get wet," Iris complained, settling back down into her seat while Avery laughed and went to the bag to get the sunscreen. Despite her constant application and the fact that she spent most of the time in the shade, her pale skin was slowly getting a little darker—and turning pinkish in some places.

"Sorry, not sorry," Avery smirked. "So, what were you guys talking about?"

"The fact that Law is probably going to wear Iris out because he went easy on her last night," Rae said quickly, skipping over any mention of Brian. Hey, it *was* the last topic of conversation.

"I think Mitch has the same thing in mind," Domi said with a happy but resigned-sounding sigh. Avery came to sit in front of Iris, handing her the bottle of sunscreen so she could do Avery's back while Avery smeared it over her arms, chest, stomach, and face. "He keeps wanting to have sex out on the beach."

"Wait, you haven't had sex on the beach yet?" Avery and Iris asked in unison before glancing at each other as they all cracked up.

"You have?" Rae asked curiously as the giggles subsided.

"The first night we were here," Avery said with amusement.

"We waited 'til the second night," Iris said. "I feel like it's mandatory at some point, though, isn't it?"

"Not for me," Rae said immediately, her hand going to her hair even though it was currently covered. "Trying to get the sand out of my braids is absolute hell. It's not impossible, but it's not how I want to spend my time."

"Just make sure you're not on the bottom," Iris retorted.

"Were you on the bottom?" Avery asked as she got up, turning to look at Iris' expression. Iris laughed.

"No, we did doggy style." She looked over at Domi. "Just do that."

"I don't want sand burn on my nipples... and don't tell me to put down a towel. Those get sandy, too." Domi made a face and cupped her hands protectively over her breasts. "At the very least, I didn't want to start the week off with sandy nipple burn, then have to deal with it all week."

"It's not that bad," Iris said, glancing at Avery.

Avery shrugged. "I was on the bottom, so I had some sand burn in... other places. Which sucked, but Nick made it up to me with lots of oral." She grinned.

It did seem a little weird to come to an island resort and not have sex on the beach, but Rae still wasn't sure she wanted to. She definitely didn't want to have sex in the water. Every time she saw that in the movies, she just had to shake her head. It was like the couple wanted to get eaten by sharks. Not that there had been any shark attacks in recent memory on this particular island, but why be the first? There hadn't been any recently, which meant the island was ripe for one.

Just saying.

But she still listened as the others weighed the pros and cons of sex on the beach. Just in case.

18

———————

BRIAN

"Do you want to have sex on the beach?"

Brian looked up from where he was sitting on the couch, reading one of the books that had been available on the shelf, and resting. Rae had had another burst of creative energy and needed to write some things down. Even though she'd asked him a question, she hadn't looked up from whatever she was writing. Dinner was an hour away, and most of their friends had gone to their own rooms to rest after the busy day.

The island heat really made everyone want to nap. Or have sex. Could be both.

"I hadn't really thought about it," he replied, closing his book with his finger between the pages to keep it in place. "Other than it might be risky."

Which was the truth. Was there something appealing about the idea of having sex outside where they might be caught? Absolutely, just like there had been when they'd hooked up in the cabana, far too close to where their friends had been.

On the other hand, he was planning on telling his friends when they got back home, anyway. Tomorrow was their last night on the island. Would it really matter if anyone caught them?

Hm. He should probably mention his plans to Rae.

"Were you planning on telling anyone we hooked up while we were here?" he asked. This time, it was her turn to raise her head and meet his gaze. It was probably something they should have talked about before they hooked up, but they had said they weren't telling anyone while they were here.

He thought. His memory of their negotiations was a little hazy, even if his memory of how hot the sex had been was still sharp.

"Yeah, but not until after we get home," she admitted. "I'll only be able to keep it from Domi for so long before I spill."

"That's basically how I was feeling. Plus, once we get home, it won't matter as much. If they bug us about it, we can avoid them a little more easily," he joked.

Rae laughed.

"Speak for yourself. Domi and I might not live together anymore, but she'll still show up on my doorstep if she thinks it's warranted."

"I don't think I'll have to worry about that with anyone." Brian chuckled. His friends didn't care that much about his love life. Thankfully. He'd much rather they didn't. "They'll let me know they think it was a dumb idea, but hey, it turned out okay, so no harm, no foul."

"Just okay?" Rae teased, and he winked at her.

"The week has been all right."

She snorted and dropped her head down again. Brian watched her for a moment, just enjoying having her there and seeing her at work. While he did wonder what she was writing, he didn't want to interfere with her process. Opening his book back up, he had just found his place again when...

"Would your week be better if I called you 'Daddy'?" Her head was still down, all of her focus appearing to be on her work, yet there was a note of vulnerability in her voice that tugged at him.

Still, he couldn't lie to her.

"Yes. That's my preferred title with a sub." He lowered the book to his lap, though he kept it open this time rather than closing it. She looked up at him, and though her expression was blank, he was pretty sure he saw the same vulnerability he'd heard in her voice reflected in her eyes. "But that doesn't mean my week hasn't been fantastic. It has. I'm not exactly glad you got kicked out of your villa, but I am glad things worked out the way they did."

He really was. He wouldn't trade this week with her for anything. It was a small taste of what he'd been craving, what he'd been fantasizing about. Now that he'd had the reality, hopefully, it would be a little easier to let go of the fantasy. Even though the reality had been pretty great, too, in his fantasies, she *had* always called him Daddy.

It was the one thing he wasn't going to get in reality, something that had been driven home this week.

"It's not that I don't want to give you want you need. It's just that... it's literally one of the biggest turnoffs I can think of. I'd rather let you pee on me."

Brian choked on laughter, despite the little pang that went through his chest. The expression on her face made it clear that she did not have good feelings about being peed on. It made her aversion to calling him "Daddy" pretty clear. There was one thing he could reassure her on, though.

"I know you're not just being stubborn about it, even if I don't completely understand why you feel the way you do. But that's okay, I don't have to understand. We all want what we want." Which was basically kink in a nutshell.

People wanted—needed—certain things, and those things didn't always align with what their desired partner wanted and needed. It just meant they were incompatible in that way, no matter how compatible they were in others. Unfortunately for him and Rae, this appeared to be a deal breaker on both sides.

"It's just... I have a Daddy. And yes, I still call him that. I mean, I didn't for a while when I was in middle school, then I realized sometime in high school that I was still Daddy's little girl, no matter how old I got, and that when I called him Daddy, I usually got what I wanted." She flashed a smile at Brian. "He's an *amazing* dad, and I would never want anyone to think otherwise."

"And you think someone might?"

"I think a lot of people assume that subs who want Daddy Doms have 'daddy' issues." She put the pen down, her gaze sliding around him now rather than meeting his eyes directly, which he understood. It was a bit of a touchy subject, but he wasn't insulted.

For some babygirls or subs into age play, that was part of it. For others, it wasn't. Rae wasn't wrong that people who didn't understand the dynamic also made assumptions.

"Does it matter what those people think?" he asked. Rae had never struck him as being overly concerned with what others thought. At least, not strangers. She only cared what those closest to her thought, or so it had always seemed to him.

He certainly never got the impression she'd ever cared what he thought until this week when they were forced together.

"Yes and no." Rae tapped the pen against her lips, hesitating. "It's not just that, obviously. I really can't imagine calling anyone but my dad 'Daddy.' But even if I could, there are a lot of people who also make assumptions about black men. My dad is amazing. I don't want anyone thinking I have 'daddy' issues, then using that to feed their stereotypes, even if my dad and I would never know. I hate the idea of it. So, that just kind of firms up the whole not calling anyone else 'daddy' thing."

Huh.

Brian had never thought about it that way.

He'd never had to think about it that way. That wasn't something he'd ever have to deal with since he was neither black nor submissive. Sitting back against the couch, he let the implications really roll over him, and... he could see her point. That didn't mean anyone had to make the same choice as her, but since she already had a reason not to use the 'Daddy' moniker, he could see how societal expectations would back that up even further.

Damn.

So much for thinking she might one day be willing to try.

He hadn't even realized he had that little tendril of hope until it died. Damn, he really needed to accept that this was not going to continue after this week. This conversation was helping a bit.

"Why do you want to be called Daddy?"

It was the first time she'd ever asked him that question. Another time, in the past, he might have put her off or given her his usual answer about how he liked to take care of submissives completely and how caretaking fulfilled a need in him... but she'd given him a very real, raw answer, and he wouldn't do her the disservice of providing less.

"Because I have Daddy issues." He gave her a crooked smile when she blinked in startlement, mouth dropping open slightly in surprise. She didn't seem to know whether to laugh, probably because he wasn't really joking. "And mommy issues. My parents were... not great. They were in and out of rehab a lot, but nothing quite managed to stick. My mom tried, at least, but my dad left us when I was six. My mom tried to keep things together for a couple years, but she ended up losing custody of me when I was eight."

"I'm so sorry." Rae's brown eyes were even wider than normal, and they were shiny with tears. Which was why he didn't usually talk about this stuff with anyone. He didn't want anyone to feel sorry for him. He was fine now.

"Thanks." He rubbed his thumb against the pages of the book he was holding, which helped ground him a little. "Anyway, I went to live with my grandmother. My mom's mom. So, she could have come to visit me there, but she never did."

His grandmother had tried to tell him that it was too hard losing him, too painful for his mom... but he'd known the truth. If his mom wanted to, she would have. She'd just cared about the drugs more.

"In a lot of ways, it was lucky. I don't know what happened between my mom and my grandmother or why my mom ended up the way she did, but my grandmother took great care of me." He shrugged one shoulder, though it didn't shrug off all the memories.

The way he'd hoarded food at first until he'd realized there was enough, and he didn't have to. The way he'd cried when he'd gotten an allowance for the first time. The way he'd started being able to sleep at night because there were no more strange people coming into his home and yelling at his mom after she'd locked him in his bedroom to keep him safe. He hadn't even been able to defend her.

Not that he would have been able to do much at eight, and logically, he knew that, but sometimes he still felt like he should have at least tried. It was one of the things he worked on with his therapist.

Rae got to her feet, and every muscle in Brian's body tensed before he managed to make himself relax. He knew his initial thought, the little part of his brain that said she was about to walk out the door because of... whatever reason she might have, was illogical. Yet he couldn't suppress the initial fear.

He'd never needed to worry. She practically threw herself at him, curling up on his lap and wrapping her arms around him in the biggest hug she could give him. Brian hugged her back, letting out the breath he hadn't known he was holding.

"I'm glad your grandma was good to you and you were taken care of, but that still sucks," she said fiercely into his chest, her voice slightly muffled by their positions, but he heard her clearly enough. "I'm so sorry you had to go through that."

He hugged her tightly for a moment before relaxing his arms—not letting her go, but not squeezing her anymore. The bands around his chest felt like they'd loosened under the warmth of her acceptance. Her weight in his lap made him feel more settled. Calmer. Reassured.

"Anyway. So, I have what my therapist calls 'abandonment issues,' but I call 'daddy' issues. Maybe some mommy issues, too." He chuckled, making it into a joke, even though it wasn't really funny. Sometimes, humor was the easiest way to deal with his past. That and ignoring it—two of his favorite coping mechanisms. "I really have always been a caretaker, but I think part of what drew me to it was wanting to take on a role I didn't have in my life."

A parental role versus a Daddy Dom role was different, of course, but there was some overlap. His therapist pointed out that it gave him a sense of control, even beyond what kink might normally. Daddy

Dom roles tended to seep into daily life rather than being confined to the bedroom, and that was a big part of what he liked about it.

"That, and this way, you get to control the relationship in a way you didn't get to with your parents," Rae said, inadvertently echoing his thoughts.

"What are you, my therapist?" he asked, poking his fingers into her sides and making her gasp before she started giggling uncontrollably, squirming to try to get away from the tickling. Of course, the squirming had an immediate effect on his dick, which should have been anticipated.

"I'm just saying!" She laughed, relaxing when he stopped tickling her, his half-hard cock rubbing against the curve of her ass where it rested against him. They might have time for a quickie before dinner... "Abandonment also comes with a desire to control the relationships you're in. It makes sense."

"I guess." It probably did, but introspection was not always his favorite thing. Especially when he had the delightful weight of a beautiful submissive on his lap and half an erection. "Are you done with your writing?"

"Yes, why— Ah!" Rae shrieked as Brian launched them both upward, his arms and hands sliding into place to hold her against his chest and lift. Her arms came around his neck, holding tight as he got to his feet with her held tightly against him. "Warn a girl before you do that!"

"Where's the fun in that?" he asked with a grin, glancing at the clock as he turned her toward the bedroom.

"Brian! We don't have time!"

They were running out of time, which was why they had to make the most of it.

"We have enough time for a quickie."

It turned out that hot, hard, quick sex was just as good a distraction coping mechanism as laughter. Maybe even better.

19

RAE

It's the last day.

That was Rae's first thought when she woke up in Brian's arms. Sure, she had one more morning of doing this, but they'd be headed to the boat to take them back to the mainland and the airport immediately after breakfast.

The unhappiness she felt at the idea that the week was ending wasn't unexpected, but it hit her harder than she wanted it to.

They weren't really meant to last. One week away from everything that was real back at home wasn't a good example of how a relationship would actually go. They didn't have anything to do here except relax, fuck, and enjoy the island. Of course, the week had gone well.

She should remember it as a special moment in time without trying to extend it. Especially after the talk she and Brian had last night.

She *wanted* him to have everything he wanted. She *wanted* him to find someone who could give him everything he was searching for. He deserved it.

Just like she deserved to find someone who could give her everything she needed.

Maybe it wasn't fair that they couldn't be that for each other, but that was life sometimes. What they wanted was close... but not close enough. She sighed, her breasts heaving, one of them filling the palm that was cupped around it, and his hand closed over the soft mound.

"Mmmm." He nuzzled the back of her neck, moving his hips forward so Rae could feel his cock pressing against her ass.

Her poor vagina practically whimpered.

She'd gone from having no sex to daily rounds. She was starting to feel a little chafed. Her clit was sore.

Yet, when he pinched her nipple between his fingers, rolling the little bud to hardness, she felt a gush of arousal as her body came to life.

Besides, it was the last full day. Tomorrow, they would need to wake up and pack, then head to breakfast. Her pussy was going to have plenty of time to recover when she got home. What she wasn't going to have was an accessible, talented dick.

Or someone holding me at night. Or helping me with my hair. Or giving me a massage or rubbing my feet or...

She cut off the voice in her head before it could get too maudlin.

Was she aware that she was trying to reduce Brian down to his dick? Yup. Because if she didn't, she was going to cry. A girl had to do what a girl had to do, and right now, she needed to think of him as nothing more than good, temporary sex.

"Open for me, babygirl," he murmured, shifting his lower body so his erect cock was pushing between her thighs. Rae lifted one leg, moving it back to rest atop his body, pushing her ass more toward him to get the angle right. The tip of his cock slid along the wet heat of her pussy, then he cursed, pulling away. "Condom."

"Just put it in."

Brian froze behind her.

"Are you sure?"

"Yes. I'm on birth control. We both know each other's test histories. Just... don't go."

It wasn't like he was really leaving her, but the words just slipped out. And they worked. He moved back behind her, one hand sliding over her leg to lift it again, giving him access to her pussy. The tip of his dick slid along her wet folds, but this time, he didn't pull away, just groaned at the sensation and moved again, sliding against her sensitive flesh until he bumped against her clit.

Rae needed more, though. She needed him inside her.

Angling herself this time when he slid forward, he pushed into her, and they both moaned.

There was a difference with no condom. His cock wasn't as slick. Wasn't as lubricated. Wasn't as uniform. She could feel the bumps and ridges as he pulled back and thrust in, working himself in deeper while filling his hands with her breasts to help him have leverage. Rae moaned, pushing back against him, reaching down to rub her clit as he began to move with more force.

The additional intimacy of having nothing between them was making her even hotter, wetter. She hadn't taken off the condoms with Damian, but... with Brian, she wanted it. Wanted to feel him fully inside her, wanted to feel everything. She might not be able to give him everything he needed, but she could give him this.

"Fuck... Rae..." He groaned again as her pussy clamped down around him, her fingers circling her clit while he massaged her breasts. "I'm not going to last long."

"Don't." She bit out the word. "I want to feel you cum in me."

It was the truth.

It was also what he needed to send him over the edge. His hands squeezed tighter, crushing her breasts and pinching her nipples between his fingers as he rolled them both over. Then he let go of her breasts, pulling her up by her hips and slamming into her from behind with utter abandon. Rae cried out, her fingers still working over her clit, her other arm braced in front of her as each hard thrust moved her along the bed.

The sex was hot and hard and ruthless. Rae's pussy clenched around him as he pistoned back and forth inside her. Her clit throbbed in response, overstimulated yet eager to cum again. When he slammed into her, filling her completely, and she felt him begin to pulse as warm heat spurted, her pussy convulsed with her own orgasm. Feeling his set hers off, making her writhe before him as she rubbed her clit harder and harder, abusing the little nub as the waves of ecstasy rolled through both of them.

"Fuck..." His voice was hoarse as he slumped over her, the grip on her hips loosening. "Fuck..."

That about summed it up.

BRIAN

"We have an announcement," Mitch declared once everyone had their breakfast in front of them. Since he'd seated himself at the head of the table, with Domi on his right and Rae on his left, everyone's heads naturally turned to look at him to find out what he was about to announce. Several seats down from Rae, with Nick and Avery between them, Brian was able to see Domi's expression and the way she rolled her eyes, even as she smiled at her fiancé's antics.

They were holding hands, forcing Mitch to eat with his left hand, but he didn't seem to mind.

"Since this is supposed to be our bachelor and bachelorette week, we've decided that tonight, we want to make sure we spend time in that manner," Mitch said with a grin, glancing at Domi and giving her hand a little squeeze. Brian's heart did a little jump in his chest.

"And because you got your beach sex last night," Domi murmured, just loud enough for everyone at their table to hear. She lifted her free hand up to her breast, wincing slightly as she cupped it.

Aw, shit. Brian knew what was coming before Mitch said it.

"So, tonight, we're going to split up. Domi's having a sleepover for the ladies in our villa. Kincaid and Zach have offered up theirs for us gentlemen to hang out in." Mitch beamed at the two of them, and Kincaid lifted his glass of orange juice in salute while Zach simply nodded. They were sitting across from Avery and Nick, and Brian had been studying them all morning to try to figure out how things were between them. He still wasn't sure.

On Brian's left, Law shook his head.

"Well, there go our plans for tonight," he joked, glancing at Iris, who shrugged.

"Nothing we can't do back home," she sassed back at him, and he leered at her.

Brian's heart sank in his chest, and he didn't know if he was glad he was on the same side of the table as Rae, so he couldn't see her expression and give away the game, or if he was sad that he didn't know if she was reacting the same way he was.

They couldn't do what they'd been doing back home.

That wasn't part of the agreement.

They were supposed to still have tonight, dammit.

But it was Mitch and Domi's week. It wasn't about him or Rae or anyone else.

Fuck.

They weren't going to get their last night together. And he had to act like he didn't care.

"What are we doing today, then?" Rae asked, her voice sounding totally normal and cheerful.

Did he buy that? No. Not after this morning when she'd had to come to breakfast with his cum still dripping out of her.

"Basically, the same plan as before for the morning," Mitch said, giving Domi an adoring look as he squeezed her fingers. "Hang out on the beach, but then after lunch, we'll go back to the villas to pack up, so we don't have to worry about it tomorrow and can just stay up late tonight and enjoy our final night doing bachelor and bachelorette party things."

Right.

Their last night together *and* the last morning were gone now.

He had to paste a smile on his face and act like it was great and he didn't care because that's how he would have felt at the beginning of the week. The fact was, he was internally cursing up a storm and wishing Domi and Mitch weren't so damn thoughtful about getting time in with their friends, even though that was technically what the week was supposed to be for.

Damn it.

"Great," he said as everyone offered up their own agreement of what a great idea it was. Just so great.

The whole morning went by without getting a chance to speak to Rae privately. Everyone had come to breakfast dressed and ready to hit the beach right afterward, and once they were there, there was no way to discreetly slip away. Especially not both of them at the same time. Even when Rae tried to go to the bathroom, all three other women announced they needed to go, too.

It wasn't until they were heading back up toward the villas that he got close to panic, though.

"Want me to come help you pack up?" Domi asked Rae. He was following right behind them, so he could hear everything.

"Don't you need to pack up, too?" Rae asked, sounding amused. "And get things ready to have the rest of us over?"

Brian relaxed. Slightly. He could only imagine how tonight would go if everyone found out that all of Rae's stuff was in *his* villa because hers had basically flooded.

"Well... yeah." Domi laughed. "But I can pack in the morning if I really need to."

"You say that now, but you'll regret it when you wake up tomorrow." Rae nudged Domi in the side. "After the drinking and the staying up late and—"

"Yeah, yeah, yeah, point made." Domi sighed as they came off the path to where the villa entrances were. "Alright, I'm going to go get my stuff packed up then. You'd better hurry your butt over, though. We've got girl stuff to do!"

Chuckling, Mitch leaned over to wrap his arm around Domi's waist and pull her along with him. Rae headed toward her villa as if nothing was the matter with it, the way she'd been doing all week. Everyone else was going toward their own, chatting with their partner.

Which was perfect.

It only took Rae a couple minutes to make it to the back door of Brian's villa, and he let her in.

To his surprise, she darted past him, heading straight for the bedroom where she grabbed her suitcase—which she'd never gotten around to fully unpacking—and started tossing any clothes outside of it back in. To say it was a haphazard mess was an understatement.

"Woah, slow down," he said, a little startled and trying not to feel hurt. He knew it wasn't that she was trying to get away from him, but the quickness with which she was moving was still a little surprising. He'd hoped they could take a few minutes to... something. He didn't know.

But their last private moments together weren't something he'd wanted to rush, even with the change in plans.

"I can't." She shot him an apologetic look but didn't stop moving as she headed to the bathroom to grab her toiletries. Brian didn't trail behind her, despite the urge. Thankfully, she didn't take long before coming back out, her arms full of her things. "Didn't you hear Domi? I'm lucky if I have five minutes before she comes looking for me, and if she goes to my villa... where I am obviously *not*..." Her voice trailed off as she dumped everything into her suitcase and pulled it close, zipping it up without any care as to how well it was packed. She shot him a rueful smile.

"And this is why it's best not to unpack everything."

Brian opened his mouth. Closed it. He couldn't think of anything to say. He couldn't ask her to stay. He wouldn't. They'd agreed to this week and this week only, and he'd already put himself out there more than once in the past... He'd promised himself he wasn't going to do it again.

He wasn't going to give her the chance to reject him. *Again.*

As she looked up at him, something flickered in her eyes. She got to her feet, and suddenly, she was pressed against him, flinging her arms around his neck.

"Thank you for this week," she whispered right before her lips met his.

It wasn't a sexy kiss. It was a kiss of desperation. Brian kissed her back with all the longing, all the pent-up emotions that he'd been holding back, all the wishes he'd had during the week...

Then she broke away.

"It was a really good week." Turning away, she hurried to her bag and picked it up, pausing only to glance over her shoulder. "Thanks for letting me stay with you."

"Anytime," he said stupidly. Stupid because it wasn't like they were ever going to be in this situation again. It was a one-in-a-million chance it had happened at all.

She gave him a half-hearted smile, then... she was gone, and he was left staring at an empty doorway. His entire chest hurt, but there was nothing he could do about it.

This was what they'd agreed on.

He just wished...

He wished they'd gotten their last night.

20

———

RAE

Leaving Brian's villa was one of the hardest things she'd ever had to do. So hard that it wasn't until she was walking down the walkway that she realized she'd gone out the front door. Immediately, she came to a grinding halt, looking around wildly... no one else was outside yet.

Another point in favor of not unpacking so she could pack up quickly.

Breathing out a sigh of relief, she pressed her hand over her heart as she quickly dragged her bag down to the main sidewalk, so she could head over to Domi's without worrying about anyone seeing her where she wasn't supposed to be. That was why her chest hurt so much, after all.

The worry.

Because she didn't want to explain things to her friends.

Not yet.

Even though obviously it would be fine, too. Everything was past. They'd be going home tomorrow, and that meant the week was over. She and Brian had both said they'd tell their friends afterward.

But she didn't want to take away from Domi's week, Domi's night with the girls. If her friends knew she'd been staying with Brian, that's what they'd all want to talk about. Heck, if she were one of them, that would be all she was able to talk about once she found out.

And tonight was supposed to be about Domi.

So, yeah. That's why she didn't want them to know yet.

It didn't have anything to do with her not feeling ready to talk about it. Because why wouldn't she be? It was just a weeklong vacation fling. No big deal. No reason for her chest to hurt or her heart to feel like it was breaking. She'd known going in what this was going to be.

It had been a fun week. A great week. So, it wasn't ending the way she'd expected it to; that was okay. Sure, okay, maybe she was a little disappointed about not getting one last night with Brian. No last chance for sex on the beach if she changed her mind about it. No last night spent cuddled up in his arms and waking up beside him in the morning.

Fuck.

Her breath hitched.

"Hey! Rae! Wait up!" Iris' voice calling her name nearly made her jump out of her skin.

Shit, shit, shit. Get your shit together, girl.

Taking a deep breath, Rae forced a smile onto her face as she turned to see Iris coming out of her villa.

"How fast did you pack your stuff up?" Iris asked with a laugh, though it seemed like there was a bit of suspicion in her eyes. Had she seen where Rae had come from?

"I never really unpacked," Rae joked. "I just live out of my suitcase when I go on trips, so it's easy to shove it all in."

"That's what she said."

Rae laughed as Iris giggled, and she relaxed a little. Maybe Iris hadn't seen her. Or if she had, she wasn't going to say anything about it. Rae could live with that.

"I do the same thing, but I didn't pack up nearly as quickly as you did," Iris admitted.

"Well, it was probably easier for me since I didn't have a man around to distract me," Rae teased, hoping that might throw Iris off the scent if she did have any suspicions.

Or maybe she had no suspicions, and Rae was getting paranoid and projecting.

"That doesn't hurt," Iris replied with a laugh.

Rae unclenched a little. She probably really *was* just paranoid and projecting.

Domi answered the door for them, beaming with excitement as she bounced around, and Rae felt a little guilty for not being more excited about girl time. Clearly, Domi wanted it badly. Rae needed to get her head on straight. She was here this week for Domi, not for Brian's dick, no matter how incredible the sex had turned out to be.

Not just his dick, either.

Go away, stupid voice.

"We're going to have so much fun!" Domi squealed, clapping her hands. "I called the front desk, and they're going to send us a whole bachelorette party package for tonight."

"That sounds fun. Does it include food, or do we need to go out?"

"It includes food, booze, and some surprises." Domi grinned as Mitch came out of their bedroom, suitcase in hand, shaking his head.

"She can't wait to get rid of me. I see how it is." He made himself sound utterly mournful and pathetic, but the little curve of his smile gave him away. "Not even married yet, and she's already tired of me."

Domi rolled her eyes even as her own smile bloomed on her face, and she went over to give him a thorough kiss. Mitch being Mitch, he groped her ass, causing her to pull away, laughing.

"Okay, get out," she ordered as she stepped back, giving his bicep a little slap. His blue eyes gleamed.

"You're gonna pay for that when we get home," he warned.

"I'm shaking in my boots," Domi called after him as he opened the door, nearly running into Avery, who had her hand up to knock. She made a small 'eep' sound and jumped back so she didn't inadvertently knock on his chest.

Two minutes later, suitcases were stowed to the side, and it was just the four of them.

"Okay, who wants some champagne?" Domi asked, heading to the fridge. "Or something else. I had an assortment sent over this morning."

"Let's do it. This is a celebration, right?" Iris replied with a laugh.

Rae managed to get in front of Domi, hip-bumping her out of the way.

"Go sit down. You're the bride. You're supposed to be relaxing. I'll get the drinks."

"Oh, is that the maid of honor's job?"

"It is now."

Besides, drinks gave her something to focus on while she got herself in the mood for an unexpected ladies' night. Everyone wanted champagne to start with, which was nice and easy. She had no doubt the evening would eventually devolve into stronger options.

"So, what did you want to do tonight?" Iris asked.

"Anything that doesn't involve my nipples," Domi said, making a face as she cupped her hands over her breasts, making them all laugh.

"Oh, come on," Rae said, bracing herself to open the champagne. It came out free easily into her hand with the customary loud 'pop.' "It couldn't have been that bad. You're a masochist, for crying out loud."

"Well, it might not have been, except Mitch decided he wanted to clamp them, too. And in the moment, it was glorious. Afterward... I had to put on a bra to keep them from rubbing against my shirt both overnight and this morning." She made a face. "It's the continuing issue I knew was going to be a pain in the ass."

"Okay, well, that makes sense." Though she couldn't help but feel a bit jealous. Her pussy was still a little sore, but she had a feeling if she and Brian had had their last night together, he would have worn her out completely. She probably would have been getting on the plane more than a 'little' sore.

"I'm sure we can come up with something that doesn't involve your nipples," Avery said with amusement, taking her glass of champagne from Rae. "Thanks."

"Welcome. And I don't know, all of my plans for the evening centered heavily around Domi's nipples." Rae shrugged, widening her eyes innocently. "I have no idea what to do now."

"Shut up." Domi threw a napkin at her, making them all laugh again. "I was thinking we could do a movie, and the resort is sending their spa package so we can do nails or masks or whatever."

"Ooh, we should watch a wedding movie." Iris brightened. "One of the really cheesy ones."

"Sounds good to me." Domi beamed all around them. "I know this wasn't the typical bachelorette trip, and I've had so much fun, but I really am so glad we're getting tonight together."

With that, all the lingering disappointment about missing out on a final night with Brian was swept away. It would have been great, but being here for her bestie was even more important. Domi was her ride-or-die, after all.

Chicks before dicks.

"We're so glad to be here with you," Rae said, putting down the champagne bottle and glass she was holding so she could envelop Domi in a big hug.

"Damn right!" Iris cheered, joining in on the hug along with Avery, who was laughing at their antics.

"I'm so happy we're friends." Avery leaned her head on Iris' shoulder. "You all made my life so much better."

"Back at you. And trust me, I am grateful you could get away from Marquis for a whole week." Domi sniffled. "I know that wasn't easy. You're the best friends a girl could ask for."

It was true. For a long time, it had been just Rae and Domi, and they'd shut everyone else out. Not on purpose, exactly. They were just so tight, they hadn't needed anyone else, and they hadn't tried to make friends outside of each other. There had been people they were friendly with, but they'd been their own little twosome. Now, their group had expanded, just a little, and they were better for it.

She would do anything for Iris and Avery, just like she knew they would do anything for her and Domi.

"Only true friends go to a kink island with you," Iris joked as they broke apart.

Rae giggled, picking up her champagne again.

"Cheers to that." Domi lifted her glass in the air, and they all clinked them together in a toast.

<u>BRIAN</u>

Being completely unpacked and having to pack everything up was good because it gave Brian time to get himself together. Time he needed. He had to get his game face on before facing his friends, all of who were far too observant on their worst days and now wouldn't have their subs to distract them. Well, except for Kincaid, who was obviously already distracted by whatever was going on between him and Zach, but that still left Mitch, Law, and Nick.

By the time he knocked on Kincaid and Zach's door, most of the ache in his chest had subsided. Logically, he knew Rae wasn't rejecting him. She was doing what was right for them by rushing out. Both of them were there for Mitch and Domi, not for each other. Reminding himself of that over and over again as he'd packed up didn't help much, but it did help a little.

He pushed a smile onto his lips when Zach opened the door.

"Hey, man, come on in."

It didn't take more than a moment to see that he was the last to arrive, which wasn't surprising. He'd been taking his time. Maybe it was just his imagination, but he felt like the mood in the room was off. Kincaid was standing by the counter, obviously mixing drinks, but Zach didn't go over to join him after letting Brian in. Instead, he went over to one of the armchairs. He wasn't glowering or sulking, but he wasn't smiling, either.

Shit.

Maybe they should have done this at someone else's villa. Too late now.

"There you are!" Law called out from where he was seated on the couch. "I was starting to think we'd need to send out a search party for you." He smiled, and Brian couldn't help but wonder if he was trying to lighten the mood.

If only Brian's mood was better, he might have been able to help more.

"No search party necessary. Just took a while to pack everything up." He couldn't think of a good joke to make.

"He actually unpacks everything from his suitcase," Mitch said, nodding somberly. "If I didn't know him better, I'd think he was a serial killer."

"Hey!" Brian shot Mitch an indignant look, setting his suitcase to the side. "You did, too!"

"The one trip we took where we had to stay in the same room," Mitch explained, answering Nick's curious glance before looking back at Brian. "Of course, I did. I was afraid you were a serial killer. I had to make you think I might be one, too."

When it came to breaking the tension, Mitch was the master, and as everyone laughed, the mood in the room lifted. Brian felt his chest unclench a little. Rae hadn't worried he was a serial killer; she'd just thought he was weird.

"I unpack everything, too," Law said, turning his head and leaning toward Mitch in a mock-threatening manner.

"Does Iris?"

"She does not." Law sighed. "She just digs around through her suitcase to find what she wants."

"Want a drink?" Kincaid asked as the conversation continued.

"Yes, please," Brian said fervently, walking up to the other man while the others argued about whether or not unpacking a suitcase while on a trip was a good indicator of being a serial killer. He had no idea. He just traveled enough that he didn't like living out of a suit-case. For the short time he was there, he wanted to be comfortable.

For the first time, he wondered if that might have something to do with his upbringing. His parents had moved them around a lot, usually after they'd gotten evicted from somewhere. Especially after his dad left. His mom would get cleaned up enough to get a job and a place, then they'd be there until she inevitably started using again, and they'd get kicked out. He'd had to be ready to go in a hurry.

He hadn't thought about that in years. Talking with Rae about his childhood must have brought up the memories.

"You okay?" Kincaid asked.

"Yeah, just... weird thought." Brian shook his head, as though he could shake the thoughts away. And maybe he could. "So, what are we doing tonight? Has Mitch said?"

"No, but he did say he contacted the resort to send us a 'surprise' later." Kincaid chuckled at Brian's groan. "Yeah, exactly. With him, who knows what we're getting."

"He does keep things interesting. I feel like I should have been the one planning the surprises for his bachelor party, though."

Kincaid shrugged. "It's not the normal bachelor party. And who knew he and Domi would want to have a totally separated night on the last night?"

No one. Brian wished he'd known beforehand; he would have planned better.

"Other than the surprise, anything?" He took the mule Kincaid offered to him. Kincaid had a near-encyclopedic knowledge of what everyone's favorite drink was.

"Dinner. Hanging out. Letting the girls have girl time." Kincaid chuckled.

"We're going to do a bonfire on the beach," Mitch called out, making them both jump. They hadn't realized he was listening in.

"Is that the surprise?" Brian asked, turning around to face him.

"You'll find out." The wink Mitch sent his way was somehow not at all encouraging.

21

BRIAN

The bonfire was not the surprise. The surprise was the stripper who showed up at the bonfire. Granted, she also brought s'mores, so she was more than welcome, but Brian was surprised that Mitch had requested a stripper... right up until he realized who the stripper was really there for.

Not for the groom... oh no, she was there for the one single man out of the group.

Him.

"This really isn't necessary," he said, sending a glare over at Mitch —who was cracking up—as the pretty brunette whipped her shirt off. "You can just chill and have some s'mores with us."

"Hey, now... I worked hard to learn these moves." She pouted at him. "Are you saying I'm doing a bad job?"

Ah, fuck. All his friends were now laughing at his expense because they knew questions like that were his kryptonite.

"No, of course not. You're doing a great job." Cue more laughter from his friends. Apparently, their laughter didn't knock her off her game. "I just... I'm not even the groom."

"The groom is taken; you aren't," Mitch called out. That was technically true, but it felt wrong to have another woman taking her clothes off for him and giving him a lap dance when he'd been spending the week with Rae.

The week they'd agreed there wouldn't be anyone else. And the week wasn't technically over. They were still on the island. Sure, they weren't spending tonight together, but...

He knew it made no sense to feel like he was doing something wrong, yet he did.

"I'm normally a club sub, but I've been taking classes... I haven't done it without a pole before, though."

Crap. He was making her feel bad.

"You're doing a really great job," he said in his best Daddy Dom voice. "I just thought tonight was going to be about the guys. I don't adjust to change very quickly."

"Oh... okay." She brightened. "Then I should keep going?"

Inwardly, he groaned, but there was only one thing his conscious would allow him to do when she was looking at him with such big, hopeful eyes.

"Yes, keep going, sweetie, you're doing great."

It wasn't like he was going to sleep with her. He just had to grit his teeth, put a smile on his face, and get through a lap dance. Thankfully, the lack of light and the flickering of the bonfire would keep anyone from being able to read too much into his expression. Especially since the dancer was right in front of him.

What was her name? She'd introduced herself when she'd brought the s'mores supplies, but he hadn't heard because he'd been talking to Zach. He also hadn't figured it would matter at that point since she'd be leaving as soon as they were set.

If he'd known she was going to be grinding on his lap, he would have made sure he at least knew her name.

"Yes, Jaclyn, show him that gorgeous booty," Mitch cheered, obviously enjoying himself at Brian's expense as the subbie rolled her hips, hooking her fingers into her very short-shorts and pushing them down.

Well, at least he knew her name now.

<u>*RAE*</u>

"Is that the guys having a bonfire?" Avery asked, pausing by the glass door that overlooked the beach. She tilted her head, leaning forward as if she was trying to see better.

"Oh, yeah, Mitch said something about doing that."

"Did he say they're going to have a stripper?"

There was a stampede to the door, all of them pressing their faces against it.

"Who is she?"

"Forget that," Iris answered Domi with a snort. "Who is she dancing up on?"

"I think it's Brian," Avery replied, the answer that confirmed what Rae thought, too, and she really wished Avery had had a different answer. Dammit.

"Well, he is the only single one." Iris sounded more intrigued than upset. Rae had to bite her tongue against saying that he wasn't.

Because he was.

Their week was over, even if the week wasn't officially over. They weren't going home together. They hadn't made each other any promises. There was absolutely no reason to feel hurt, much less jealous. She was definitely going to need to get over the jealousy before they got back home because, at some point, he was going to scene with someone else, and she was going to have to deal with it.

Was she going to dance with anyone else?

It didn't look like it.

No one else was getting that treatment.

Rae gritted her teeth and pulled away from where she was watching. Just because it was happening didn't mean she had to watch.

"Everything okay?" Iris asked, turning slightly as Rae stepped back to see where she was going.

"Yeah, I'm just not invested like you all," she managed to say teasingly. After all, *she* was the only single one. And even when she admitted to them that she and Brian had been hooking up during the week, she needed them to know that it really hadn't meant anything... which meant she couldn't react now to him getting a lap dance. From a stripper. On kink island.

And she definitely couldn't storm down to the beach and smack him across the face the way she wanted to. He didn't owe her anything.

Meandering over to the counter, she picked up the bottle of vodka she'd been making her drinks from. Nothing to do with what was going on down on the beach. She'd needed to freshen up her drink, anyway.

"I don't think she's dancing for anyone but Brian," Iris said after another minute of watching.

Rae took a big swig of her freshly made drink, only grimacing a little at the burn as the alcohol slid down her throat. That was definitely not something she needed to see.

"Are you worried she's going to dance for Law?" Avery asked.

Iris shrugged. "Not really. I trust him. We see plenty of hot naked people at Marquis and Stronghold. I am surprised they got a stripper, though."

Domi coughed. "Right... well... about that..."

As if the universe was working entirely in her favor, there was a knock at the door before she could finish her sentence. All of their heads swiveled as they turned to look at the door. Then, all of them turned back to look at Domi.

"You didn't..." Despite her words, Iris was already darting to the door to open it. The others were right behind her.

The door opened, and there was a very buff, beefy, beautiful man on the other side. His skin was a little darker than Rae's, and he had startling amber eyes that gleamed when the light hit them and a full head of wavy black hair that came down to brush his shoulder tops. He grinned at them, a flash of white, as he looked them over. He was wearing a very tight staff uniform. Much tighter than most of the staff uniforms she'd seen anyone wearing.

"Hello, ladies," he said. "I'm Alejandro." His voice was deep and smooth, and if Rae hadn't just spent the week with Brian, she might have melted a little.

Okay, maybe she melted a little, anyway.

Damn, he was fine.

"Hello," they chorused back at him, which made him laugh.

"Can I come in?"

"Yes! Sorry." Iris stepped back to give him room to enter. Her hand swung up to point at Domi. "That's the bride."

"Hi." Domi waved at him cheerfully. "He's not here for me, though."

Oh.

Oh, no.

Mother fucking…

She was going to murder her best friend.

Domi pointed at Rae.

"That's our single lady."

The smile on Alejandro's face widened. "Hello, single lady."

Well, fuck.

Rae

Packing up the night before had been the right decision.

They were a pathetic stumbling line of hungover wrecks from the villas to breakfast to the boat. Well, everyone except Law, who took charge of the whole group with a smile on his face. He seemed pleased with himself. From the little conversation over breakfast, she gathered that he'd enjoyed waking the guys up with a bit of fanfare.

Thank goodness no one had done that in Domi's villa. They were all in similar sorry states this morning.

"Excuse me, Miss Rae Whitley?" Her name sounded even better with the gorgeous accent. Rae turned, blinking and holding her hand over her sunglasses, wincing a little because the aspirin still hadn't kicked in.

Holy Silver Fox Zaddy.

The man striding toward her with ground-eating steps was even more beautiful than Alejandro had been. *Does the island just grow them or something?* Tall, broad-shouldered, with a full silver mane that waved back away from his face, styled perfectly and a neatly trimmed beard and mustache, he looked like he'd just stepped off a movie set or something. He was brimming with confidence, as though he lived and breathed Dom swagger with every move he made.

"Damn..." Iris whispered behind her, echoing her thoughts.

The man came to a halt in front of Rae, smiling down at her in an odd way.

"Miss Rae Whitley?" he asked again.

"That's me."

"Ah." He held out his hand, and she took it automatically. "My name is Javier Francisco. I'm the owner of the Hideaway Resort, and I wanted to come personally apologize."

"Apologize for what?" Domi asked from behind Rae.

If she wasn't so hungover, Rae might have been quicker on the uptake, but at the moment, she just stared at him, trying to figure out what he was talking about.

Which was her undoing.

"For the issue with her villa," Javier said, glancing over Rae's shoulder at Domi with a charming smile before refocusing on her. "I understand you were able to stay with another member of your party, but I wished to personally apologize for the inconvenience. And also apologize for not coming to see you earlier. There were some things on the resort that needed my immediate attention. I'm so glad I caught you before you left the island."

"Really, you shouldn't have," she said before she could think about what she was saying. But damn. Did he really need to put her whole business out there?

But, of course, he would assume she'd let the others know what had been going on with her villa this week. Why wouldn't she? That's what would normally happen.

"No, no. We will make it up to you. Obviously, you've been refunded for your stay, and any time you would like to come down again, you will be able to do so free of charge for the same amount of time. A note has been made in your file."

Right now, all she wanted to do was get off this island and never come back, but she managed to smile at him and thank him, all while the back of her neck was tingling. She was pretty sure she could feel everyone staring at her.

Javier finally said goodbye and let go of her hand. Turning around to face her friends was incredibly painful. Domi was standing with her arms crossed over her chest, glaring at her. Beside her, Avery and Iris were more blank-faced. The guys were all in the back, Mitch saying something very quietly and very earnestly to Brian, who was staring off into the distance and completely ignoring him. The only people not paying attention were Kincaid and Zach, who had gone on ahead and were presumably already on the boat.

Mother fucker.

This was going to be the worst trip home in the history of trips home.

"So, who were you staying with, Rae?" Domi asked, drawling out the words, even though it was pretty obvious who she'd stayed with. Though she supposed she could claim Kincaid and Zach, but that lie would be revealed the moment they were asked.

"You know who I stayed with," Rae replied irritably.

"I want to hear you say it."

"Brian, okay? I spent this week sleeping with Brian." She practically shouted the words, making all the guys turn toward her. Including Brian.

"I knew it!" Iris punched the air as she shouted, jumping up and down. Turning in a circle, she pointed at everyone other than Brian, starting with Domi. "I told you. I told you. I told you. I told you. You all said I was crazy, that there was no way, but *I fucking told you.*"

Avery was laughing, Domi was shaking her head and looking annoyed, and Brian... Rae looked at him, but he was still staring out to sea with an unreadable expression. Dammit. This was not at all the way she wanted the trip to end.

The boat's horn sounded, rolling through the air, reminding them that they were supposed to be boarding.

"Guess we should get on the boat," Rae said, lifting her chin and stepping forward as if she hadn't just dropped a mini social bomb on their group.

"Oh, just like that?" Domi asked, falling into step beside her.

"Just like that."

"You wish I would let it go that easy."

"Yes, I do."

"And that's why you're delulu."

Yeah. She probably was.

22

———————

BRIAN

As much as he wanted to curse Rae for shouting the truth to the world, he understood why she'd done it. It wasn't like there was a whole lot of choice. He'd just hoped to tell the guys on his own terms after they got home, when he wasn't stuck with them on a boat, then a plane.

Avoiding them was completely impossible.

They'd made him sit down with them on a couple of bench seats out on the deck while Domi dragged Rae into the interior with Avery and Iris trailing behind them. The interior had huge windows so the occupants could see out, which meant everyone could see in, too. So, he knew Rae wasn't doing any better with her friends.

However, it didn't look like Avery and Iris were talking much. Iris was still too jubilant about being right—which would have been hilarious under other circumstances—and Avery was listening quietly while Domi did all the grilling.

Unlike his friends, who were taking it in turns. The only ones who didn't care what was going on were Kincaid and Zach, who were having what looked like their own terse conversation at the stern of the boat.

"All week and you didn't tell us." Mitch huffed, crossing his arms over his chest. "I can't believe you kept it a secret."

Brian shot him a look. "Really? You can't?"

As Mitch huffed again, Nick raised his hand like he was in class.

"I still don't understand. Why *did* you keep it a secret? I mean, not the sleeping together. I understand why you didn't want to tell all the nosy Nellys, but why did you keep what happened to her bathroom a secret? I mean, obviously, if you'd told us, we'd all have offered her a place to stay..." His voice trailed off, obviously figuring it out.

"Because then he wouldn't have had the excuse to sleep with her," Law said. He sighed. "I can't believe Iris was right, dammit. Do you know how long I'm going to have to hear about this?"

"Hopefully, at least as long as me," Brian muttered unsympathetically. He cleared his throat and shook his head. "It wasn't about trying to sleep with her. That just... happened." He looked at Mitch. "This week was about you and Domi. It was supposed to be relaxing and enjoyable. You weren't supposed to have to worry about a thing, so we didn't want you to know because we wanted it to be entirely stress free."

"That is a load of bullshit," Mitch stated. He leaned back against the bench he was seated on. "We would not have been that stressed."

"Well, we didn't want you to be stressed at all. Rae knew Domi would want her in the villas near us. She didn't want to interrupt any of the couples or end up being a third wheel, and obviously, then we'd have to tell someone else. I just happened to be there when everything happened, so I said she could stay with me, and that way, she didn't have to bother anyone. She was still in the same grouping of villas as us, and you and Domi got to have your vacation stress free." He crossed his arms over his chest, glaring back at Mitch. "You're welcome."

"Oh, yes, having sex with Rae was about doing *me* a favor." Mitch shook his head, the corners of his mouth quirking up. "Dude, you are the Simone Biles of mental gymnastics right now."

"Yeah, you could have just slept on the couch," Nick pointed out.

"But it sounds like you spent the week actually sleeping with her. I didn't think you two really got along."

"We don't," he said, but Mitch was already talking over him, explaining. At least explaining based on his own point of view.

"They've got a 'will they, won't they' thing going on," Mitch said, focusing on Nick and ignoring Brian's glare. "As in, they both want each other, but they stay away from each other for stupid reasons."

"It's not stupid reasons," Brian snapped. Mitch was finally starting to get under his skin. "I'm a Daddy Dom. Rae doesn't want a Daddy Dom. It's that simple."

"No, Rae doesn't want a Dom she has to *call* Daddy. She needs a Daddy Dom." Mitch arched an eyebrow at him as if daring him to disagree.

"I'm confused," Nick said, looking back and forth between them.

"Rae won't call Brian 'Daddy,' so Brian refuses to even try anything with her," Law explained.

Brian opened his mouth to protest, but Mitch was already talking.

"Also, Brian handles rejection really poorly, and Rae's done that, like, twice now." He shook his head again. "I can't believe you set yourself up for another rejection from her. You rarely even give anyone a second chance, much less a third."

"I wasn't setting myself up! We agreed it would only be for this week. She couldn't reject me because we had a mutually agreed upon end date." As the words came out of his mouth, he slapped his palm against his face. Yeah. Now that it was out there, said out loud... "Yeah, I hear it. Just... shut up."

There was silence for a long moment.

"So, who's going to inform the pool?" Law asked.

"The pool?" Poor Nick. He was the newest to the scene and the club, and since he was often working on the weekends as Marquis' executive chef, he tended to be at the very end of the gossip train.

"The betting pool on whether Brian and Rae are ever going to get their heads out of their asses and get together." Mitch stroked his chin, looking up thoughtfully. "Hm. Yeah, I might need to change my day. The question is, is this going to move things along faster or push them back?"

"I hate you all." Brian dropped his head into his hands. Theoretically, he'd known about the pool. People were way too up in each other's business at the clubs. It was all in good fun, but sometimes...

"I think I'm going to move mine up," Mitch mused. "Y'all are getting worse at keeping away from each other."

"Because you put us on an island together, and her bathroom flooded! That's not going to happen at home!"

"None of that required you putting your penis in her, and you know it."

<u>*Rae*</u>

"Why didn't you just tell me?"

"Because this week was about you. Not me. And Brian was there, and he offered to let me stay with him, which meant I didn't have to move to a totally different area or be a bother to anyone else." Rae huffed. "You know, if the situations were reversed, you wouldn't want to stress me out at my bachelorette party."

Domi scowled at her because she knew she was right. And immediately changed tactics.

"So, who was the masked Dom? Was it Brian?"

"It was Brian; he just wasn't masked."

"And now you guys are going to go home and just go back to pretending you don't feel anything for each other. Is that it?"

"Exactly, except we won't be pretending," she snapped, but her heart clenched a little even as she said the words. Okay, so she might be pretending not to have feelings for him a bit, but it would fade. It was just that island magic. It had made everything shiny and great. "We don't go together. The only reason it was good this week was because we agreed on an end date. There was nothing to fight over, and he only had to go a week not being called Daddy, which I'm never going to call him, so there's no reason to start something up that can't end well."

"Call him something else. You two act like 'Daddy' is the only thing in the world that you can call him." Domi threw up her hands. "Call him 'Papi' if it matters that much. But you haven't even suggested anything. You see one roadblock, and instead of trying to work around it, you just decide it's not worth the work at all."

"That's not true! I just don't think either of us should have to give up the things we want!" She said the words, but Domi's accusation hit her in the gut. She and Domi didn't usually argue, so it was making her stomach churn in an uncomfortable way.

"It's called compromise. That's what you do in a relationship. You have a fight about what you both want, then you find a compromise. Sometimes, you even get to do it without the fight, but a fight is not the end of the world. You are not always going to agree on everything, but you have to be willing to work through that!"

"You and I don't fight," Rae retorted.

"We are fighting right now." Domi threw her hands up in the air. "I can't with you."

"We're disagreeing. It's different. And we're not in a romantic relationship." She looked back and forth between her friends. Though Iris and Avery had seemed content for Domi to be the interrogator, they were obviously invested in the conversation. "I just want what my parents have."

"She thinks they never fight," Domi told the other two.

"They don't!"

"I think they just don't do it in front of you. Or one of them is always getting their way, and the other one never gets what they want." Domi shook her head. "But I think it's the first thing."

"I would know if they fought," Rae insisted. "But they never needed to fight. Good relationships don't. You and Mitch don't."

"Of course we do. I just don't tell you about it because the moment I tell you I had a fight with a guy, you're all 'dump him, dump him,' so I stopped telling you when I have a fight."

Rae's mouth dropped open. "What?" She... she'd had no idea.

Domi huffed, running her hand over her curls as if she would be able to smooth them back while the wind was whipping them around.

"Yeah. Domi told me not to tell you when Law and I had a fight, too, unless I wanted to hear a whole bunch about how I needed to break up with him," Iris put in tentatively. "Which... I didn't want to break up with him. I just needed to vent so I could get my anger out before we figured out our next steps."

"I can't talk to you about fights if I want you to support my relationships." Domi didn't sound so mad anymore. She sounded sad. "The moment I told you about a fight with one of my boyfriends, you never saw them the same way again. Everything they did, even if it was small, was just another reason to break up. It's like you think relationships can't work if everyone's not getting along all the time, but it's just not true."

"I... I don't think that. I'm sorry I made you feel like you can't talk to me. I just... I want what my parents have. I don't think everyone else has to want that."

"Maybe not consciously, but you get super judgmental about couples who don't act like your parents. So, it's better to just not tell you about fights. I don't want to hear about how I need to dump my fiancé, who I love, just because he and I were both cranky one day and took it out on each other. We got through it, and we were better for it. But you don't do that. You just leave."

"Well, I'm glad that works for you, but now you're sounding kind of judgmental about what I want." Rae crossed her arms over her chest. "Just because that works for you doesn't mean it would work for me."

"It definitely won't if you're not willing to try."

Avery cleared her throat, finally speaking up and breaking up the argument. "I feel like we've gotten a little off-topic. So... you and Brian were just for this week, and that was it?"

"Yup. What happens on the island stays on the island." Rae nodded firmly, though her stomach clenched. Then she rolled her eyes. "Well, other than the gossip."

"We don't have to tell anyone," Avery reassured her.

Oh. That was cute that she thought that would work.

"Fuck that," Iris said. "I'm telling everyone I was right." She grinned unrepentantly, proving Rae right, though even if her friends would have been willing to try to keep it quiet, she knew it would get out, eventually.

"There's too many people on this trip, anyway," Domi said. "It'll come out sooner or later. Someone will accidentally say something or make a comment in passing, then it'll take on a life of its own. It's better to get the truth out there first. Stronghold and Marquis run on gossip."

Sad but true. At least, sad for her now. It wasn't as if she'd minded in the past. That didn't bother her so much, though. People liked to talk. It didn't mean anything.

What smarted were Domi's words and knowing her best friend had kept things from her. That Domi had felt she couldn't share certain things with her. And... well, Rae couldn't even blame her. Looking back, she knew exactly what Domi was talking about.

The second Domi had a fight with a boyfriend, Rae was no longer willing to put up with any of his bullshit, even if Domi was. It wasn't as if she'd ever forced Domi to break up with anyone, but she always felt like it was a long time coming when Domi finally did. As though she should have known after that first fight.

And she did leave relationships as soon as there was a big fight. Because she didn't want that. She wanted what her mom and dad had.

She could see the fight with Brian coming.

Just call him Papi.

Was it even worth making the suggestion when he'd already told her what he wanted? It wasn't what he wanted, so why bother?

Because maybe the fight would be worth it.

23

———————

Opening the door to what he expected to be his quiet home, Brian did not think to pause to see what Morgan and Asad were up to. He knew they were there because their cars were out front, but that hadn't meant much other than knowing they were around.

He was hopeful the gossip hadn't flown too fast, though. After the hellacious boat ride, then an uncomfortable plane ride he'd pretended to sleep through, all he wanted was quiet. Since he couldn't have quiet, he wanted some time with people who didn't know he'd been sleeping with Rae all week.

So, he wasn't expecting to walk in on Asad and Morgan in the middle of the living room playing hide the pickle while dressed as what looked like Aragorn and an elf lady. Asad was wearing a wig. Morgan, with her long red hair, was not, so he couldn't call her Arwen—and wasn't he a giant nerd for even knowing that.

"Shit." He clapped his hands over his eyes. While he'd seen both of them naked and even having sex at the clubs since they'd gotten together, it was a little different to walk in on it unexpectedly.

"Shit! Sorry!" Morgan squealed, then Asad grunted.

Brian wasn't sure exactly what they were doing because he was still covering his eyes, inwardly sighing.

Asad made Morgan very happy, and that was the biggest thing, but...

"You two couldn't do this at Asad's house?" he asked plaintively.

"Morgan has to film this afternoon," Asad answered. "Her room at my place isn't ready yet."

Morgan had an even more tragic backstory than Brian. She'd been raised by heinous parents who threw her out when she was a teenager after they found out she'd had sex, and she ended up with the man who groomed her until he basically sold her to an abusive so-called 'Dom.' Since she'd been rescued, she'd gone right back into kink, this time learning about consent, limits, and being able to make her own decisions rather than being someone's sex slave.

He didn't want to squash that, but he also hadn't really wanted to come home to see her boyfriend balls deep in her while they were doing nerdy role-play.

"Sorry, Brian," she apologized.

He let his hand drop from his face so he could see them straightening their clothes. Morgan's expression was a mix of contriteness and defiance.

"You should have texted to let me know when you were on the way."

"I did."

"Oh." Heat filled her cheeks, turning her pale skin bright pink. She glanced at Asad, who didn't look sorry at all—although maybe sorry they'd been interrupted before they could finish. "Sorry, I must not have heard the alert go off."

"It's fine." Now, he just needed to retreat to his room. He gave Asad a half-hearted wave. "You two just keep on as you were. Sorry for interrupting. I'm going to go rest. It was a long plane ride."

"Are you sure?" Morgan asked, just as Asad spoke up.

"We can move it to her room." They gave each other a little look, one of those looks that two people who were connected by more than physical attraction gave each other. The kind of little look that couples shared, where they didn't need to speak to know what the other was thinking.

The kind of little look that Brian so desperately wanted to share with someone.

That he'd almost felt like he'd had with Rae the last week.

"Thanks. You can do what you want, but I'm definitely going to my room." He needed to be alone for a while. He gave them a wan smile, trying his damndest to make it seem like he was tired from traveling and nothing more. "I just want to lay down and sleep until tomorrow."

Surely, tomorrow would be better. Or at least, he'd be a little further away from it all. He could mope around the house. Hopefully, Morgan and Asad would decamp to Asad's, then he'd be ready to go back to work on Monday. A buffer day to let himself recalibrate and reacclimate to reality.

And the reality was that he and Rae were never going to work.

"Okay," Morgan said, nodding. "Do you want me to make some food for you for dinner, so you don't have to?"

That was one of the best things about having Morgan as a house-mate. She tended to take things at face value. While Asad was looking at him with curiosity, as if he'd realized there was something more going on, Morgan just heard that he was tired, accepted it, then did what she could to offer help. Thankfully, he and Asad weren't close enough for Asad to feel comfortable questioning him.

"Only if you were going to make some for yourself and will have extra. Otherwise, I can just order in."

"Well..." Her voice started to trail off, and she glanced at Asad, who nodded encouragingly. "I was going to make you a welcome home dinner, but if you feel too tired to come eat with us, that's okay."

Dammit. He was an ass. He pushed another smile he didn't feel onto his face.

"I just didn't want to intrude on your plans, but if you were planning for me..."

"She was," Asad confirmed, shooting him a grateful look, as if he knew Brian really wanted alone time but was adjusting for Morgan. "You do look tired, though. We won't keep you up late."

"Oh, no, definitely not." Morgan's expression had lit up now that she knew Brian was going to have dinner with them. "I can't wait to hear about the week and the resort."

Great. Now, he really needed to go sit in his room and figure out what highly edited version he was going to tell her. Or if he could tell her a highly edited version. Somehow, he didn't think it would be better to let her hear about him and Rae hooking up through the grapevine, and it would reach her, eventually.

Hell, probably sooner rather than later, now that she was with Asad. He was very close friends with Law.

"Great. I just need to rest my eyes for a bit, then I'll tell you all about it." He nodded his head and headed to his room. Yeah, he'd have to tell her all about it, though he'd emphasize that he and Rae were not getting into a real relationship or anything like that.

She and Rae had gotten off on the wrong foot when they'd been in the Intro for Submissives class together, and things had only marginally improved since then. He didn't think she'd be upset or anything, but who knew? Morgan could also be very protective of him, so he'd have to ensure she understood there really were no hard feelings between him and Rae. He didn't want to accidentally exacerbate the divide that already existed between the two women.

As he was headed down the hallway, he heard the chime of Morgan's phone going off. It practically echoed down the hall. She must have turned it up after realizing she'd missed his text message.

He'd just opened the door to his bedroom when he heard the screech.

"You spent the week hooking up with Rae, and you didn't tell me?!"

Ah, fuck.

---

*R*AE

Home sweet home.

Except it was more like home lonely home. Not that she'd ever been an extrovert, but she had lived very happily with Domi and her daughter Ana for years. Now Domi lived with Mitch, and when Ana wasn't with her father, she was over there. At first, Rae had liked the quiet.

Now, she was semi-grateful for the quiet because she didn't really want to put up with any more of Domi's interrogation about Brian, but...

She'd gotten used to living with Brian during the week.

Which was crazy because it had only been for a few days, but she couldn't explain why else she felt lonely. And she wasn't thinking of Domi or any of her other friends when she was wishing she wasn't alone—in fact, she was relieved to get away from their questions for a bit. It was Brian who kept popping into her head. Which was maddening for a number of reasons.

Unpacking meant throwing everything into her laundry machine and turning it on. Then she just... wandered around the house. She tried to write, but she couldn't get her head in the game. She turned on the television but couldn't find anything to watch.

Her phone pinged several times, including a threatening message from Domi that said, 'You can't avoid me forever.'

After she moved her clothes into the dryer, Rae gave up and headed out to the place she really wanted to go to get reassurance on what she wanted from her future—her parents' home.

What Domi had said about her parents just hiding their fights from her... she didn't really believe it, but she couldn't stop thinking about it. As much as she was thinking about the week with Brian, she was also thinking about that.

She texted her mom that she was on her way and got back a thumbs up. It wasn't unheard of for her to drop by for dinner with little notice. With her parents living only twenty minutes away, it was easy, and they had an open-door policy for any family members. Well, anyone except her mom's sister, Aunt Deirdre. The two of them always needed at least a day's notice before seeing each other so they could prep for the inevitable clash and get their best comebacks ready. They always got into a fight, so Rae knew her mom could; she just didn't with Rae's dad.

It did keep the holidays interesting.

"Hey, babygirl," her dad said as soon as she walked in the door, striding down the hallway like he'd been waiting to hear the door open.

Nearly a head taller than her, his closely cropped hair liberally sprinkled with grey and a beard to match, he was broad-shouldered and carried just a bit of extra weight around his middle. She always felt like he was a giant teddy bear. Rae beamed at him, stepping into his big bear hug and sighing as some of the tension leeched from her body.

"How was your trip? I didn't think we'd be seeing you today. Too tired to cook?"

"Something like that." As close as she was to her dad, boy problems were not something they talked about. That had always been kept between her and her mom, and she wasn't going to change that now. Neither of them knew anything about Hideaway Resort, though, other than she'd gone to an all-inclusive resort for Domi's bachelorette party.

"Well, it's good to see you." He gave her another little squeeze and let go, turning to head into the living room where the television was on. It was always on during the weekends of football season. Her dad followed both the colleges and the pros, and her mom tolerated it. "Wanna come watch the game with me?"

"Yeah, in a few. I wanted to talk to Mom real quick." At least, she assumed it would be a quick question.

Do you and Dad hide your fights from me?

No, baby, of course not.

The reason she couldn't ask her dad was because she knew that even if they did, he'd never admit it to her. And he was a good enough actor that she might not know. It had served him well during many a practical joke while she was growing up.

Her mom, on the other hand, had a terrible poker face.

That was also why Rae felt so sure her parents hadn't been hiding fights from her. Her mom had never been able to hide anything. She'd figured out that Santa wasn't real when she was only four years old because when she'd asked her mom why Santa had the same wrapping paper as them, her mom froze. Her dad had jumped in to cover, something about Santa also wanting to support the neighbor's kid's school fundraiser, but it had been too late.

Thus had followed the pattern—if she wanted to know the truth just by an expression, ask mom.

Her dad might have been able to hide fights from her over the years, and she could totally see him doing that to try to protect her, but mom? Nope. There was no way.

But she just needed it confirmed. For her own peace of mind. To know that what she'd been wanting was something she could actually have. Because if she didn't ask, she was never going to get Domi's voice out of her head.

"Mom's in the kitchen," her dad said with a wave of his hand, settling down into his favorite chair, his gaze already on the game.

Following the smell of home-cooked chili, Rae headed on in and wasn't the least bit surprised to find that her mom was not actually cooking but was sitting at the island counter, nibbling on an apple slice and reading a book. The cover looked like the latest by Leslye Penelope, her mom's favorite author. She looked up as Rae walked in, smiling and sliding her bookmark into place so she could put it down. She was dressed in colorful, comfortable clothing that she called her 'house clothes' and a headwrap to keep her hair out of her face. She always said she didn't feel like messing with it on weekends.

Rae had a lot of memories of weekends at home with her mom looking exactly like this when she was younger—then the flurry of activity that would happen if they needed to leave the house for some reason.

"Hey, babygirl." Her mom greeted her in the same manner her dad had, getting to her feet and enveloping Rae in a warm hug. "I guess you were too tired to cook tonight, huh? How was your trip?"

Both the greeting and the question were completely natural, and she couldn't help but think that her parents were two peas in a pod. It wasn't just the words of the greeting or the inquiry. It was the way they said it, with the exact same intonation. She relaxed a little more.

"It was good. Domi had a great time, and that was the most important thing."

Her mom smiled as she sat back down, gesturing for Rae to take the seat next to her. Her parents had opted for very comfortable bar seats with backs for the kitchen island because the kitchen was her mom's favorite place to sit and read. Sometimes, she did it in the window seat next to the big bay window, but when she wanted to eat and read, she preferred the counter where she could lean on her elbows and prop her book up.

Rae got her love of books and reading from her mom, though her mom didn't read the same kinds of romance as Rae did. She didn't think her mom had gone down the kink rabbit hole, but if she had, Rae didn't want to know.

"I hope you still enjoyed yourself, too," her mom teased. "I didn't expect to see you today, though."

"Right... well. Actually, I had something to ask you." She felt odd. Was she sweating? No. She just felt... strange, as though her body was a little out of sync with the rest of the world. Domi was wrong. She must be. Yet, it was hard to get the words out.

"Of course, honey, what?" Her mom raised her eyebrow, the little signal that said *spit it out.*

"Did you and Dad hide your fights from me?" The words came out in a rush, barely any space in between them, almost unintelligible... and her mom froze, eyes widening, the exact same way she had when Rae had asked about Santa's Christmas wrapping paper.

No! Fuck!

Domi was right.

24

———

Rae stared at her mom, and her mom stared back at her. Somehow, her mom seemed to know that the answer had been very important, even though she didn't know why Rae had asked the question and that she'd given the wrong answer.

"Um... why do you ask?" her mom said after a long moment, with too wide a smile.

"Mom!" Rae threw her hands up in the air. "Why did you hide your fights from me? What did you and Dad even fight about?"

Her mom sighed, as if she was giving up.

"Oh, everything." Her mom waved her hand with a snort. "Anything. But... well, my parents fought a lot when I was growing up. Big, loud, screaming fights. It drove me nuts. And I was always having the same with Deirdre, which also drove me nuts, and I couldn't help it. Your dad and I tried not to because he knew it bothered me, but sometimes it happened anyway. When I was pregnant with you, I made him promise me that we'd never fight in front of you. I wanted us to be a united front and didn't want you to have the same kind of childhood I did."

"Oh..." Rae didn't know what to say. It made sense, yet she suddenly felt like the carpet had been ripped out from underneath her feet, as if her entire childhood had been a lie. "But... when? When did you fight? It should have been impossible to hide anything like that from me."

Her mom eyed her like she was trying to figure out why Rae was so invested in this, and Rae knew that it was going to be her turn to be questioned soon, but she still had things she wanted to ask. Things she needed to know.

"Well, you know those after-dinner walks we took that you never wanted to go with us on?"

Rae's jaw dropped open.

"And there was that one time when your dad went on that impromptu fishing trip with his buddies right after one of those walks." Rae's mom shook her head. "That man. I almost didn't let him back in the house after that one."

"But what were you fighting about?" She knew she'd already asked the question, but she still didn't understand what her mom meant about everything and anything. How could she? They'd never shown her. As far as she knew, they'd always gotten along perfectly.

"Like I said, anything and everything. That weekend he went on the impromptu fishing trip... I don't remember. Something about how much time he spent watching football." Her mom snickered, glee sparkling in her eyes. "He ended up at his mom's, so no football over there."

No, Mimi had a 'no football game' rule in her home.

"So, he wasn't even out fishing?"

"Nope."

And she'd never known. She remembered that weekend being a fun one with her mom. Though now she understood a little better why her mom had been so energized about having a 'girl bonding experience' while her dad was away. At the time, Rae hadn't suspected a thing. She'd been excited by her mom's seeming excitement.

Looking back now, with full knowledge of what had actually

happened, she could see that her mom had probably been covering one high-energy emotion with another.

"Baby, what's going on?" Her mom reached out to put her hand over Rae's, concern no longer blooming in her eyes—it had taken full root. "What's wrong?"

"I thought you guys didn't fight!" The words burst out of her like an accusation of wrongdoing, startling her mom, though she didn't pull away.

"Of course, we fight. Everyone fights."

"I don't!"

"What?" Her mom frowned at her. "I mean, you've always been easygoing, but I wouldn't say you don't fight. We've had some fights."

"With other people, though, outside of my own family, I don't fight. I especially don't fight with my boyfriends. If I fight with a boyfriend, it's over. That's it. And literally, no one would call me easygoing except you." Her frustration was growing, as was a strange pit of anger in the ball of her stomach that she didn't know how to deal with.

Not only had her faith in her parents been a lie, but that lie had been the reason for so many decisions in her life, so many break-ups. It had been the reason she hadn't been willing to have it out with Brian about whether or not she really needed to call him 'Daddy' or why even Domi's suggestion of 'Papi' had made her hesitate because she hadn't wanted to fight about whether it was a suitable replacement.

She didn't know how to fight and make up with a romantic partner.

She'd literally never done it.

Her mom's mouth dropped open in surprise, her gaze losing its focus like she was going back through her own memories. It wasn't like Rae hadn't brought boyfriends around before. She'd had a few semi-serious ones... all that had ended with one fight.

"I... I'm sorry, baby. I thought you'd realize we were fighting, just not around you."

"Well, I didn't. I thought you were perfect." The urge to run was growing, just like it did with her boyfriends. Just like it had any time she and her mom *had* had a fight. The reason her mom thought she was easygoing was because Rae usually had found it easier to just give in, then do what she wanted in secret. If she got caught, she accepted the punishment because she'd known it was going to happen and already accepted the consequence as a possibility.

"Baby, no one's perfect... Rae... Rae, come back here!"

Her mom's voice followed her down the hallway and out the door, her dad's voice joining in, filled with confusion. But she had to get away. Everything was falling apart. Everything she'd been so sure of was an illusion, and she didn't know where she went from here.

BRIAN

The only joy he got out of having to explain everything to Morgan and Asad was that he'd cock blocked Asad pretty thoroughly. Which wasn't really joy so much as petty vengeance for the joy Asad appeared to be getting out of having first-hand access to such a big topic of gossip. He was beaming the entire time Morgan questioned Brian, listening closely and appearing to be taking mental notes.

At least he wasn't actually getting out his phone and texting people right in front of Brian's face. He looked like he was reaching for it at one point, and the glare Brian had sent him should have singed his hair off. After that, he sat quietly with his hands in his lap, listening intently and letting Morgan do her thing.

She was a pretty relentless questioner. If there was something she didn't understand or was unsure of, she did not hesitate to ask.

"I don't understand why Mitch and Domi would prefer not to know about Rae's shower." Her face creased in a frown, Morgan tapped her fingers against the table, a sure sign she was agitated because she felt like there was something she was missing. There were a lot of social cues she'd had to learn after escaping the abusive households she'd experienced as a child, then as an early adult.

"It's not that they would prefer not to know. It's that Rae didn't want to bother them because she thought it would stress them out. And I agreed."

"It wouldn't stress them out to find out that they didn't know?"

"Well... not in the same way. And we figured the trip would be over by the time they found out." He shifted in his seat, trying to think of a way to explain that didn't sound ill-conceived. Because the more he had to talk about it, the more he had to face that he and Rae had done some pretty impressive mental gymnastics to land them together that first night. Granted, they had really had good intentions, but it wasn't like anyone's trip would have been ruined... except maybe theirs because all eyes would have been on them if they'd insisted that he stay with her rather than with one of the couples.

"So, it was better to find out after?" Morgan still seemed confused, though like maybe she was accepting that part of the explanation. Asad's eyes danced with mirth at Brian's discomfiture. Yeah, Brian didn't mind having cock blocked him at all.

"Plus, Rae didn't want to bother anyone else or end up being a third wheel in someone else's villa, so she probably would have ended up in mine, anyway."

"And this way, you wouldn't have to put up with anyone asking about what you two were doing in there." Asad spoke up for the first time with a wink.

Brian clenched his jaw as he fake smiled and replied through gritted teeth.

"Exactly."

Morgan looked back and forth between the two of them.

"I'm not sure I understand. Asad and I didn't tell anyone about us because everyone had told him not to hook up with me, and I didn't want to get him in trouble. Would you have been in trouble?"

"No, we just would have had everyone in our business. Wasn't it nice to get a start to your relationship away from everyone who might have an opinion about it?"

Morgan opened her mouth. Closed it. Tilted her head to the side as she thought. She looked over at Asad, whose laughing smile had faded to something more rueful. He gave her a soft look that made Brian's heart clench again in raw envy. The two of them had found love, despite all the improbabilities around their relationship—the socially awkward submissive with the overly charming club manwhore had been a surprise match to everyone.

Why not me?

Then Morgan turned back to Brian and asked a question that hit him like a punch to the gut.

"You were starting a relationship with her? I'm confused again. I thought you said you were going to hook up for the week."

"Well, to be fair, that's what we said, too," Asad interjected.

This time, Brian was thankful for him jumping in because Morgan's question had taken his breath away. No, he hadn't been starting a relationship with Rae... except in some ways, that was exactly what they'd done. They hadn't kept emotions out of it. At least, he hadn't. Maybe he'd meant to, but he was hurting too much now to believe he'd been able to stay cold.

Deep down, even at the beginning, he was pretty sure he'd known it was going to be like that. Though he hadn't thought it would be this difficult. He hadn't anticipated it would hurt this much.

It was supposed to be easier, leaving everything behind on the island and returning to real life. Though, of course, it would help if real life didn't insist on talking about her. He wasn't sure who had sent Morgan the text, but when he found out...

"So... are you and Rae in a relationship now?" Morgan asked, turning her attention back to Brian.

"No," he said shortly, his tone clipped. He pushed himself up to his feet. As much as he didn't want to hurt Morgan's feelings, he was done with this conversation. He needed to be alone and to rest and to get some distance from all of it. "And we're not going to be. For us, it really was just for the trip. Now, I need to go rest."

Morgan looked like she was about to say something, but Asad reached out and put his hand on her arm, and she subsided. The last Brian saw of them, Asad was leaning over, speaking softly into her ear. Maybe trying to explain, maybe trying to distract her. It didn't really matter as long as Brian didn't have to talk about Rae anymore.

Hideaway Island had been the very last and final hurrah.

It was time to leave behind the fantasy once and for all and find a babygirl who actually wanted something real with him.

25

———————

RAE

Somehow, she ended up at Marquis. She hadn't had a plan when she'd started driving. She definitely hadn't thought, *Oh, I should go to the center of the gossip hub for the club.*

She just... needed somewhere familiar to go. Somewhere she felt safe. Somewhere she knew the rules. And, for once, that hadn't meant Domi's. Was it partly because she didn't want to admit to her friend that she'd been right about Rae's parents?

Yes.

Eventually, she would, but she needed a little bit of time, so it wouldn't smart so much when Domi said, "I told you so."

Her parents had lied to her. As much as she understood her mom's motivations and why they'd done it, she still felt deceived. Wildly misled.

And incredibly stupid.

That was it—she felt stupid. She couldn't believe she had just taken their lack of fighting at face value. That she'd built up a whole romance around how they never fought. That she'd based her own decisions about romantic relationships off that fiction.

Putting the car in park, she headed into the restaurant portion of the club. The second floor was where all the kinky stuff happened. The first floor was a regular restaurant and bar. On the first floor, there was nothing to indicate what was happening overhead. Plenty of customers went in and out of the restaurant for a good meal without ever being the wiser.

That was where Rae was headed now. She shook her head at the hostess as she walked in, angling toward the bar instead. While she was hungry, and part of her was regretting questioning her mom before dinner because that chili had smelled amazing, she didn't want to sit at a table and eat. It felt too formal. Too confining.

Instead, she went to the bar. As a member of the club upstairs, they had a card on file for her. If she felt the need to flee again, she'd be able to do so and tip the bartender later. They all knew her because she came here often for girls' nights with Domi and Iris. Avery worked in the kitchen, so that allowed her to come and join them when her shift was over.

Tonight, there were several bartenders since it was a weekend and the bar was crowded. Thankfully, there was a solo seat open between two couples, and Rae slid right in. On the other side of the bar, Shane, one of her favorite bartenders, gave her a smile.

He was a Dom, though she never saw him around the club. He and his wife tended to play in private, but everyone knew he was a Dom. If they didn't, and they misbehaved in his bar, they'd figure it out soon enough. In his fifties, with a bald head and a salt and pepper goatee, he wasn't very tall. In fact, he was about the same height as her, with a fit figure and a kindly smile that made him seem like a thinner Santa Claus.

But step one finger out of line and it was like something inside him shifted. He'd give the offending subbie a *look* that would have them meekly falling back in line. She didn't know how he did it; she just knew that it was impressive to watch—and slightly terrifying to be on the receiving end of.

"Welcome back home, Rae. What can I get for you?"

"The pretzel and a dirty martini."

Shane's eyebrows rose. Yeah, she came here often enough that he knew her 'something is bothering me' order. Putting a napkin down in front of her, he went to put in the order. When he came back, it was with both the martini and a glass of water. She couldn't help but roll her eyes, but she didn't protest.

She knew better.

"Want to talk about it?"

The couples on either side of her were completely involved in their partners, and she didn't recognize either of them from the club, which probably meant they were regular restaurant goers rather than members. And while the club ran on gossip, Shane himself was like a vault. He heard everything, knew everything, and told no one anything.

And he never, ever said, 'I told you so.'

Not that he could in this case because he'd never offered her relationship advice before. But he'd offered other people advice, and it always turned out well.

So, she took a sip of her martini and started to talk.

The best thing about talking to a bartender was that there were natural breaks as he needed to tend to other customers, which also gave her the chance to think. And drink. The alcohol definitely loosened her tongue because she found herself telling him about *everything*—including the fact that she hadn't gone to Domi because she didn't want to hear her friend's 'I told you so.'

Shane listened without a hint of judgment on his face, which was another thing she loved him for. The only time he gave her anything other than a kind expression was when she tried to order her second martini. Lifting one eyebrow, he gave her water a pointed look.

As soon as she'd drunk half the glass, the second martini appeared in front of her. This time, Rae did roll her eyes and got another stern look from Shane, though he didn't say anything.

"Is it so bad to be wrong?"

"I don't like it."

"I don't think anyone does. But you don't have to let it make you feel bad, either. Everyone is wrong sometimes. It's part of life."

"Even you?" she asked.

He smiled enigmatically.

"I've been wrong a time or two. The important thing is that you don't let being wrong change where you want your life to go. What's worse—being wrong or not getting what you want because you don't want to admit that you're wrong?" With another little smile, he turned to go take care of another customer, leaving her there with that extremely uncomfortable thought.

While she was sitting there, Olivia appeared behind the bar, crooking her finger at Shane. The redheaded Domme was the manager for Marquis and a serious badass. Rae watched with interest as the two of them had some kind of intense conversation, then Shane shook his head. Olivia sighed and turned away, shaking her head as well.

Oh, intrigue.

"What was that about?" Rae asked when Shane returned. Hey, it didn't hurt to ask, right?

To her surprise, he actually answered.

"Mistress Julie got another gift delivered here to the club. Olivia just wanted to check in and see if I saw anything or anyone out front."

"Oh... well, better here at the club than at home, right?"

Shane's lips twitched. "I believe that's how everyone feels, yes. Olivia's main concern is trying to figure out how the admirer knew Julie would be at the club tonight. They've been keeping her schedule under lockdown ever since she got the present to her home."

"Why did Olivia think you might know something?"

"I actually delivered the first gift. It came to the front instead of to the back." He smiled ruefully, shaking his head. "Granted, I had no idea at the time that it was going to turn into such a thing."

There was something about his tone, the way he was acting, that was different from everyone else. Law was freaking out about the admirer, Olivia was concerned, quite a few of the Doms were on edge, and... Shane was completely blasé. Not indifferent, but unconcerned.

"You know something," she accused, pointing her finger at him. It wavered a little in the air, and she leaned forward so she could rest her elbow on the bar to keep her arm steadier. "You know who the secret admirer is."

"No." He said it so firmly, so sincerely that she believed him, and her heart sank a little in disappointment. He gave her a wink. "But I have a strong suspicion."

"What?" She managed to keep from falling over, mostly because she was already partially braced on the bar. "Who?"

"I'm not going to say. Not while it's just a suspicion. And if I do ever get confirmation, there are other people I'll be telling first."

"What if things escalate?"

"If it's who I think it is, they won't. And if it's not, then casting suspicion on them won't help anything." Clearly, he'd already thought it through.

Damn. He really wasn't going to tell her anything. She threw her balled-up napkin at him, and he caught it, chuckling.

"You're a tease."

"Sadist," he said with a wink and just a hint of that Dom gaze that was enough to make her want to hide under the bar. Just a little. "Now drink your water and eat your pretzel so you can drive home in a bit."

Obediently, Rae tore a piece of pretzel off and dunked it in the beer cheese. Mm. So good. And she did actually feel a little better, even if she didn't know where she was going to go from here.

BRIAN

It turned out a quiet house wasn't any better than Morgan's questioning. She knocked on his door to let him know food was in the kitchen and that she and Asad were heading out.

He ate alone. Sat alone. Thought alone. Normally, that wouldn't bother him. He was used to being alone. Liked it. Was happy for company but could take or leave it. Right now, though, it chafed. He wanted a distraction, yet he couldn't think of where he would go to get away from everything... because what he really needed to get away from were his own emotions.

He wished he could call his grandma and talk to her. She always had the best advice. She would have loved Rae.

After dinner, he sat on the couch, staring at the television he wasn't really watching, replaying the last week in his mind. He understood why Rae didn't want to call him 'Daddy,' he did, yet he also couldn't help but think... *is it really that big a deal?*

But then, of course, his brain twisted it around on him.

If it's not that big a deal, then why am I insisting on needing it?

Hypocrisy, thy name is Brian.

But once he had the thought, he couldn't escape it. It zoomed round and round and round his head.

If he wanted her to give in to calling him 'Daddy' because it was what he preferred, why was that more important than her preference for not doing so?

It wasn't.

In fact, by all standards of what he felt made a good Dom, first came her needs, then his needs, then her wants, then his wants.

Was being called 'Daddy' a need on his part, or was it a want?

And... he wasn't really sure.

It was how he'd imagined his life, how he'd imagined his relationship for so long, he wasn't sure he could let that go. He wanted to be his submissive's Daddy. He wanted to take care of her, to support her, to have her give up control to him.

Does she have to call me Daddy to do all of that?

He didn't know.

He used to know. He used to be sure.

Now, he was questioning everything, and it didn't even matter because he and Rae were over, anyway. He wasn't going to put himself through that again. But it was an important question to answer for himself, especially if it came up again. Maybe the lesson he was supposed to learn here was that he needed to be more flexible if he wanted to find his perfect babygirl in the future.

Maybe she wouldn't want to call him 'Daddy,' either.

Or maybe he was supposed to learn that he wouldn't be happy without it?

He'd felt pretty damn happy with Rae the past week.

Was it sustainable?

His doorbell ringing made him jump. His heart leapt in his chest.

Surely... no.

It couldn't be.

But he found hope surging inside him as he pushed himself to his feet.

Hope that he tried to push away because he knew the right thing to do, even if it was Rae on the other side of the door. She'd used up all her chances.

He still hoped, though. That stubborn, gritty hope that refused to be tamped down or eradicated, that clung on through every one of his vows to himself. And when he opened the door to see Zach standing there, he felt nothing but disappointment.

Though the disappointment was quickly swept away by concern as he took in the other man's appearance. He looked disheveled. Which was a big fucking deal because Zach never looked disheveled. When they'd gotten off the plane today, he'd been the only one walking through their airport looking like he had just arrived for his flight instead of leaving it, and that had been with a hangover.

His hair looked like it had been raked through multiple times, he had a five o'clock shadow covering his jawline, and the skin around his eyes was swollen and pink. When he blinked and met Brian's gaze, Brian could see that his actual eyes were bloodshot.

Brian's mouth dropped open.

Holy shit.

"Kincaid and I just broke up. Can I stay here tonight?"

"Of course, man." Brian didn't hesitate. He opened his arms, and Zach stepped into them, bursting into noisy tears as Brian hugged him as tightly as he could.

26

Brian

Apparently, misery really did love company.

And Zach was good company. For starters, he was too wrapped up in his own shit to care about Brian and Rae hooking up. Secondly, since he had his own things he didn't want to talk about, even if he had cared, he wouldn't have brought it up.

He was also the perfect distraction.

With him moping around, vacillating wildly back and forth between pretending like everything was fine and that he was just visiting or slumping on the couch and staring into the middle distance, it wasn't like Brian had too much time to think about Rae. Morgan was a champ. She immediately ceded her room to Zach for as long as he needed it, though he promised he wasn't going to take too long. Just long enough to figure out what he was going to do next, he said.

Not that he seemed to be looking.

Which suited Brian just fine.

Having someone to take care of around the house soothed a lot of his agitation.

Something his therapist would have a field day with when he

confessed it on his next visit, he was sure. He was self-aware enough to realize he was focusing on Zach because that meant he didn't have to focus on himself, but he also wasn't doing anything to change the situation. Helping his friends made him feel good.

Helping someone who was out of control to gain control made him feel fulfilled.

And yes, he understood that he was getting a sense of control by proxy, but hey... much easier than facing his own problems.

He also talked to Kincaid on the phone. Zach had been adamant that everyone stay friends. He didn't want to make things worse, even though he wasn't ready to see Kincaid yet. Kincaid had also assured Brian that he wanted everyone to remain friends... even though he wasn't ready to see Zach again just yet. But he was relieved Zach had somewhere to stay.

From what it sounded like, Zach wasn't ready to come out to his family, and Kincaid was tired of feeling like a secret that was never going to be revealed. They loved each other, that much was evident, but they hadn't been able to find a compromise, and trying to plan for the upcoming holidays had blown everything out of the water.

"Are you sure you don't want to come to Stronghold tonight?" Brian asked over dinner. They'd eaten together almost every night that week. "Kincaid won't be there."

"I know." Zach stabbed at a piece of lettuce, not meeting Brian's gaze. He wasn't disheveled anymore, but he had kept the five o'clock shadow growing, and it was starting to turn into real facial hair. "It's a work trip for that security firm he's going to work for. But no, thanks. It's not just him I want to avoid."

"I get that." Brian was still struggling with making himself go tonight. The gossip was probably going to be rife. But... if he didn't show up, everyone would assume he was avoiding Rae. They'd draw all sorts of conclusions.

It was probably best to meet things head-on and get it over with, anyway. Like pulling off a band-aid. The longer he waited, the more speculation would run rampant and the worse it would be.

While he had the ready excuse of keeping Zach company, he

really didn't like the idea of anyone thinking he was avoiding the clubs because Rae might be there.

Okay. Not 'anyone.' Rae. He didn't like the idea of her thinking he was avoiding the clubs because she might be there. He didn't want her to know that she'd hurt him. Was it to spare her feelings or for his pride? He wasn't sure, but the end result was the same.

He needed to go to one of the clubs. Since he didn't have a reservation for Marquis, it had to be Stronghold.

Unless...

"Do you want me to hang out here with you? I don't have to go." If anyone asked, he could honestly say Zach had needed him.

"No, you can go." Zach sighed.

Well, there went that small hope, but he knew it was better this way.

"I should probably take the time to think. I've been avoiding thinking all week."

"Do you want to talk about it?" He wasn't going to push the issue, but Zach was looking as though he might be ready to actually spill rather than avoid it.

"I don't know." Zach dropped his head down again. "It's not like I can do anything to fix it other than man up and tell my family."

"Do you think they'd take it badly?" They'd been friends for a while, so Brian knew a little about Zach's family, but he'd never met them, and it wasn't like they'd had deep conversations about whether or not their families were homophobic. Brian tended to avoid talking about his childhood and his family, so he didn't ask questions about anyone else's. Everything he knew about Zach's were things Zach had said in passing.

"I don't know," Zach said again, even more morosely this time. "I mean, yeah, I know how they vote, and they say they support gay rights and everything, but I also remember my dad being super pissed off when my sister dressed me up and put makeup on me as a kid. My mom... she doesn't mean to be rude, but she just doesn't get a lot of stuff. Again, she'll say people should be able to love who they love, but she also complains about all the changes to 'that pronoun stuff.' So, I don't know. I just don't know." And the not knowing was clearly the hardest part for him.

Brian didn't entirely know how to sympathize because it's not like either of his parents had cared enough about him to care what his sexuality or gender identity was. But if his grandma was still alive, and he'd realized he was bi or enby, he might have been afraid, too. She'd been loving but old school, and he wasn't sure how she would have taken it.

"What about your sister?" he asked since she was the only one Zach hadn't mentioned.

"I think she'd be fine," Zach said immediately. "She had it out with my mom last year because my mom said something along the lines of trans people needing to accept that people were going to ask them invasive questions." He chuckled, looking a little lighter. "After Krista went to town asking her a bunch of questions about how she knew she was straight and cis, and immediately followed it up with questions about her and dad's sex life, I think she understood a little better."

Brian burst out laughing.

"Your sister sounds like fun."

"She is. She's straight, but she's always been super into politics and human rights, and she tries to be a good ally. She's working in D.C. right now."

"Why don't you start with her, then?" Brian asked. "It's not like you have to come out to the whole family all at once. Unless you think you and Kincaid are completely over, and you're only going to date women from now on. Then it's kind of a moot point."

Looking up from his plate, Zach met Brian's gaze for the first time, his dark eyes a little hopeful.

"Do you think just telling one of them would make a difference to Kincaid?" he asked eagerly, making it clear he wasn't ready for things to be over yet, which was good to know. Brian really hadn't been sure which way that was going to go. Zach could have easily decided he'd rather never come out to his family as anything other than straight.

"I think it would show that you're moving in that direction. Especially if she could meet him. Why not focus on the person you think will be the most supportive? She might even have ideas for how to prep or tell your parents."

Granted, he knew that Kincaid probably wanted Zach's entire family to know about him. They wouldn't be able to celebrate holidays together otherwise. But at the same time, he could see why Zach would find that daunting.

Just telling one of them would be easier on Zach, and it would show Kincaid that he wasn't being completely shut out.

Compromise.

Just like you could find a compromise with Rae, right?

Fuck, he hated that little voice in his head sometimes.

<u>RAE</u>

Stronghold was hopping, and so was Rae, though she was hopping from nervousness. Every time the door opened, she looked up, wondering if it was going to be Brian. Even though she wasn't sure what she was going to say to him yet. If she was going to say anything at all.

But this week had sucked without him.

She hadn't realized how used she'd gotten to having him around. Not just for the sex stuff but also for the day stuff. More than once, she'd wanted to tell him something... but it would have been really weird to text him when they'd never done that before Hideaway.

She kept thinking maybe she was hyping things up too much in her head. Maybe she was too deep into writing romances—even if she'd had writer's block all week despite all the ideas that had been flowing on the island—and she had built up a fantasy. Once she was faced with the reality, it would go away.

So, she hoped he showed up.

Even though she was really nervous about it.

"You are making me want to jump out of my skin. Will you sit down?" Iris said, tugging on Rae's arm to pull her back into her barstool. "I'm already nervous enough with Noelle constantly glaring at me."

"Sorry. Sorry." She hadn't even realized she'd jumped up. Master Will looked a bit like Brian, and she'd... yeah. Rae sighed, tossing her hair back over her shoulders. She'd dressed like a babygirl tonight, the way she often did at Stronghold. It didn't mean anything. She had just felt like wearing her purple tutu skirt and the corset with all the fun ribbons and lace because she felt good in them.

Not because they were something she saw other babygirls wearing.

Then she frowned.

"What do you mean she's glaring at you?" Rae leaned to the side so she could see around Domi, who also turned in her seat.

"Wait, don't look... ah, shit." Iris sighed.

Rae had already made eye contact with Noelle, who looked startled to suddenly be at the center of their attention. She turned away from Rae's glare and started talking to the others she was with, gesticulating wildly. Sam dropped her head into her hands while Amy reached out, focusing on Noelle like she was trying to soothe her. The other two, Marissa and Carolyn, turned to look at Rae and Domi... and probably Iris, although Iris was staring at the ceiling and taking deep breaths.

Marissa raised her eyebrow, and Carolyn smirked before they both turned back to whatever Noelle was saying. Wait, was Noelle crying? Good grief. It looked like she might be. Amy had her arm around Noelle's shoulders and was patting her knee with her other hand. Sam looked over at Iris with an apologetic expression on her face.

Great. She was sure that couldn't be good.

"What on earth is she doing?" Rae murmured, watching with consternation as Noelle suddenly jumped up, Amy trailing after her.

"Who the fuck knows," Domi said, shaking her head. "To cause trouble, probably."

"I wish you guys hadn't looked. Now she knows I was talking about her." Iris sighed.

"Yeah, because she was glaring at you."

"I didn't want her to know it was getting to me. And now she knows I said something about her, just like she's always telling everyone I do. Look, she's going to tell Patrick."

Sure enough, Noelle was knocking on Patrick's office door, ignoring whatever Amy was saying to her. Back in the Lounge area, where Marissa, Carolyn, and Sam still were, the three of them were looking at each other with what appeared to be confusion. They didn't know what Noelle was doing either.

Well, this should be interesting. Law was in there with Mistress Julie, having a meeting with Patrick about the upcoming round of classes. Rae didn't think any of them would appreciate a specious interruption.

"What's going on?" Mitch had come back from the bathroom, making all of them jump. He frowned at them, obviously picking up on the tension. "What are you all looking... Oh. Noelle." The disapproval in his voice made it clear what he thought of her.

The door to Patrick's office opened, and as they watched, the big man himself appeared in the doorway, towering over Noelle. The big black man took up most of the doorway, and his expression said he did not like being interrupted. But if she found him intimidating, she didn't act like it. She immediately started gesticulating wildly, waving her hand at Amy like she was trying to hush anything the other woman said.

"What is she doing?"

"We're not sure. Iris said she kept glaring at her, so Domi and I both looked over, then she started waving her hands and acting upset, and then she jumped up and ran over to start knocking on Patrick's door." Rae shrugged. She wasn't sure what had set Noelle off, but clearly, she was looking to cause some kind of scene.

Patrick looked up and over at their table. There was no point in pretending they weren't watching what was going on, so they just all looked back. Even from across the room, Rae could see him sigh, then he nodded. Noelle stepped back, dramatically wiping some tears away.

As Patrick headed over to their table, Noelle and Amy on either side of him, Law and Julie came out of the office behind him. There wasn't a total hush in the club as he moved, but more than one person looked up and started watching where he was going. Over in the Lounge area, the rest of Noelle's friends got to their feet and started to come over as well.

Great. It was going to be a whole little party.

"Ladies, Mitch." Patrick nodded his head when he reached them. Noelle stood at his side, still sniffling, though Rae was pretty sure she saw satisfaction glowing in Noelle's eyes. "Sorry to interrupt your evening, but I have to ask you a couple of questions. Mitch, have you been with the ladies all evening?"

"No, I just got back from the bathroom." Mitch sighed. "Sorry."

"I see." Patrick looked disappointed. "Okay, then. Ladies, can you tell me what, if any, interactions you've had with Noelle this evening?"

"They—" Noelle started to say, her voice shrill, but Patrick's hand was already going up in the air to make the 'stop' sign. She was smart enough to cut off whatever bullshit she'd been about to start spouting off.

"I asked *them*," Patrick said sternly. Noelle glared, but she subsided, and Patrick turned his attention back to the table, his gaze sweeping over Iris, Rae, and Domi in turn. "Ladies?"

27

Walking into Stronghold, Patrick headed across the club to a table where Rae was sitting, which was not what Brian had been expecting to walk into. There were two other women with him, and behind him were Law and Julie, who Brian recognized immediately. At least, he'd spent enough time with Law on the island that he knew the back of that bald head, and it wasn't hard to figure out that Julie was the one next to him—not too many FemDoms at Stronghold had her petite stature, and none had the combo of her stature and long black hair.

There was a sense of tension in the air, of drama, and he picked up his pace to find out what was going on.

"Iris was feeling uncomfortable because she said Noelle kept glaring at her." Rae's voice floated above the crowd, clearly heard as Brian slid around to the side so he could see a little better. Mitch glanced over and saw him, but the others didn't seem to.

Rae looked cute as hell in a purple corset with lace and ribbons that she wore a lot, her braids in pigtails tied with matching ribbons. Her expression said 'ready to fight,' though, and her arms were crossed over her chest, pushing up her breasts.

"So, Domi and I looked over at Noelle to see what Iris meant and saw her glaring at Iris. She started waving her hands around and saying something to the rest of her group, then she jumped up and headed over to knock on your door."

"And that was it?" Patrick asked.

"That was it," Domi confirmed with a nod of her head and a glance to Patrick's left. Leaning around, trying not to draw attention, Brian noted that's where Noelle was standing. He couldn't see her expression.

Patrick turned to his right.

"Amy, did you notice anything else from this group?"

"Um... well, no... but I wasn't really watching them," Amy said in a rush, sounding extremely uncomfortable.

"So, the first time you noticed them looking at Noelle was when Rae indicated?"

"Um, yes?"

Patrick turned.

"Sam? Carolyn? Marissa? Did you notice anything else?" he asked, his tone long-suffering. Clearly, he felt a certain way about this, but he was making sure to cover all the bases.

The three women shook their heads.

"They were looking at her when we looked over," Carolyn offered up, sounding more amused than anything else.

"Only because she was glaring at Iris," Rae retorted back. "We wouldn't have looked at you at all if she hadn't started it."

"That's not true! Iris has been shooting hateful looks at me all night, then she was obviously talking about me to you!" Noelle butted in tearfully, sounding like she was on the verge of breaking down.

"Yeah, because she told us that you were glaring at her. Which you were," Rae retorted. "I haven't seen her shoot one look at you. Why would she? She just wants to be left alone. You're the one who's obsessed with her."

"Because she's trying to ruin my reputation here and drive away all my friends! Or steal them from me!" Noelle sounded close to hysterical, and she leaned into Patrick's side as though she was appealing to him to take pity on her... unfortunately for her, he wasn't buying it.

He frowned down at her. It was a good thing his submissive, Lexie, wasn't here to see this. She wasn't super possessive, but she would have drawn the line at the way Noelle was trying to manipulate Patrick.

Noelle seemed to realize she was losing her audience. She sniffled again.

"I'm sorry, I'm sorry. I know I must sound crazy. I'm just so on edge because of all the rumors going around about me here. I don't want to lose my friends. I don't want everyone talking about me. I just want to be able to come here and have a good night and not be bullied or harassed or talked about." She gulped in air, as if she was about to start sobbing.

"Maybe you should stop glaring at people then," Rae said.

Patrick shot a look at her, but it was too late.

Noelle let out a wail and ran for the exit. Quite a few heads turned as she went, concern rippling through the crowd of people. No one liked seeing a submissive running from the club upset. A few frowns turned back in the direction of Iris and the others, and Brian frowned back at them. If they didn't know what was going on, they needed to keep their opinions to themselves. Noelle's dramatic exit was only a tiny slice of the story.

"Noelle!" Amy called out before running after her. Sam hesitated.

"I don't think they did anything. She's just... sensitive," Sam said before heading quickly after Amy and Noelle. Marissa went with her, leaving Carolyn behind. Patrick turned to look at her.

"What do you think? Is Noelle sensitive?"

"She's a drama queen, is what she is, but it's fun, right?" Carolyn flashed him a smile and laughed when he shook his head in disgust. There were quite a few people in the club who didn't like Carolyn for various reasons, and she seemed to thrive on it. She was honest about it, though.

Patrick sighed again and turned back to the table. Law was now standing behind Iris, his arms wrapped around her for support, while

Mitch stood between Domi and Rae, an arm draped over each of them. Brian had to resist the urge to go and replace his friend's arm on Rae with his own.

Yeah.

Totally didn't have any lingering feelings for her.

Not.

Not any that he was going to act on, at least.

Rae spread her hands wide, giving Patrick a challenging look. There was the inner brat coming out. Also her protective side. She was never going to back down from protecting her friends.

"What?" she asked Patrick.

"Just... try not to look at her." He sighed again. "Yes, I know how ridiculous that sounds. I can hear it. But..." He looked around as if remembering that he was out on the main floor, where everyone could hear him. Tilting his head back, he looked up at the ceiling, probably begging some higher deity for patience, before he returned his gaze to the three women. "Just try not to look at her, okay?"

He couldn't kick Noelle out for being dramatic. All he could do was try to mitigate the drama.

"Are you going to tell her not to look at Iris, too?" Rae challenged.

"Yes, I am," Patrick replied firmly. "If everyone could just not look at each other at all, that would be great."

Well, that was going to be interesting to enforce.

Not that Patrick was assigning any particular consequence. He was just making a request. But Brian didn't know what he expected to do if it wasn't followed. This was hardly a usual situation.

Giving them all a look, Patrick turned around as if he was going to head outside to follow after Noelle... but her friends were already back inside. Sam headed straight for the bathroom with Marissa and Carolyn on her heels. Looking slightly miserable, Amy walked up to Patrick. Brian was about to join his own friends when she happened to glance over him, and her expression lit up. She held up her hand with one finger raised, asking if he could wait a minute for her.

Brian nodded, rocking back on his heels. Considering everything that had just gone down, he would wait to join the table of friends, which wasn't the worst thing. It would give him a little more time before he had to face Rae for the first time since their trip and pretend he was completely unaffected.

Was she watching him?

He wasn't sure.

He tried to sneak a peek, but when he looked, she wasn't looking at him.

Maybe she had been, though.

Maybe you're full of wishful thinking.

After having a low-voiced discussion with Patrick, who patted Amy's shoulder before he headed back to his office, Amy wheeled around and hurried up to Brian. Cute and curvy, she was pretty in a girl-next-door kind of way. Her long brown hair had been pulled up into messy buns on either side of her head, giving her a vaguely Princess Leia look, and she was wearing a cute little black dress that hugged her curves.

"Hi, Brian. How's Zach doing? Is he okay?" She bounced slightly in place as she clasped her hands in front of her.

"He's good. Mostly. Sort of. I mean, it's kind of hard to define." Watching her practically vibrating in concern was making him uncomfortable. Taking her by the arm, he pulled her over to two of the empty chairs in the Lounge so they could sit down.

"He just loves Kincaid so much, you know?" she said earnestly, brushing an errant strand of hair out of her face. "He wants to tell his family. He's just afraid."

Amy and Zach had become good friends because she was a masochist in a vanilla relationship, though her fiancé was understanding about her needs and was fine with her scening platonically at Stronghold. It worked for Zach since he was both a sadist and a switch in a committed relationship as well. They'd been scening regularly to get their needs met almost from the very beginning.

Brian wasn't surprised that Amy knew as much as she did about the situation. He was a little surprised at how distressed she appeared to be. Then again, she had a soft heart. As evidenced by the way she'd run after Noelle. Just knowing someone she cared about was hurting was enough to distress her.

"I know. And even Kincaid knows that," Brian said gently. "It's just something they have to work through themselves." He reached out and took Amy's hand in his, squeezing it gently. "Are *you* okay?" It had suddenly occurred to him that maybe part of her distress wasn't just over Zach but a reaction to everything that had just happened.

She took a deep breath, getting herself under control and confirming some of his suspicions.

"Yeah... Noelle was just so upset. And angry. And... Sorry. You shouldn't have to worry about this."

"No, it's okay. You can tell me. Sometimes, it helps to unload on a third party who doesn't have anything to do with the situation. And, to be honest, you look like you could use a hug."

Looking up to meet his gaze, Amy's hazel eyes were full of unhappiness as she burst into tears. Brian reacted immediately, without thinking, reaching across and pulling her from her chair onto his lap.

"I'm sorry," she hiccupped, trying to get herself under control.

"It's okay," he murmured, rubbing her arm. "There's nothing wrong with a good cry now and then."

"I'm just so stressed out from the wedding, and I thought with my new medication that I'd be losing weight by now, but I'm not. And Noelle is always so upset about things going on with Iris, but she won't listen to reason, and she can be so nasty when you tell her that you don't see what she does... I know it's just because she feels hurt and betrayed, but it doesn't make it easier to deal with. And Jeremy has been spending all these extra hours at work, and I really needed a good cry tonight, but Zach is going through it, and he's not here, and I don't want to scene with anyone else, and that makes me feel horrible because I should be more concerned about what he's going through—"

"Breathe," Brian murmured, rubbing her back. He wasn't sure she'd actually taken a breath while she was talking. He'd understood all the words she'd said, but not exactly why she was upset about all of it. There was one thing he could reassure her about. "There's nothing wrong with wanting to have your needs met. You're not horrible for needing a scene."

She sniffled again, taking a deep breath the way he'd told her to.

"I'm sorry for word vomiting all over you."

"That's okay. Word vomit is easy to clean up."

Self-high-five. He'd managed to make her giggle.

---

*R*ae

"I'm gonna kick her ass," Rae muttered.

"What? Whose ass?" Domi's head swiveled around, finding what Rae was looking at immediately—Amy wrapped up in Brian's arms on his lap. "Amy's?"

"No, Noelle's. If she made Amy cry, I'm gonna kick her fucking ass."

It didn't matter that they weren't really friends. There were a few people in the club everyone liked, including Rae, and Amy was one of them. She was sunshine and rainbows and puppies and kittens, and right now, she was crying. It made Rae want to punch someone. The fact she was pretty sure the person who had upset Amy was someone Rae already wanted to punch was just icing on the cake.

"Oh. I thought maybe you were jealous because Amy is sitting on Brian's lap."

"Sitting on his lap because she's crying." If she'd just started sitting on his lap for no reason, Rae might have felt jealous. If anything, right now, she felt envious. She wanted to sit on Brian's lap and cuddle up. But she was also concerned about Amy and whatever the fuck Noelle might have said to her. She definitely didn't think there was anything going on there other than a distressed submissive and a caring Dom.

"What do you think Noelle said to her?" Iris asked nervously. Law's fingers stroked up and down her arm, obviously trying to soothe her.

"Whatever she said, it's not your fault," he said sternly.

"I know," Iris huffed, looking a bit mutinous. Even if she did know, she sometimes took Noelle's behavior onto herself, as if it was her fault Noelle was a shit-stirrer. "I just..." She sighed.

"You can't control her behavior. The best thing we can do is ignore her. Next time, we'll make sure you're seated so your back is to her. That way, even if she's shooting you looks, you won't have to see them," Domi said.

"Plus, she really hates being ignored." Rae shook her head. "I think she got off on causing drama tonight. She enjoyed making that little scene. She wants the attention."

"You think she enjoyed it?" Iris asked, looking pained.

Domi and Rae exchanged a glance. Yeah, Rae thought Noelle had been enjoying being the center of attention and having all eyes on her. Iris sighed when neither of them answered and put her hand in her hands.

"I think you're right. I don't know how I ever considered her a friend. She really was a good friend sometimes, though."

"Of course she was. No one toxic is toxic all the time. That's what makes them toxic. The fact is they're really good at pretending to be a kind, caring person for a lot of the time, usually when they're getting something they want from you or to make themselves look good." The way Law broke it down so quickly was impressive.

Rae's fingers itched, wanting to make notes for her book, but she didn't have any paper with her.

Turning her head, she found herself staring at Amy and Brian again. They'd gotten to their feet, and Brian was giving her a hug and a forehead kiss. Her heart ached. Was she really going to give up such a sweet, caring, good guy so easily?

Was it time to learn how to fight for someone?

28

RAE

"Are you going to go over and talk to him?" Iris asked.

"To who?"

"To the man you keep staring at." Iris raised her eyebrows at Rae. "Brian, obviously."

"Do you think that's such a good idea?" To Rae's shock, it was Mitch who asked the question—and he was frowning at her. Mitch hardly ever frowned. It looked weird and slightly unnatural on his face.

"Why don't you think it's a good idea?" she retorted rather than answering. She really didn't know if it was a good idea for her, but she didn't like the idea that Mitch thought it was a bad idea.

Mitch hesitated, his gaze darting around the table.

"Look... I don't know how much you know about Brian after Hideaway, but he's not really someone who gives second chances. He's very much a 'you're in or you're out' kind of person. It's not always cut and dried. The last girl he dated didn't show up for a date, called him after it was supposed to be over and said that she'd had car trouble and her phone had died. He wasn't happy, but he accepted it. The next time she didn't show up for a date, we don't even know why she didn't show because he never bothered to find out. He was done. Refused her calls and blocked her number. For all we know, her mom died or something." Mitch shrugged, but the concern in his eyes was clear.

Wow. Okay, that was brutal. And yet, because Brian had told her about his childhood and his parents, Rae got it. He wanted reliability and someone who was going to be there for him. Someone who made him a priority. And he didn't give people extra chances to prove to him that he wasn't.

"Except you." Mitch eyed her, and Rae almost jumped because it felt like he was answering the thoughts she was having in her head. "You, he's given multiple chances. Which makes me think that it's because he has even deeper feelings for you than he wants to admit."

Oh.

Oh.

Yeah.

Rae had turned him down a number of times. Walked away from him more than once now.

Yet he'd still offered up his villa on Hideaway. Had still fallen into bed with her. Had still agreed to be exclusive roommates-with-benefits for that whole week. But he'd cut off a girl he was dating without even getting an explanation the second time she didn't show up for him.

Rae was getting special treatment, and she hadn't even realized it.

As she was turning that revelation over in her head, Sam walked up to their table. Her eyes were a little pink, as if she'd been crying, too. The urge to go hunt Noelle down and impress upon her how people were supposed to be treated surged again. Sam gave them all a small smile before focusing on Iris.

"I'm so sorry. I had no idea she was going to do that tonight."

"No, how could you? It's not your fault at all," Iris reassured her immediately. "I should have just ignored her. Or at least told Rae and Domi not to look before I told them she was looking at me."

"No, you shouldn't have to ignore her." Sam shook her head. "I just wish I could have stopped her. But she's been so edge on, and she's not listening to anyone."

"Well, if I shouldn't have to ignore her, you shouldn't have to stop her," Iris retorted with a little smile of understanding. "And trust me, if anyone understands what she can be like, it's me."

Sam huffed a little sigh.

"Yeah. Well. Did you all happen to see where Amy went?"

"She's over there crying... Brian's got her, though," Rae said, pointing past Sam, who half turned to see before Rae's next question drew her back. "What did Noelle say to her?"

"Oh, it's not just Noelle, though I don't think that helped. Noelle did snap at her about taking Iris' side, but there's a lot more going on with her fiancé and... yeah. It's just a hot mess. Sorry, y'all, I'll have to talk to you later." Sam rubbed her forehead.

"Go, go," Domi said, making a shooing motion with her hands. Amy obviously needed some friend support, and none of their group was close enough with her to truly count as that.

Rae felt a little disappointed that she didn't have an excuse to go after Noelle now. Seriously, someone needed to slap some sense into that girl.

Why not me?

If wishes were fishes...

Speaking of wishes, she watched as Sam sat down to the side of Amy and Brian. Amy threw herself into Sam's hug, but Brian didn't get up to go anywhere. Of course, he wouldn't. Not until he knew Amy was okay.

Rae sighed.

As much as she wanted to go over to him, as much as she wanted to talk to him, she knew Mitch was right. She needed to be one hundred percent sure what she wanted from him before she tried to talk to him. It wasn't fair to either of them for her to keep going back and forth.

This time, she wasn't going to be impulsive.

She was going to think first. Then she was going to decide what to do.

What a freaking night. Brian leaned back in the chair he'd made his own for the evening. He didn't feel any desire to try to find a play partner from the submissives in the Lounge, though some of them were shooting him inviting looks. He didn't feel even remotely tempted.

He felt drained.

Not just from taking care of Amy—in some ways, that had made him feel a little better to be able to help someone who needed him— but he hadn't been able to fix everything. And he'd spent a lot of the night with one eye on Rae.

After the showdown with Noelle, she seemed quieter than usual. Had something about it bothered her? Had she been bothered that he was consoling Amy?

If it was the latter, he wasn't sure how he felt about that. Because while part of him liked the idea that she felt possessive of him, he knew he would be better off if he _didn't_ like that idea. He shouldn't want her to feel possessive. He needed to get past her. Get over her. Stop thinking about her. Stop thinking about their week together.

"Hey, are you okay?" Connor, one of Law's good friends who had eventually shown up with Q, clapped him on the shoulder, peering at him with concern. They'd been focused on Sam and Amy after they'd arrived, but when Brian glanced over now, it looked like the other three had disappeared somewhere. Connor was a mountain of a man, looming over him with a frown that wrinkled his brow. A lot of the same subs who liked being coddled by Brian also flocked to Connor. At first, Brian had thought he might be a Daddy Dom, too, but he didn't seem to be drawn that way.

There were a few people in the club who still seemed like they were looking for what they really wanted, and Connor was one of them. But he was a good guy, and Brian appreciated the lookout.

"Yeah, I'm good. Just tired." As he said the words, he found himself yawning and quickly covered his mouth with his hand while his jaw cracked. Ouch. Damn.

Maybe he needed more sleep than he'd thought.

Connor gave him a crooked smile as Brian held out his hand in a request for help to his feet. The big man pulled him up like he weighed nothing. Connor was a wall of muscle, yet he never seemed bulky or like he was going for a bodybuilder physique. He was just *strong.*

No wonder the subs liked him.

"Where'd Amy go?"

"Sam and Q are walking her out. She's gonna head home for tonight."

So, she wasn't getting her scene. Poor thing. Though he had a feeling what she'd needed the most was a good cry, and at least she'd gotten that. Still, eventually, she would probably need a scene. Maybe he'd mention it to Zach when he got home. It wasn't like Kincaid had shown up tonight, and helping out Amy might give Zach some sense of normalcy.

"I think I might be headed that way, too," he admitted. "I wish I'd realized. I could have walked her out."

"You were off in your own little world." Connor chuckled. He turned, his eyes tracking someone across the room, but when Brian turned to look, he couldn't figure out who Connor might be watching. The club had gotten crowded while he'd been tending to Amy.

"Are you going to scene tonight?" Brian asked curiously. He couldn't remember the last time Connor had done a scene with someone. He wasn't surprised Connor hadn't offered to do one with Amy—or if he had, she must have refused.

The two of them would be incredibly mismatched. Amy needed pain, and Connor tended to more sensual scenes and pleasure Dom scenarios. He could administer a spanking or flogging when he had to, but he rarely did, even though he watched them almost religiously. Brian sometimes wondered if he was just too afraid of hurting someone with his strength. Connor was definitely not a sadist.

He'd figure it out eventually, though. Maybe Brian could offer to mentor him. On another night, when he wasn't already feeling so tired.

"No, I don't think I'm scening tonight. Mistress Julie is supposed to do a demonstration on using Florentine flogging. I was going to go watch that." Connor's eyes lit up, the way they always did when there was a flogging demonstration. No wonder he was interested in the two-handed technique.

Yeah, Brian was going to have to work on confidence with the big man. He was sure there were any number of submissives who would happily offer to be his test subject to try out flogging techniques.

Things for Brian to think about later.

Things to distract yourself from Rae, you mean. While still having an excuse to show up at the club regularly to see her.

Brian ignored the thoughts that kept bubbling up, mocking him. Fake it till you make it, right? If he kept making himself come to the club and act like it didn't matter she was here, eventually it wouldn't.

That was how he'd gotten himself through a lot of his childhood. He'd kept pretending he didn't care that his parents had both abandoned him until he really didn't anymore. Well, unless he got a better suggestion from his therapist this week. He was self-aware enough to realize this was probably not the best coping method.

Time for him to get going. He looked around and didn't see Rae and had to resist the impulse to go looking for her. Was she somewhere in the club, scening with someone else?

It doesn't matter. You're not supposed to care.

"I'm heading out," he announced with enough firm fervor that Connor gave him a startled look. Thankfully, the other man didn't ask.

"Hope you get some sleep." Giving him a little nod that Brian returned, Connor headed off toward the Dungeon. Which meant Brian definitely couldn't go down there to see if Rae was there. Which was good.

He made himself walk to the door.

He'd just gotten into the lobby area when the door to the outside opened, and Mitch and Domi came in.

Brian frowned.

"What were you two doing out there?" he asked. He could have sworn they were in the club earlier. Was he losing it? Maybe he really did need more sleep if he was imagining things so vividly.

"Walking Rae to her car. She decided to make it an early night." Mitch eyed him with suspicion. "You, too, huh?"

It took Brian a moment to realize what Mitch suspected, then he had to laugh because it was so far from the truth.

"I'm just going home to bed. Alone." He said firmly, aware that Tracey—the subbie working the front desk this evening—was listening avidly to every word being said. He had no doubt it was going to do the gossip rounds along with everything else. "It's a coincidence."

Mitch nodded his head, though he didn't seem convinced. Brian was aware that his friend was regarding him with a lot of concern.

"Trust me," he said with a snort. "I've learned my lesson. There's nothing between me and Rae."

Giving them a wave, he headed out the door, too distracted and tired to notice the way Domi was watching him as he went.

29

———————

R_{AE}

I've learned my lesson.

"What does it mean?" Rae muttered. It didn't sound good.

"I don't know," Domi admitted, crossing her arms over her chest and leaning back against her chair. "I'll be honest, I thought I'd find him here with you this morning."

"Is that why you brought so much food?" Rae couldn't help but be amused. Domi had shown up on her doorstep about twenty minutes ago with a bag full of takeout breakfast and a dangerous gleam in her eye. She'd barely paused before barging past Rae and running around the house, looking in every room. Bemused, Rae had just watched her until Domi was done and ready to explain what the fuck she was doing.

That was when she'd found out that Brian had left Stronghold right after her, and her first thought was, '*I wish he'd been coming to secretly meet me.*'

Then she'd immediately realized that wasn't true.

She didn't want him to secretly meet her at all.

Had running around and secretly hooking up on Hideaway Island been fun? Absolutely. But it wasn't what she wanted. Not here at home. She didn't want to be sneaking around. She didn't want to have to pretend they weren't together.

She wanted… him.

If he'd have her. If he could accept a compromise on the whole 'Daddy' thing.

If she could be brave enough to ask.

The fact he'd said he'd 'learned his lesson' when it came to her did not inspire hope.

For all that she liked to think she was a strong, confident woman who always went after what she wanted, she'd quickly started to realize when it came to matters of the heart, she was far more used to waving the white flag. Asking for a raise at work? No problem. Making herself vulnerable to Brian? *I want to hide.*

"I was kind of hoping he'd be here." Domi sighed. "Even with what Mitch said. I think you guys would be really good together. I think you just need to convince him to give you another chance."

"What makes you think he'd want to give me one?" Rae's heart clenched as she sat down at the table across from Domi. "You heard what Mitch said about him giving chances. And it's not exactly like I'm able to go and offer him everything he ever wanted." She sighed. It really did sound hopeless.

Domi made a face and began to unpack the food, sliding some of the containers in front of Rae.

"What if *you're* everything he ever wanted?"

"He's always wanted to be a Daddy Dom. That's something I can't do for him," she argued. She popped a piece of cantaloupe into her mouth, using some of the sweetness of the fruit to wash away the bitterness of the truth. If she couldn't offer him everything he wanted, why would he say yes?

Just to have her?

She didn't like the insecurity she felt or the way it sounded as though she thought she wasn't enough, yet wasn't that exactly what she was afraid of?

"I still think you should call him something that means 'Daddy' and call it a day. *Papi,* Papa—"

"I don't know." It felt like not the same. Maybe for Domi it would be if she used 'Papi,' but for Rae...

"Pop. Old man. Pater." Domi said the last one with a terrible British accent, and Rae cracked up.

"Oh my God, stop."

"Does he have to be a Daddy Dom? Can he be a Pop Top?"

"Oh my God, stop. I can't breathe!" Rae wheezed out.

She wanted to call him a Pop Top. She wanted to call him a Pop Top so bad. Would she get an even better expression than when she'd called him 'not the mama'?

Except she couldn't. Shouldn't. Because she wasn't his babygirl, and he wasn't her Daddy Dom. Or her Pop Top. God, she was never going to be able to look him in the face again without wanting to call him that, just to see how he reacted.

"What about Father Figure?"

"I. Will. Murder. You." If she could ever stop laughing hard enough to actually take a deep breath. The tension that had been riding her was seeping away, though, unable to hold up against the rockslide of laughter that cascaded through her.

"I'm just saying. You don't know what he'll be willing to compromise on until you talk to him. Maybe you guys can skip the fight and get straight to the compromising. Nothing wrong with that." Domi raised her eyebrows at Rae, who sighed and finally admitted the truth.

"You were right, my parents fight, okay? They just didn't do it in front of me because my mom wanted to protect me from all the fighting."

"Ha!" Domi pumped her fist in the air. "I knew it!"

"Iris has been a bad influence on you," Rae retorted, referencing Iris' reaction to Hideaway when Brian and Rae's secret hooking up had been revealed.

"She would say she's been the best influence." Domi stuck out her tongue in a move that was more reminiscent of her daughter than of Iris, and Rae had to shake her head and laugh again. Also, because

Domi was right. Iris would definitely say she was the best influence. "So, does this change everything for you?"

"I don't know about *everything*." Rae sighed again as she nibbled her bacon. Her delicious, delicious bacon. Sadly, bacon did not bring clarity. "It's made me kind of mad at my parents." She'd talked to them the day after she'd run out on them—they'd known to give her some space before reaching out—but she couldn't help the lingering feelings of resentment, despite knowing where her mom was coming from. It was like they'd been so determined not to do one thing, they'd overcorrected in the complete opposite direction.

You mean the way you do?

Yeah, but she came by it honestly. Like mother like daughter.

The problem was that now that she'd noticed it, she did want to course correct. Again. But she didn't want to overcorrect. Somehow, there had to be a way for both her and Brian to get what they *needed,* even if they didn't get everything they *wanted.*

Right?

"I'm just saying. You were really happy on the island. Happier than you ever were with Damian. I thought it was just getting away from everything, but now that I know it was also partly Brian..." Domi let her voice trail off, giving Rae a Significant Look.

The truth was, Rae had also felt happier on the island than she had in a long time. Other than the 'Daddy' thing, she and Brian fit together. She missed him. She was pretty sure the reason she couldn't write right now was because of him, just like he'd been the reason her ideas had been flowing while they were at Hideaway.

"He said that he'd learned his lesson, though, right?" Rae let out a long, slow breath, trying to hide the ache that she felt at those words. "That sounds like he's done with me."

"You just have to show him that it's worth giving a relationship with you a real shot. For once. You guys don't need a second chance for that. Neither of you have ever really given it a first chance," Domi pointed out.

She was right. Rae had definitely never really given her and Brian a real shot. There had always been roadblocks and reasons not to and hard-end dates. How was she supposed to convince him?

"Seriously? You're a romance author. You have read nothing but romance for the entire time we've been friends." Domi raised her eyebrow. "How do you think you're going to convince him?"

"Are you reading my mind?" Rae demanded to know because she had definitely not said that out loud.

"Yes. Duh." Domi snorted. "Like I didn't know exactly what you were thinking. Now... what are you going to do?"

That was the question.

BRIAN

Marquis on a Friday night. Well, not night, exactly, more like early evening. Dinner would be starting soon, then the show, but it wasn't quite time yet except for the earliest arrivals.

He'd actually been planning on staying in this weekend and not going to either club. He'd made his point last weekend by being at Stronghold. This weekend, he was going to hang out at home with Zach... but then Zach went out to lunch with his sister on Thursday and told her about him and Kincaid. Then he'd called Kincaid today to tell him he'd come out to his sister, and they'd ended up agreeing to meet for drinks.

Zach had texted Brian and told him not to wait up. Which was a message Brian was thrilled to get. He hoped it meant good things for Kincaid and Zach. He'd even looked forward to having the evening to himself, and that meant he'd be on call in case things between the couple took a turn.

But then Law had messaged him, asking if he could come give his opinion on a new addition to Marquis' pink room, formerly known as the Little Girl's room. They'd started calling it the 'pink' room after one of their nonbinary members pointed out that they weren't a little girl but still enjoyed that room. It had been an easy switch to include everyone, and now they had the pink room and the blue room, and no one felt like they couldn't enjoy either room. Brian hadn't known they were getting anything new, and he'd been both flattered to be asked for his opinion and curious about what they could have added.

"Hi, Brian." Olivia was standing behind the front desk of Marquis, looking at something on the computer. She straightened when he reached the top of the stairs and the lobby. He was rather surprised to see her there instead of Law, even though she ran the place. She had her bright red hair down rather than pulled back, and it fell in waves around her shoulders, down to the top of her black leather corset. Intimidation, thy name is Olivia.

"Hi, Olivia. Law asked me to come by to see something in the pink room." He managed to sound pretty confident as he spoke rather than nervous, which was a feat in and of itself. Olivia had taught the class he'd taken when he'd wanted to become a Dom at the clubs.

It was hard to stay confident with someone who had heard you squeal when she pushed a plug up your ass. Brian definitely had a better understanding of what he was putting a submissive through after taking the class.

"I know." Olivia smiled enigmatically. "I asked him to text you. I'm very interested to see what you think."

"Oh... well, great. I'll be happy to give you my thoughts." He couldn't help but feel even more chuffed, knowing Olivia had specifically asked for him.

Her smile widened.

"Do you know how Luke and I got together?" she asked.

As eager as Brian was to head over to the pink room and see this surprise, there was no way he was going to cut off Olivia. Even if he didn't understand why she was suddenly bringing this up.

He'd been new to the club when she and Luke had gotten together, not really part of anyone's inner circle other than the so-called "Baby Doms." There was a new set of Baby Doms now, but he, Mitch, Kincaid, and Zach had been the first to be titled that. They'd heard plenty of gossip when they were the Baby Doms, but back then, they never had any idea how accurate any of it was.

"I heard he was a silent partner for Marquis, so you guys had to spend a lot of time together, then he signed up for the new submissives class because you said it was the only way you'd consider being with him." It hadn't been all that juicy of gossip, other than the fact it had to do with Olivia.

She laughed.

"Almost right. He signed up to prove to me that he could handle being a submissive and to force my hand into giving him a chance." She leaned her hip against the desk, smiling at the memory, her grey eyes unfocusing.

Well, that was certainly playing with fire with a Dominant like Olivia... but it had worked out for them in the end. He still wasn't sure why she was suddenly confiding in him... unless she was expressing an opinion on him and Rae. Olivia had a bit of a reputation as a meddler when it came to relationships, though she was usually more blunt. He'd once heard Law say it was like being hit with a fairy godmother's two-by-four rather than a magic wand.

Subtle was not her thing.

"Anyway. The main thing is to keep an open mind. Sometimes what we think we want isn't what we actually need, and sometimes, what we need shows up in a way we didn't expect." The unfocused look in her eyes had disappeared entirely, sharpening into something... more. Okay, she had to be talking about Rae, right? "Anyway, I'll be interested to see what you think. Here's the key card. Go on to the pink room. It's all set up."

"Right. Um, thanks." More confused than ever—had she been talking about Rae or about whatever new addition they'd made to the pink room—Brian took the key card from her with a nod and headed through the door into the club. The main area of Marquis was set up completely differently from Stronghold, where everything was public. Everything here was far more private.

The main room was set up around a stage with deep booths to watch from, each with its own set of curtains that could be closed for extra privacy. There were sheers if the booth occupants wanted to watch the show but remain hidden, and thicker velvet curtains if they wanted to be totally in their own little world. Each of the booths was equipped with all sorts of restraint options, and all sorts of implements and toys could be ordered from the menu along with dinner if you didn't bring your own.

On the opposite side of the room, there was a door that led to the themed rooms, which were also hotel rooms. Each one was set up as a suite, with the theme room being the first room, then the bedroom and bathroom beyond that. The pink room was the first on the left, and it had always been Brian's favorite room.

He'd spent one very memorable night in there with Rae... back when he'd hoped to convince her that she really did want to be his babygirl.

So much for that.

Regardless, he still loved the room, even if he hadn't used it again since that night. It wasn't because the last time had been with Rae. It was just that a night at Marquis was... special, and he hadn't had anyone special to use it with.

He didn't know what he was expecting to see when he opened the door, but he knew one thing that he *wasn't* expecting—Rae standing in the middle of the room dressed in a pink corset and tutu that went down to mid-thigh with white trim on both and white bows holding her braids in pigtails.

Brian ground to a halt and blinked as Rae gave him a tremulous smile.

What the fuck?

30

Big romantic gesture.

Easy, right?

Except what do you get for the guy who wants the one thing you can't give?

The answer—everything else you can think of and hope it's enough.

It was clear he wasn't expecting to see her when he opened the door. She'd been on pins and needles waiting for him, even though Olivia had told her what time he was supposed to be coming in, and she'd never known him to be late to anything. For some reason, even though he hadn't known she was the reason he'd been invited in, she'd convinced herself he wasn't going to show.

She hated thinking that he might not have come if he'd known she was the surprise.

"Hi, Papa." Ew. Nope. Rae wrinkled her nose at the exact same time as Brian. That one wasn't going to work. Shaking his head, Brian stepped into the room, letting the door close behind him. Well, at least he hadn't gone running. That was something, right?

"Hi, Papi."

Nope. Not much better. Maybe a tiny bit better in some ways, but worse in others.

None of these were comfortable.

Brian put his hands on his hips, his expression caught somewhere between exasperation and amusement.

"What are you doing, Rae?"

"Trying to find a compromise, Pop." She snorted. Nope, that one not only felt weird, but she couldn't take it seriously with Domi's voice echoing in her head. *Pop Top.*

Pointing a stern finger at her, Brian shook his head vehemently.

"Absolutely not that one."

Which, of course, meant she had to do it.

"What? A Pop Top is basically the same thing as a Daddy Dom." Well, that was one way to keep him in the room. His jaw dropped at the same time she saw his hand actually twitch.

He wanted to spank her *bad*.

Thanks, Domi.

Wanting to spank her would probably keep him from running off before she could get her words out. She took a deep breath. Bratting wasn't what she was supposed to be doing, though she didn't think it was hurting her case.

"I want to date you."

Brian frowned.

Okay, that didn't quite cover it.

That was not a grand gesture. *Be vulnerable. Open yourself up. Give him what he needs. Fight for him.* Rae took a deep breath.

"I'm falling in love with you." The words had been so hard to say, yet they felt like such a relief to finally get them out there. And they worked.

Brian froze. The look of astonishment was even better than when he'd walked in the door and saw her standing there, but not quite as satisfying because she didn't want astonishment—she wanted reassurance. She wanted to hear that he was falling for her, too, but she knew that when it came to their past, he'd put himself out there more than once for her... and she'd walked away every time. It was her turn.

"I think I have been from the very beginning. I kept walking away from it because... because I don't know how we're going to make this work. I saw a fight about the whole 'Daddy' thing, and it was just easier to avoid it than to face it. But I don't want to keep avoiding it... I don't want to keep avoiding you. I want to see if we can find a way to make it... to make us work. If you still want to."

With her hands twisting in front of her as she spoke and her heart pounding like a stampede of elephants inside her chest, she felt almost like she was going to throw up. But she got the words out. They weren't as polished as she'd hoped or sound as good as she wanted them to, but she'd gotten them out.

Hopefully, that was the important thing.

But Brian wasn't responding. He was just standing there, staring at her, poleaxed.

"Um, feel free to chime in any time... otherwise, I can just, like, go back there,"—she jerked her thumb over her shoulder at the door to the bedroom—"and you can leave, and we can pretend like this never happened." And she would cry herself to sleep here tonight, then never talk about this with anyone again. Sounded like a plan. But if that was the way it was going to go, she really needed him to get out now before she started to fall apart.

Rather than answering, Brian looked around the room. What, did he think someone was going to jump out at yell 'Pysch!' at them?

"You rented the room for tonight? To tell me that?" he asked in a hushed voice.

Okay, that sounded promising. He seemed touched. Touched was good. She could work with touched. Hope started rising up inside her.

"Yes?" It came out as more of a question than a statement. The question was whether he would stay. Whether or not she'd done enough.

Whether or not *she* was enough.

He didn't answer her. Instead, he strode forward, reaching her in two steps, his hands coming up to cup her face, and he caught her lips in a searing kiss. Rae's lips parted with a sigh of relief, and his tongue delved between them, claiming her mouth as his own.

But they hadn't finished talking.

Rae pushed at his chest, squirming back.

"I'm still not calling you 'Daddy,' though." Dammit. Did it have to come out sounding like a challenge? She hadn't meant for it to. Brian didn't move his hands from her face, though. His thumb made a slow sweep over her lower lip, holding her right where she was, with her hands on his chest.

"I think..." He took a deep breath. "Would it be okay if I called myself 'Daddy'?"

She frowned, not because it sounded bad but because she wasn't quite sure what he meant.

"Like, talk about yourself in the third person?"

A rueful smile twisted his lips.

"I know it might sound a little silly—"

"No, no, I'm just trying to understand what you're saying." Even if it did end up sounding a little silly, she could live with that. The important thing was that he was right here with her, wanting to find a way, looking for a solution. A compromise.

Maybe they couldn't have it all, but they could have *enough*. That was life, wasn't it? Nobody ever got one hundred percent of everything they wanted. Yesterday, the woman who ran Human Resources at Rae's accounting firm had told her a fun fact about job hiring— they looked for the candidate who came the closest to getting ninety percent of the qualifications they wanted. They could work on the other ten percent from there. Trying to find someone who fit one hundred percent was an impossible task.

That's what Rae had been doing. She'd been trying to find one hundred percent, but that wasn't life. That wasn't people. But she thought she and Brian were well above ninety percent. They could keep working on whatever percent they had left.

"What do you mean, call yourself 'Daddy'?" she asked, prodding him when he didn't answer right away. He took a deep breath, and she realized this was a moment where he was making himself vulnerable, the way she had.

To her amusement, a blush was reddening his cheeks. Whatever he was going to say, she might agree to it just for that. It was incredibly adorable. He cleared his throat, his expression altering just a bit, as though he was trying to make himself appear surer of himself than he actually was.

"Well, when we were on Hideaway, I had to hold myself back from speaking the way I normally do. Normally in bed, I would say things like 'Be a good girl for Daddy' or 'You're taking Daddy's cock so well.' I didn't while we were there, but since we're talking about it, I wondered if calling myself 'Daddy' would also be a hard limit for you." The blush on his cheeks darkened as he spoke, but his gaze never wavered from hers, taking in her reaction.

No disgust rose, no immediate rejection of the idea, nothing that made her think 'absolutely not.' In fact, there was an odd little tingle between her legs at the sentences he'd apparently been holding back for her.

"I think I'd like that," she said, almost wonderingly. She wouldn't have expected to, but hearing Brian actually say them... it was hot. Maybe it really wouldn't hurt to try it herself. "Daddy."

Oops. Nope. She ruined it. The second she called him that, her entire body flinched.

Ironically enough, so did his. The horror in his expression was almost enough to make her laugh. See? He didn't want her calling him 'Daddy' either.

"That just sounded wrong," he complained. "You don't say it right."

Rae bristled. She'd just wanted to try it, to see if she could. She didn't like how it sounded, but she also didn't like hearing that she'd done something wrong... even if it was better that he didn't like hearing her say it. Yeah, she was a mass of contradictions. So what?

Before she could express her disgruntlement, Brian must have noticed her reaction, and his expression softened.

"It's not going to mean to you what it does to me," he said. "It's better for both of us if you call me Brian or Sir. I can call myself Daddy if I really need to hear it... and yes, I know what that sounded like. You can just let it go." He raised his eyebrow at her, giving her a stern look as a warning not to ruin the moment.

She closed her mouth again, pressing her lips together to keep from making a joke. They were finding a compromise, and that was more important than making fun of Brian for talking about calling himself Daddy. At least for now. Maybe she'd get another opportunity in the future.

It really was a good compromise. While it didn't feel right for her to say it or even think it, somehow, Brian made it sound good when he said it.

"So, we have a compromise?" she asked wonderingly. Was it really that easy? Just talk through the things she thought were insurmountable, and—since they were both willing to bend—they found a solution that worked for both of them. It seemed almost *too* easy. Or maybe it just made sense. They'd been fighting this for so long, and it had been so hard, giving in was just naturally easier.

"We have a compromise. Thank God." He closed his eyes briefly before opening them again, the bright blue boring into her. "Because I'm in love with you too, Sunshine."

Rae's heart jumped in her chest, her heart thrilling to the words, but she didn't have a chance to respond before his lips claimed hers again. This time, she kissed him back with all the fervor of her emotions as they surged up within her.

This.

This was it.

This was everything she'd been wanting and who she'd really been wanting, and just letting herself finally feel it all and be swept away by the emotion was an ecstasy as good as an orgasm. Though she knew she was going to get at least one of those, too.

Then, suddenly, she was being spun around, and she squealed as his lips were pulled away from hers.

"Hey!"

"Hey, yourself, Sunshine. You didn't really think you were going to get away with calling me a Pop Top, did you?"

"It wasn't my idea, it was Domi's!" Did she throw her bestie under the bus in a heartbeat? Absolutely. In situations like this, it was every brat for herself. Besides, Domi wasn't here, so she was safe. And Mitch would probably think it was hilarious when he heard about it.

He was a sadist, so it wasn't like it would be hard for Brian to convince him to give Domi a punishment. But Domi was a masochist, so she'd like it.

Not that Rae was going to hate it. She already knew that as she was turned to face the spanking bench, which was so helpfully set up right behind her. It was a cutesy-looking bench with pink leather and light wood, but that didn't detract from what it actually was... and as soon as Brian had her skirt down, he started bending her over the bench.

She wasn't actually protesting, though. She wanted his hand coming down on her ass. She wanted the spanking and the heat and the pleasure. She wanted all of him.

31

———

Brian

Pop Top.

He was never going to get that out of his head. He didn't know whether to laugh or cry. One thing was for certain—he was going to take it out on Rae's upturned ass. Not that she minded, from the way she was wiggling it at him as he bent her over the spanking bench.

His cock was hard as a rock, but he didn't want to skip the fun stuff to get straight to the main event.

She'd set them up in this room for a reason. It didn't feel right to move right past it into the hotel room beyond, no matter how much he might yearn to pick her up and carry her off in his arms so he could fuck her senseless. They should make use of this front room.

Especially because he needed to pay her back for 'Pop Top.' If nothing else, he was going to do his best to make sure that particular monicker never made it around the club. Although, since Domi had been the one to come up with it...

Well, he'd do what he could.

Though he'd almost rather 'Pop Top' than hear her call him 'Daddy' again. That was the first time he'd ever had an adverse reaction to a sub calling him Daddy. He'd thought he'd wanted to hear it from Rae's lips. He'd thought it would be a fantasy come true.

As much as he appreciated her trying, he almost wished she hadn't. That particular desire was now very, very dead. He didn't even get to hold on to the fantasy that it would be everything he'd ever wanted. The crushing reality was also something he was never going to be able to erase from his brain, unfortunately. It had sounded so, so wrong coming from her lips.

"I didn't actually call you a Pop Top," Rae argued, even as she slid herself into position on the spanking bench, squirming to get comfortable, which had the happy effect of making it look like she was shaking her ass at him. "I asked if that would be better. I was just looking for alternatives that might appeal to you!"

Brian snorted and brought his hand down on her ass, giving it a little smack that made her jump and squeal.

"You knew exactly what you were doing, little girl." She was such a brat. He shook his head in semi-exasperation. If nothing else, she was going to keep him on his toes.

Fuck, that felt good. Finally, being able to let go and give in to his emotions. To admit to both himself, and to her, that he loved her. He'd been fighting his feelings for so long, he wasn't entirely sure when he'd fully fallen, but the moment he didn't have to fight them anymore, he'd realized how completely gone for her he was.

"How was I supposed to know you wouldn't like Pop Top?"

God, she was going to keep saying it, wasn't she? Brian shook his head, a rueful smile curving his lips, as he brought his hand down on her ass again. Rae yelped, wriggling in place as her cheeks jiggled from the impact. In her current position, he could see that her pussy was already wet and glistening, ready for his cock... but he was going to make both of them wait.

"Do you want to call me Pop Top?" he asked, just to see what she would say.

Silence.

Yeah, that's what he thought.

He brought his hand down on her ass again, spanking her in

earnest now, darkening her cheeks with every crisp swat. Rae moaned, dropping her head down and lifting her ass up to receive the spanking. With the corset still on, hugging up her upper body, all the focus was on her ass and pussy... He teased around the latter, letting his palm and fingers strike right next to that tender spot without actually connecting.

Moving his hand up and down her ass, he covered the entirety of her bottom, from the rounded top down to her sensitive thighs. She cried out, the wood creaking as she rocked on it, gripping it tightly, pressing the front of her mound against the supportive leather.

"No cumming until Daddy says you can," he murmured, pausing between swats to make sure she could hear him.

She moaned in response, and he grinned.

Was it unusual for her not to call him Daddy but for him to say it? Sure, but it worked for them. Every kinky couple was different in how they operated, and all of it was valid as long as they were both getting their needs met. And not having to hold himself back from calling himself Daddy while they were scening was apparently all he really needed.

And when he said it, it sounded *right*.

Even Rae liked hearing him say it.

"I don't think I like that rule," she muttered, squirming back against his hand as it came down again. She moaned. He chuckled and rubbed his hand against the sensitive skin of her ass, as though he was rubbing the swat in.

"But you're going to follow it, aren't you?"

"What if I can't help myself?" she asked, lifting her head to look over her shoulder at him. She fluttered her eyelashes, her gaze filled with false innocence.

Brats. Always having to push the envelope.

"Then you'll spend the evening tied to the hotel bed with a vibrating wand pressed against your clit, so we can see how many orgasms I can force out of you," he said amicably.

The expression of horror that his suggestion was met with was a good indicator that she was not into forced orgasms as a punishment.

She immediately dropped her head back down like any good brat when met with a line she didn't actually want to cross.

"I was just asking."

He laughed again, caressing her ass and giving it a rough squeeze before lifting his hand again.

"Be a good girl, Sunshine, and you'll get your orgasm soon enough."

Rae

Did her pussy clench when Brian called himself 'Daddy'?

Yes, yes, it did.

Did it make her want to try calling him Daddy again?

Nope. Not even a little.

She didn't know why this dynamic seemed to work for both of them, but she was glad it did. The relief pouring through her was nearly as strong as the pleasure growing inside her with every slap of Brian's palm against her ass. It stung in the best way, the heat rippling through her, warming her insides and fueling her desire.

Was he spanking the sass out of her? Maybe a little. It was hard to feel sassy when she felt this good, especially with the threat of the vibrator hanging over her head. She didn't want a vibrator. She wanted him... above her, inside her. She wanted the connection again.

She'd missed him so much, even though they'd only been 'together' for less than a week. Even though they hadn't been apart all that long after getting home.

With every slap of his hand against her ass, she wanted him more.

Dropping her head, she gave herself over to the sensations, submitting to the spanking and to him. She could feel his fingers caressing her in between each smack, dipping dangerously close to her pussy, teasing her and stimulating her. Making her yearn.

"Please... Brian... Sir..." *Fuck.* His fingers brushed over her pussy lips, a featherlight touch that made her want to scream in frustration. Her clit pulsed in response, begging for more.

His hand came down on the backs of her thighs, making her scream as her pussy clenched in response. It hurt, it burned, yet it made her insides hotter.

More, please.

Fuck me, please.

Suddenly, she could take a deeper breath than before.

He'd loosened her corset.

Rae whimpered as he pulled her to her feet and spun her around, pulling the corset from her body while running his hands all over her. Their lips came together in a tumultuous kiss, clothing falling to the ground. She heard something rip and was pretty sure it was his shirt—*oops*—but he didn't pause.

Scooping her up in his arms, he carried her from the pink room into the hotel room. Which surprised her—she'd thought for sure he'd want to make use of the frilly white and pink bed that was in the front room. But when he tossed her down onto the bed, re-igniting the heat in her bottom as it came into contact with the sheets, she realized this was the right choice.

The big bed was so similar to the one they'd shared on Hideaway, yet while they'd leave this bed behind, they would go forward from this room together. It was like a redo of their final night—the night that they'd missed out on when Domi and Mitch had decided to separate everyone.

She expected Brian to climb on top of her, but instead, he bent over to bury his face between her thighs. His arms wrapped around her legs, prying them wide apart for his oral assault, his tongue delving between her pussy lips as he began to feast like he was a starving man.

"Oh, fuck!" Rae's fingers weaved through his hair, her lower body trying to levitate off the bed—partly from the discomfort of her seared cheeks being pressed against it and partly to get more of her pussy on his mouth. All the stimulation she'd been craving was suddenly hers for the taking, and the shock made it hard for her to assimilate.

It was a glut of pleasure, of sensation, where there had been nothing, and the suddenness of it made her brain fritz.

Her knees bent, heels digging into the backs of his shoulders as she rubbed herself against his questing tongue. When he sucked her clit between his lips with a low hum that vibrated straight up her spine, Rae felt herself coming apart at the seams. She cried out again, muscles tightening and releasing, clenching and loosening, as pure ecstasy exploded inside her.

Who needed a vibrator? Not her. Brian's tongue was sending her soaring without any extra help, her body quaking as he kept suckling, kept licking, sending her on another paroxysm of pleasure. She might try to levitate, but he leaned into her, keeping her pressed against the bed, right where he wanted her.

"Please, please, please..." She didn't know if she was begging him to stop or to keep going. All she knew was that she was drowning in pleasure, her most sensitive spots rapidly becoming *over*sensitive. She couldn't take anymore, yet she could feel another orgasm building, swelling inside her, and she thought she might die if he stopped before it released.

Then he pulled away... no, he was moving upward, his mouth sliding over her stomach up to her breasts, leaving her pussy wet and wanton and begging.

"Brian!"

He covered her mouth with his own, the taste of her arousal coating his tongue as he thrust it between her lips with filthy confidence. The tip of his cock slid over her swollen folds, rubbing against them, seeking out her opening. She moaned as he deepened the kiss, pushing up against him to help his dick find what it was searching for.

They both shuddered as he found it, and the head of his dick pushed into her, stretching her. Fuck, it felt so good. So right. Rae slid her hands up his chest to his shoulders, digging her nails in when it seemed like he hesitated. If he stopped now, she would murder him. She wanted—*needed*—him inside her.

Then his hesitation—if that's what it was—disappeared, and he thrust in hard enough to make her cry out. The thick length of his cock split her open, stretching her deliciously as her slick flesh parted for him, and he slid in deep. The change-up of sensation was enough to have made her orgasm begin to recede, but now her passion mounted again as new pleasures rippled through her.

He pounded into her, her heated bottom bouncing off the bed with each one of his thrusts, and she cried out as she clenched around him. They moved together, her hips lifting to meet his thrusts, his body rubbing against her swollen clit every time their bodies came together. She clung to his shoulders, shuddering as her climax swelled, swirling higher and higher.

"Oh, fuck..."

"That's it, Sunshine. Come for Daddy. Come all over Daddy's cock."

Brian's growling voice did it. The most powerful orgasm Rae had ever experienced surged through her, sweeping over her like a tidal wave. She was thrown into the maelstrom of ecstasy, crying out as he slammed into her to the hilt, rubbing his body against her clit as his cock pulsed inside her.

It was everything she'd ever wanted and more.

32

BRIAN

"I knew it!" Iris danced around, pointing at him and Rae the moment they walked into the kitchen of Domi and Mitch's house, holding hands. She was the first one to spot them. "I knew it, I knew it, I knew it!"

"No, I knew it," Domi corrected, shaking her head with a smile as she scooted around the dancing Iris to put some dip out on the counter.

The whole surface was covered in food, and it smelled amazing. Clearly, she'd been cooking all morning in preparation for having people over for the game in the afternoon. Most of them were in the other room where the television was, just past the kitchen, but Mitch, Domi, Law, and Iris were all standing around the counter. Well, and Zach was behind Brian and Rae because he'd driven over with them.

"You only knew because I told you," Rae retorted from next to him.

Brian gave her hand a little squeeze, shooting her a sidelong glance. Everyone was staring at them, and not just because he was in silver and blue while Rae was in red and gold. When he'd pulled out his jersey this morning, he'd thought that she might actually leave him over it, but she'd decided she loved him more than she hated a football team.

He'd had some fun spanking her over the smack talk, though.

They hadn't told anyone other than Mitch and Domi for a week, wanting to have some time to themselves before having to deal with their friends. Brian was pretty sure Zach had suspected something was up before Brian had given him the news this morning, but he'd been embroiled in his own relationship drama. He and Kincaid weren't exactly officially back together, but they weren't *not* together either.

They weren't doing the holidays together, and Zach was still living with Brian, but he'd also spent a few nights back at his old place with Kincaid. He swore up and down they hadn't been doing more than talking for now. Which after seeing Zach and Amy scening last night at Stronghold, Brian believed. They'd both apparently needed an outlet because he'd been rough on her, and she'd cried her eyes out but had also obviously needed every bit of it. Afterward, Zach had cried, too, while he held her.

Then Sam had taken Amy home, Brian had taken Zach home, and Kincaid had already been at home. Today was the first time they'd be back in the same place with all their friends since breaking up, so Brian and Rae were really kind of taking one for the team by announcing they were officially together.

"I knew," Zach said with a wink, sliding by Brian to get farther into the kitchen, heading for the snacks that were lining the counter in front of Iris.

"Knew what?" A little voice asked as a tiny hand reached up from the other side of the counter to grab a chip. Brian almost jumped. He hadn't realized Domi's daughter was also in the room since she was totally hidden by the counter.

"Ana, you need to eat some veggies, too," Domi said sternly, looking down on that side of the counter. Another little hand reached up to grab a carrot stick.

"Knew what?"

"Knew that Aunt Rae has a boyfriend," Domi answered her daughter.

"She does?" Ana, Domi's daughter, came around the counter, chip in one hand, carrot stick in the other, big brown eyes wide. She was wearing a pink dress with a tutu skirt featuring two cartoon dogs, one blue and one orange, hugging each other on the top part of the dress. Her gaze locked onto Brian and Rae's hands and somehow got even wider. "Rae-Rae! You have a boyfriend?"

"I do," Rae confirmed, letting go of his hand and crouching down to open her arms. "Can I have a hug?"

Squealing, Ana ran into Rae's arms, giving her a huge hug. She was a seriously cute kid. Brian had met her quite a few times, but he hadn't been given a hug yet. As she pulled away from Rae, he held up his hand.

"High five?" That was their usual greeting. To his surprise, Ana gave him the high five, then threw her arms around his legs. She was a short kid for her age, which wasn't surprising given Domi's petite stature. Her cheek pressed against his thigh, which made trying to lean down to hug her a little awkward, but he attempted it anyway. "Aw, thank you for the hug, Ana."

Apparently, being Rae's boyfriend got him special treatment.

"You're welcome," she said to him very seriously, tilting her head back to look up at him with her arms still around his legs. "Treat her right, or I will end you."

She said it with total seriousness, in her cute little high-pitched voice, which made it a thousand times creepier than if an adult had said it. Next to him, Rae grinned widely. Iris and Domi were both muffling their own laughter. Obviously, he was on his own with the tiny terror.

"I plan to treat her right," he promised seriously.

"Good." She nodded and let go of his legs, wandering off toward Mitch and Domi's living room where the tv was, now munching on her chip. He looked across the counter at Domi and raised his eyebrow. She just grinned at him and pushed the tray piled with vegetables and dip toward him.

"Can you take this into the living room with you?" she asked.

"Sure."

But he didn't get a chance to because the rest of their friends were suddenly streaming into the kitchen from the living room, leaving the television behind. Avery was in front, with Nick and Zach right behind her, Kincaid and Mitch bringing up the rear.

"What's this we hear about Rae having a boyfriend?" Avery asked, her eyes widening when she saw Brian standing there next to her. Apparently, Ana had gone and immediately announced the news to everyone else.

"Hi, I'm Brian, Rae's boyfriend," he quipped, waving his hand at them. Mitch snickered and shook his head while the others gaped at him.

Well, this should be fun.

Rae

"Yes, we're together, yes, it's for real this time, and no we don't care what you think," Rae said, answering the obvious questions. Only the last one was untrue. It wasn't that it was entirely untrue, but she also wasn't going to let what their friends think affect her and Brian's decision, and he agreed. Of course, they cared what their friends thought, though. Just not enough to change their minds.

At least she already knew that Domi and Mitch were supportive. And Ana. God, that kid cracked her up.

She stepped closer to Brian, slipping her hand back into his so they could present a united front.

"I'm so happy for you!" Avery squealed, rushing forward to give Rae and Brian a hug, which they returned. Out of the corner of her eye, Rae saw Iris leaning forward across the counter, pointing her finger at Law.

"I told you!" Iris crowed. Obviously, she was more concerned about being right than anything else, which worked for Rae.

Law just rolled his eyes and shook his head, coming forward to join Iris behind the counter. On his way, he clapped Brian on the shoulder as if to say 'congratulations.'

As she lifted her gaze over Avery's shoulder, she met Nick's. He shrugged and smiled at her, but he wasn't as invested as the other guys, the Baby Doms, who had been friends with Brian since the beginning.

Brian's friends were the real possible barrier.

Zach wasn't looking at her, though. He had turned away to nudge Kincaid in the side. She couldn't quite see what he said, but it looked like it might have been 'told you so.' Which it might have. Brian had told her that he was pretty sure Zach suspected something was going on, even if he wasn't as vocal about it as Iris.

They shared a cute little smile that wasn't quite like the looks she'd seen them share before but gave her hope for them for the future. After all, if she and Brian could make things work, Zach and Kincaid surely could as well. They loved each other, she could see that... they just still needed to find the right compromise, the right piece of the puzzle that hadn't fallen into place yet.

They would. She had faith.

"I care a little bit about what they think," Brian said, bringing her attention back to her grand announcement. She looked up at him, narrowing her eyes. He chuckled. "You do too, Sunshine. Don't even pretend you don't."

"Her name's not Sunshine, it's Rae." Ana peeked out from behind Mitch and Kincaid's legs. She must have gotten curious about why everyone had stormed into the kitchen. Her comment got a laugh from everyone around the kitchen.

"I know." Brian's smile down at Rae widened, and he didn't take his eyes off her as he answered Ana. "I'm calling her that because she's my ray of sunshine."

The filthy things this man did to her.

He'd made her name into a pun, and she loved it.

"That was terrible." She smiled widely back at him, her heart beating in her chest. "You should absolutely say that in front of my parents next weekend." They'd give him a hard time, but they'd eat it up too. In fact, she was surprised her dad had never thought of it before. That kind of cheesy but affectionate joke was right up his alley.

"Oh ho, he's meeting the parents already," Nick said. "It's serious!" His tone was joking, but he was right.

They weren't going to pretend that it wasn't. They'd been dancing around each other too long for that. This was the real deal, which was why they'd wanted to make sure their friends knew it was official, and they'd come to announce it together.

"Damn right, it is." Ignoring their friends, Brian leaned in toward her, dipping her back slightly as he lowered his lips to hers. Reaching up, Rae wrapped her hand around his neck to help her keep her balance, well aware that they looked like something out of a movie. It was one of the most romantic moments of her life, and her heart thrilled at the physical demonstration.

All around them, their friends literally started clapping and cheering as they kissed. Laughing followed as Brian straightened back up, bringing her with him, and took a bow. Cracking up, Rae elbowed him in her side.

This was her happily-ever-after, and it was nothing like what she'd thought it would be, but everything she needed it to be.

EPILOGUE

"John got another promotion."

Another phone call from her mom, another update on her ex-husband's terrific life. If only her parents were as proud of her as they were of their former son-in-law, but of course—according to her parents—she'd peaked when she'd married him, then lost it all when she'd divorced him.

"That's great, Mom, but I asked how Dad is doing." Julie rubbed her forehead. Forget that her father had a procedure today to check out some suspicious shadows on a recent scan. Talking about her ex's recent promotion was far more important. Why John didn't stop picking up the phone when her mother called him, she didn't know, and she probably never would since *she* refused to ask him to stop talking to her parents. Again.

Family is family, Julie. His snide, superior voice echoed in her head from the first and last time she'd asked him to stop answering her mom's calls. She ground her teeth as she waited for her mom to answer her.

"Oh, your father is fine. John saw to him personally, even though that's beneath him now that he's going to be the hospital director."

Her mom sounded breathless, as if she was swooning over the fact that John was just *so* gracious to be personally involved.

Which she probably was.

With only one girl child who had no interest in becoming a 'real' doctor—her master's in psychology didn't count—her parents had been thrilled when she'd married a 'real' doctor. In retrospect, she'd finally realized that a big part of her attraction to John had been knowing she'd finally have her parents' approval. The hardest part of divorcing him had been losing that.

She loved her parents, but she also understood their relationship with her was not the ideal adult-child relationship. It didn't stop her from yearning for that. Julie felt like it helped her with her own work, though.

"I'm glad to hear that Dad is fine. I have to go now." This was Julie's work with herself, setting firm boundaries with her parents, and that included stepping away the moment they brought up John. It didn't surprise her that her mom used her father's health to find a way to sneak in news about him. That was par for the course. But now that her mom had, it was up to Julie to reinforce the boundary and step away from the conversation.

"Oh, I thought you were calling because you wanted to talk to me. It's been forever since we've really talked." This was the hardest part because she could hear the genuine disappointment in her mom's voice.

She didn't doubt that her parents loved her; it was just that their love came with expectations that veered dangerously close to outright conditions. They didn't understand why she didn't want the same things for herself that they wanted for her. They were utterly convinced they knew best what would make her happy, and they were baffled by her resistance to that happiness.

"I know, Mom, but I told you I'm not available to talk about John. I'm glad to hear that Dad is doing well, and I will talk to you later." She hung up the phone over her mother's protests that she was being too sensitive and overdramatic, then bent over the desk so she could gently bang her head against the hard wood several times.

The first few times, she'd made the mistake of wavering, of believing her mom was right that she was unreasonable for hanging up after 'just one slip-up.' She quickly learned that giving that inch meant being knocked over for a mile. The only way she had any success with getting her mom to respect her boundaries was by enforcing them constantly and consistently without even a hint of leeway.

She already knew the next time she talked to her mom, she'd get an earful about how rude she'd been this time, and her mom wouldn't acknowledge why Julie had hung up on her, but she also wouldn't bring up John again for at least another five to six phone calls. That was up from three to four phone calls, which was last year.

Maybe one day, it would finally be the end, and Julie wouldn't have to hear about John at all. She doubted that, though. While her parents were thoroughly invested in him, that was due to the fact they thought she and John still belonged together. Why the man just couldn't find someone else to date, she didn't know... unless all the other women in the area were smarter than her and saw through his charming exterior to the hidden misogynist who would do his best to crush their dreams and personality in favor of being his sweet little wife.

Julie had nothing but respect for stay-at-home spouses and parents, but she'd never wanted to be one, and she vehemently rejected the idea that she should be one just because she was an Asian woman. Granted, at least her parents were supportive of her having her own job, but they insisted that, *of course,* John's career came first.

He was a *doctor,* after all, and she *was* a wife. Was she looking down on stay-at-home wives and mothers?

It was insidious, that kind of gaslighting.

Sometimes, she wondered if her parents' manipulations were why she'd gotten interested in psychology in the first place when she'd realized that not everyone's parents were like that.

Someone knocked on the open office door, which she probably should have closed, but she'd known the call wouldn't take long. And it wasn't like this was her day job. She spent most evenings at Marquis, the kink club she belonged to and where she was also a kink educator.

"Everything okay?" Olivia, Marquis' manager, asked from the doorway, sounding both concerned and amused.

The other Dominatrix had become one of Julie's best friends, so she didn't hesitate when answering, knowing Olivia would immediately understand.

"Call from my mom." That was all that needed to be said.

"Ah. Well, I've got something that could either cheer you up or make things worse." As Olivia approached the desk, Julie lifted her head to see what she was talking about. There was a huge box of cookies in her arms. Not just any box. Julie's favorite box. The ones that were available only in the lead-up to the holiday season.

They could only be from one person.

"Another secret admirer gift?"

Was it sad that having a secret admirer perked her up so much? Maybe. But it felt nice to be admired for who she really was. It felt nice to have someone pay attention to her likes and dislikes and act on them. It was even nicer not to have any kind of reciprocity expected.

She knew it drove Law, her co-instructor for the classes at Marquis, absolutely nuts. He was convinced there was something nefarious behind all the gifts. Julie had been a little nervous at first, along with flattered. Part of her had even wondered if John had finally decided to step up and try to win her back with something more than an admonishment.

It's time to stop being ridiculous, Julie. You've had your little tantrum, done your little show. I know you're serious now. If working really means that much to you, I won't stand in your way.

Julie gave herself a little shake. She knew the reason John's voice kept popping into her head was because her mother had brought him back. He'd quiet down by the time she went to bed tonight, then stay that way until the next time her mom gave her an update.

"These are your favorite, right?" Olivia asked, putting them down on the desk in front of Julie.

She was relieved it was Olivia here tonight and not Law. Even though she appreciated his concern and knew he had a few valid points, she couldn't deal with his particular brand of overprotectiveness right now. Especially over something she had become more and more convinced was harmless over the months as gifts kept arriving.

That was also what had ultimately convinced her they were definitely not from John. He'd never be able to go so long without getting recognition for his effort. The man expected to be applauded for the bare minimum. She couldn't imagine what kind of adulation he'd want for going above and beyond.

"They are." Julie stared at the card on top of the box. It was bigger than the cards that normally came with her gifts. Normally, she got very short notes. "And they're only available at this time of year."

"Interesting. What's the note say?" Olivia perched on the edge of Julie's desk—well, the desk she shared with Law in their office—and peered down at it with interest. The pencil skirt she was wearing meant she had to cross her legs to do so, making her look like a very prim, redheaded librarian. Since she was clearly more interested than judgmental, Julie didn't mind her sitting there as she opened it.

It really was longer than the previous ones.

"What does it say?" Olivia asked again after a moment. Julie closed the card and looked up at her friend contemplatively.

"I'm not going to tell you."

Olivia's eyebrows rose.

"That good, huh?" she asked, though her tone hadn't changed.

Julie knew her well enough to know her feelings weren't hurt by being kept out of the loop. It just made her even more curious. But she also understood the importance of keeping secrets, especially at Stronghold and Marquis.

"Maybe." Julie tapped the outside edge of the card as she cradled it in her hands. "I'll be able to tell you more after next weekend."

Curiosity lit a flame in Olivia's grey eyes. Then she nodded her understanding.

"I look forward to hearing about it." She got to her feet, brushing her skirt down. "Law will be here soon." Olivia sauntered out with that little reminder.

Yeah. Julie and Law had their own private spaces within their shared office, and she quickly stashed both the cookie tin and the note in hers. She knew Olivia wouldn't mention it, and hopefully, no one else had been there for the delivery.

She didn't need to worry about thinking about John or her mom anymore. Her thoughts for the rest of the night were going to be consumed by the note... and trying to decide what she was going to do.

Dear Mistress Julie,

I want to apologize for any fright or distress I might have inadvertently caused you. I don't think I have, but just in case. I didn't mean to worry you when I sent the gift to your house.

If you'd like to know who I am, I am willing to meet.

I haven't revealed myself before because I've been unsure of what you would think. Of what everyone would think. But I'm tired of hiding.

I'll be at Marquis next Friday in a booth by myself. I'll have a bouquet of roses for you. If you would be open to joining me, I would love to try serving you for the evening. If not, I understand. I hope, at the very least, that I've given you some pleasure over the past year.

Yours, ever in admiration.

Mistress Julie will find out who her secret admirer is in Secret Submission...

ABOUT THE AUTHOR

Golden Angel is a USA Today best-selling author of heart and bottom warming romance.

She is happily married, old enough to know better but still too young to care, and a big fan of happily-ever-afters, strong heroes and heroines, and sizzling chemistry.

When she's not writing, she can often be found on the couch reading, in front of her sewing machine making a new cosplay, hanging out with her friends, or wandering the Maryland Renaissance Fair.

www.goldenangelromance.com

BB bookbub.com/authors/golden-angel
g goodreads.com/goldeniangel
facebook.com/GoldenAngelAuthor
instagram.com/goldeniangel

OTHER BOOKS BY GOLDEN ANGEL

Contemporary BDSM Romance

Venus Rising Series (MFM Romance)
The Venus School

Venus Aspiring

Venus Desiring

Venus Transcendent

Venus Wedding

Venus Rising Box Set

Stronghold Doms Series
The Sassy Submissive

Taming the Tease

Mastering Lexie

Pieces of Stronghold

Breaking the Chain

Bound to the Past

Stripping the Sub

Tempting the Domme

Hardcore Vanilla

Steamy Stocking Stuffers

A Sassy Christmas

Entering Stronghold Box Set

Nights at Stronghold Box Set

Stronghold: Closing Time Box Set

Masters of Marquis Series

Bondage Buddies

Master Chef

Law & Disorder

Switch Play

Legally Bound

Shallow Submission

Hidden Away

Secret Submission

Third Wheel

Dungeons & Doms Series

Dungeon Master

Dungeon Daddy

Dungeon Showdown

Dungeons & Doms Boxset

Daddies Everywhere

Chef Daddy

Foosball Daddies

Taco Daddy

Cheese Daddy

Garden Daddy

Little Villain

Historical Spanking Romance

Domestic Discipline Quartet

Birching His Bride

Dealing With Discipline

Punishing His Ward

Claiming His Wife

The Domestic Discipline Quartet Box Set

Bridal Discipline Series

Philip's Rules

Gabrielle's Discipline

Lydia's Penance

Benedict's Commands

Arabella's Taming

Pride and Punishment Box Set

Commands and Consequences Box Set

Deception and Discipline

A Season for Treason

A Season for Scandal

A Season for Smugglers

A Season for Spies

Desire and Discipline

A Season for Bliss

A Season for Desire

A Season for Christmas

Bridgewater Brides

Their Harlot Bride

Standalone

Marriage Training

The Duke's Pursuit

Rogue Booty

Sci-fi Romance

Tsenturion Masters Series with Lee Savino

Alien Captive

Alien Tribute

Alien Abduction

Standalone

Mated on Hades

Shifter Romance

Big Bad Bunnies Series

Chasing His Bunny

Chasing His Squirrel

Chasing His Puma

Chasing His Polar Bear

Chasing His Honey Badger

Chasing Her Lion

Night of the Wild Stags

Chasing Tail Box Set

www.ingramcontent.com/pod-product-compliance
Lightning Source LLC
Chambersburg PA
CBHW070444200726
48293CB00007B/2114